What
Kind
of
Girl

ALYSSA SHEINMEL

ATOM

First published in the US in 2020 by Sourcebooks
First published in Great Britain in 2020 by Atom

13 5 7 9 10 8 6 4 2

Copyright © 2020 by Alyssa Sheinmel

The moral right of the author has been asserted.

Quote by Kate DiCamillo on p. 364 printed with permission.

*All characters and events in this publication, other than those
clearly in the public domain, are fictitious and any resemblance
to real persons, living or dead, is purely coincidental.*

A CIP catalogue record for this book is available from the British Library.

ISBN: 978-0-349-00329-0

Printed and bound in Great Britain by Clays Ltd, Elcograf S.p.A.

Papers used by Atom are from well-managed forests
and other responsible sources.

Atom
An imprint of
Little, Brown Book Group
Carmelite House
50 Victoria Embankment
London EC4Y 0DZ

An Hachette UK Company
www.hachette.co.uk

www.atombooks.co.uk

What
Kind
of
Girl

Also by Alyssa Sheinmel

What

Kind

of

Girl

the girls

PART ONE

Monday, April 10

one

THE POPULAR GIRL

It's hard not to want to defend him. He's one of my best friends. I've known him since we were little kids. The whole school knows how sweet he is. It's hard to believe he would ever do what he's accused of doing. And if he did, maybe he didn't mean it. Maybe it was an accident.

Or maybe it was justified, somehow.

Okay, okay, I know—no girl *deserves* to get hit by her boyfriend, no matter the circumstances, it's never okay, et cetera, et cetera. I'm as much of a feminist as the next girl. I'm all for the sisterhood. I'll wear my pink knit you-know-what hat with pride to march for women's rights, and when I turn eighteen next year, I'm going to vote for female candidates, or at least male candidates who support us. Rah-rah, feminism. *Women's rights are human rights and human rights are women's rights.*

But I'm not sure what that has to do with what's happening now. What's happening *here*, at my school.

What had been happening for *months*, according to the rumor mill. Though I don't know how that particular detail got out.

Which kind of makes you wonder why someone would wait so long to say anything.

Which kind of makes you wonder how long a person can live with something like that. If maybe it doesn't really hurt that much. If maybe a person can get used to being hurt.

Which kind of makes you wonder if maybe—on some level, deep down or right at the surface, I don't know—someone might actually *like* it.

two

THE GIRLFRIEND

It was my eye that did it. It wasn't quite a black eye, not at first, but there was an undeniable bruise. More of a pink eye, though not in the way that kindergarteners get pink eye. I guess I could've tried to cover it with makeup, cut school until it faded—I'd have had to pretend I had some viciously contagious strain of the flu to keep anyone from visiting—but honestly at this point, that seemed like more trouble than telling the truth.

Or maybe I just didn't *feel* like covering it up. Covering for him.

So I went to the principal's office this morning.

It happened on Saturday night. All day Sunday, the skin around my eye stayed light pink, barely noticeable. Not that my mother—the only person who saw me on Sunday, since I spent the day at home studying—ever looked that closely. Sometimes I think we live more like roommates than mother and daughter, each keeping to her room and doing her work and reading her books and watching her shows.

But this morning, the skin around my eye had turned dark pink, almost but not quite purple. I got dressed in the clothes I'd laid out the night before: jeans and a North Bay Academy T-shirt in red and white—our school colors—because Mike has track practice after school today and I always cheer him on. I pulled my wavy brown hair back into a tight ponytail. I grabbed a sweater because even though it's April there's still a chill in the air, and I left the house early without saying goodbye (or even good morning) to Mom. She might have noticed the eye now that it's darker.

And, I wanted to be gone before Mike arrived to drive me to school like he usually does.

I walked to school through the morning fog. At some point I realized that the cardigan I was wearing over my T-shirt used to belong to Mike. He lent it to me once when I was at his house late, and I never gave it back.

I walked straight to Principal Scott's office. (*Never trust a man with two first names*; where had I read that? What about a woman with a regular woman's first name and a man's last name—could you trust her? And if she were a married woman who'd taken her husband's last name—and Principal Scott had definitely taken her husband's name—then you knew that her husband had two first names. Did *she* trust him?)

Anyway, I arrived in the office before Principal Scott, so I sat on the uncomfortable bench outside the office and waited. At eight fifteen on the nose—Principal Scott is a very on-the-nose sort of principal—Principal Scott breezed in. She didn't seem to notice the girl sitting on the bench at first.

But when she unlocked the door to her office, I followed her inside.

◇◇◇◇

"That's a very serious accusation," Principal Scott said carefully. She'd offered to get me an ice pack from the nurse's office, but I said no, it didn't hurt anymore, though I could still feel a tiny thrum of pain beneath my eye.

It's not that she didn't believe me—or anyway, it's not *exactly* that. I had a bruised eye, after all, and our school is the sort of place that prides itself on empowering its students to speak up for themselves; it's literally in the brochure. She knew I'd been hit, it's just that she couldn't believe Mike—*her* Mike, the student who worked in her office during his free periods for extra cash (he isn't on scholarship like I am, but his parents aren't rich like some of our classmates'), the humble track star, the guy who blushed when his best friends made naughty jokes (not that Principal Scott knew that about him)—was the one who did it.

I almost felt sorry for her, trying to square that circle. I tried to imagine her thoughts:

There is a student in my office who claims her boyfriend is hitting her.

Always give the victim the benefit of the doubt.

And yet: *Not Mike, right? It was some other kid, some other boyfriend, who did this.*

What's a neutral response—something that will let her know I don't disbelieve her, but I'm not 100 percent all-in either?

Until finally, out loud: *That's a very serious accusation.*

I nodded. On the walk to school this morning, I decided that no matter what Principal Scott said or did, I would do my best to stay calm, appear reasonable. Because maybe she wouldn't believe me if I seemed hysterical, unhinged. Sitting in her office, I hoped she couldn't hear the way my heart was pounding, couldn't see the sweat pooling at the base of my neck, just beneath my ponytail.

"Was this the first time Mike—" She stopped herself then, looked off to the side for a moment, and finally said, "Has this happened before?"

I nodded again.

"Have you discussed this with your parents?" she asked. I shook my head. "With any of your friends here?" I shook my head again. "Why not?"

It was about then that I began to wonder whether I'd gone to the wrong person. I probably should've gone to my mother first. Maybe even to *his* mother. It was weird, wasn't it, that I'd told the principal before anyone else? I tried to remember *why* I'd chosen her. I thought—I guess I thought—that she'd be able to make it stop. Isn't that what teachers and school administrators are supposed to do, step in if a student misbehaves?

Anyway, it was too late to take it back and do it differently.

10

Then Principal Scott said, "Have you thought about going to the police?"

My mouth went dry then, too dry to explain that going to the police seemed like too much, too big a step to take. Even just hearing the principal say the word *police* felt like too much. The sort of thing my mother would call *a bridge too far*, if I'd given her a chance to say anything at all.

Oh god, was the *principal* going to call the police? My heart beat even faster. She couldn't do that, could she, not if I didn't want her to? The only things I knew about the police came from TV shows, and I vaguely remembered some official-looking actress telling another, much less official-looking actress, that *she* had to the be the one to file a complaint with law enforcement. But if I told the principal I didn't want to go to the police, would she think I was lying about what happened? I slid my hands beneath my legs. My palms were so sweaty I worried she'd be able to see it. Weren't sweaty palms considered a sign of lying?

As though telling the truth is any less nerve racking.

"You understand, of course, that I'll want to discuss this with your parents," Principal Scott said. I had to hold my breath to keep from sighing with relief. Calling my parents didn't exactly sound *good*, but it sounded better than if she'd said she was calling the cops. She continued, "And Mike's parents." Okay, that made sense. It was only fair, if she was going to talk to my parents. "And I'll have to discuss this with Mike, of course."

I nodded again. Isn't that what I'd wanted? How else did I think she could stop it?

She added, "And the way rumors spread around here—I can only imagine your classmates will begin to hear about it too."

She said it like she was sorry that she couldn't keep it a secret. I pressed my palms into my jeans, trying to wipe away the sweat without letting the principal see that I was sweating in the first place.

Maybe I shouldn't have worn my hair in a ponytail today. Maybe it looked like I was trying to draw attention to the bruise. I decided that as soon as I left the principal's office, I would let my hair down, so I could tilt my head to hide the bruise behind a few strands. But then maybe Principal Scott would think I'd done that on purpose too: pulled my hair back for her, let it down for the kids in the halls.

I wanted to pull my legs up and rest my chin on my knees, making myself as little as possible. But I kept my feet on the floor. I even tried not to slouch. Could Principal Scott tell this was Mike's sweater? I looked at my feet. I wondered when the floor had last been vacuumed and who decided the principal's office would be carpeted, unlike the floors in the rest of the school, which are hard, cold linoleum. I was wearing a particularly beat-up pair of sneakers. Maybe I'd done that on purpose too, trying to look that much more like a victim: *See, even my* sneakers *are beat up.*

Or did it make me look that much more to blame: *You can't trust a word that girl says, even her* sneakers *are beat up. Clearly, she doesn't know how to take care of herself. Clearly she can't handle having nice things.*

Mike was a Very Nice Thing. I fell in love with him the day he asked me out. I mean, literally, at that moment. Until then, I didn't think he knew I was alive—no, that's an exaggeration, and I should be careful about exaggerating, given the circumstances. Of course he knew I was alive; we'd been going to school together since kindergarten and had most of the same friends. We'd gone to the same birthday parties when we were little and the same blowouts as we got older. But—until he asked me out—I never would've guessed he thought of me *that way*, so I didn't bother thinking of him *that way* either. I mean, I'm not blind; he's the most handsome boy in school. (In my opinion. But believe me, I'm not the only one who thinks so.) Sandy brown hair, tall, tan, toned. I'm not even the prettiest girl among our group of friends. I'm not the funniest or the smartest, and I don't have the best body. I'm average—I looked it up once and my height is *literally* the average height for a girl my age. My eyes and hair color (brown) are average too. Mike could've had anyone, so there would've been no point to thinking of him *that way*.

But then he asked me out—and no one ever asks anyone out like that. It's always a group hanging out or a hookup or whatever, but Mike actually *asked me out*. I felt like I was in a movie from the 1980s and he was captain of the football team and I was head cheerleader. (Or would that be a movie from the fifties? Should I have realized then that he was old-fashioned? Should I have recognized it as a warning sign?)

Anyway, when he asked me out on an actual date, I fell. Just like that. Like this whole time I simply hadn't noticed that I was

13

madly, desperately, completely in love with him. He stood over me while he waited for my answer, close enough that I had to tilt my head up to face him and tell him that yes, of course I'd go out with him. My heart was pounding so hard and so fast that I was sure he could hear it. It didn't even pound that hard in the principal's office this morning, and that should have been so much more nerve racking than accepting a date, shouldn't it? Maybe when all this is over, I'll need to have my heart checked.

"Are you sure about this?" Principal Scott asked, crossing then uncrossing her legs. She isn't one of those teachers who tries to act like *one of the girls*. She keeps her blond hair cut bluntly just below her shoulders and wears thick black headbands. She wears sensible flat shoes almost every day. On field day this year, she wore khakis that were pleated in the front and sneakers so clean, it looked like they'd never been worn before.

She didn't sound unsupportive. More *concerned*.

After our first date, that was that. We've been together ever since—six months. I don't remember exactly when Mike started saying that we'd be together forever. He said we'd go to the same college (wherever they recruited him to run track), that we'd live in the same dorm, that we'd end up working in the same city after graduation.

Doesn't every girl dream that her boyfriend will love her like that?

three

THE POPULAR GIRL

I wonder what the deal will be at lunch today. We—my best friend and I—sit with Mike and his guy friends pretty much every day. Maybe today it'll break down gender lines—girls on one side and boys on the other. Or maybe everyone will act like nothing happened because of course, no one's supposed to know that anything happened, because of course, this isn't any of anyone else's business. But (of course) by lunchtime everyone at school knows, as easily and quickly as if they'd announced it over the loudspeaker:

Sad Girl accuses Golden Boy of abuse.

Mom called this morning. We're not supposed to talk on our phones in the halls, but I figured the teachers would make an exception today, considering everything that was going on. Mom was sympathetic and concerned, saying the things I guess a parent is supposed to say at a time like this—*how are you, do you need anything, do you want to come home early*, et cetera. But as the conversation went on, I couldn't help thinking that she also sounded kind of relieved that at least it had happened to two people who were too young to have been married.

To be fair, my parents went through a tricky divorce recently. There wasn't any abuse or anything like that, but there were lots of entanglements where money was concerned, because Mom and Dad owned a company together, and when things were finally settled, Dad moved all the way to New York just to get some space. Mom tends to see the things that happen to other people through the lens of her own experience, so she couldn't help comparing what was happening with Mike to her own breakup.

"At least there's no shared home, or kids to fight over, or financial dependence to figure out." She spoke very fast, like she was trying to convince me—or maybe to convince herself—that everything would be okay.

She continued, "And it's only high school. This doesn't have to change *everything*. You and Mike and everyone else still have your whole lives ahead of you, right?"

"Right," I agreed, because it seemed like she wanted me to reassure her. But I didn't really see why it was less significant because it happened in high school, when we all had our lives ahead of us. If we were talking about anything else—drugs, drinking, sex—it would've been a bigger deal *because* we were only in high school, *because* we had our whole lives ahead of us, *because* the things that happened now would impact our futures.

"What does Mike say?" Mom asked, speaking at a normal

pace now. Mom always loved Mike. To be fair, everyone loves Mike. But Mom loves any male who comes around the house, because ever since the divorce—and Dad's subsequent departure across the country—she acts like having a man in the house is a complete novelty to her. Whenever Mike stopped by, she'd ask him to change light bulbs and dust cobwebs she couldn't reach on her own. I had to explain that Mike wasn't there to see *her*. In front of Mike, I'd tell her she was embarrassing herself. (A fact Mike always disputed when Mom could hear—*No trouble at all!*—and agreed with me about when Mom couldn't hear—*A woman needs a man in the house*.)

"I haven't talked to him yet," I said.

"Of course not," Mom agreed, talking fast again. She was probably picturing him sequestered in the principal's office until this all blew over.

"It's just such a mess," I said, and then I hung up because even though I wanted Mom to know what was going on, I didn't really want her opinion about it, because it's not like Mom knows anything about anything.

I didn't tell Mom that Mike wasn't actually in the principal's office. Principal Scott's assistant had pulled him out of homeroom, I assume taking him to the office, where she told him about the accusations—but then they'd let him go back to class. Being accused of hitting your girlfriend is no reason to miss third-period physics lab, right?

I have history third period, but I know Mike has physics. (Everyone in our friend group knows everyone else's schedules.)

17

I follow the lunch crowd outside after fourth period. We're California kids—spending as much time as possible outside is practically written into our DNA. The school has an indoor cafeteria in case of inclement weather, but even when it's pouring out, it's mostly empty. We'll picnic in the halls and in empty classrooms before we'll eat in the cafeteria. But as long as it's dry, we crowd onto the tables outside anyway, even though the old wooden benches have splinters so sharp they'll stab right through your jeans.

I text my best friend that I have to study through lunch—**I'll be in the library, text if you need me**. I miss lunch at least a couple times a week—everyone knows that I'm very studious. I have to get straight A's so I can get into any college I want and follow my dad across the country.

He's not the only one who wants to get the eff out of Dodge.

four

THE BURNOUT

"Man, this shit is messed up," Hiram says, playing with his lighter. I inhale, hold my breath, exhale.

"Yeah, it is," I agree, though I wonder how Hiram even knows what's going on. As far as I can tell, he never steps foot inside the school.

Hiram's fingers brush against mine. I don't mind. It's not like I don't know Hiram has a crush on me. I'm stoned but I'm not stupid.

"What's it like in there?" Hiram gestures vaguely to the school across the parking lot. I look up and gaze at all the cars. The school building seems farther away than it did before.

We're in Hiram's car. I don't know why he bothers driving to school every day. From what I can tell, he only goes to class about half the time, if that.

But I'm grateful he's here. I'm not the only one who sneaks

off to his car between classes. I wonder if anyone would bother hanging out with him if it weren't for the chemical incentive. After all, that's why I started coming here in the first place, months ago.

"It's not good," I answer finally. I squint in the yellow April sunlight, wishing I had sunglasses. "Everyone's on edge, Hiram."

What a funny name: *Hi-Ram.*

High Ram.

Hi, Ram.

I run my fingers along the window. I feel like laughing.

"Bad energy, man." Hiram shudders, like he's literally shaking off all that badness. Hiram doesn't ask if I'm on edge. He doesn't ask how I feel about everything that's going on. He's understood, from the first time I knocked on his car window, that I'm not interested in talking about things like that. Instead, he looks at me and taps the car keys, which are in the ignition even though the car isn't turned on. "You wanna get out of here?"

He's never offered that before. It was always a very *wham, bam, thank you, ma'am* sort of exchange.

I look back at the school. Inside, no one is talking about anything but Mike and his girlfriend. Everyone from the geeks to the jocks to the stoners (like me). The teachers and the administrators. The coaches and the guidance counselor.

If I leave, I'll get a call from the guidance counselor later.

I heard you weren't in your afternoon classes. We should talk.

I roll my eyes. They feel sandy inside my head. I blink

slowly—who knew it was possible to blink so slowly?—and fix my gaze back at the school.

Somewhere inside that building is a boy who beat up his girlfriend. If I weren't so stoned, maybe I'd be angry that they didn't expel him on the spot. Screw innocent-until-proven-guilty and all that BS. Doesn't the victim deserve protection? It's the twenty-first century.

No, I remind myself. I don't care. That's why I came to Hiram's car in the first place. To not care.

Because here, I'm not that kind of girl. Here, I'm chill, I'm cool. Here, I don't have to care about anything.

It must be the bad energy, like Hiram said a few seconds ago. (Seconds? Minutes? Who cares?) The bad vibes must be seeping out of that building and heading straight toward me like they're made of iron and I'm a magnet.

If I take Hiram up on his offer to get out of here, they could suspend me for cutting class.

I could miss a pop quiz and the big fat zero will bring down my GPA.

Colleges would frown at the blot on my transcripts.

Well, maybe I won't go to college. Hiram isn't going to college, right? He's a senior, he'd be waiting for his admissions letters right about now if he'd applied anywhere, which I'm pretty sure he didn't. Not that we ever talk about that kind of thing. Anyway, he seems a hell of a lot happier than I do.

I'm not, like, a stoner. If my mom knew, if my dad knew, if my best friend knew—they'd be shocked, probably alarmed.

Maybe they'd insist on sending me to rehab or something. In fact, maybe I should tell them. Because at least rehab would be a way out of here.

But then I remember that Hiram just offered to get me out of here, even if it's only for the afternoon.

"Yeah," I say finally. "Let's go."

"You got it," Hiram says. He turns the key, and his old car roars to life. It literally sounds like a lion, making all that noise so that the rest of the jungle knows he's there.

Or knows he's leaving.

five

THE GIRLFRIEND

I don't look at my mom. Instead, I stare at my beat-up sneakers just like I did in Principal Scott's office. I'll have to throw these shoes away. Every time I look at them from now on, I'll remember this day.

"There's nothing to explain," I answer finally. The question was: *Tell me how things went this far.* Not like it's my fault that it happened in the first place, Mom isn't *that* insensitive, but more like why did things have to get so bad—black-eye bad—before I said anything.

We're sitting at the kitchen table, something we pretty much never do because Mom rarely cooks, and even when she does, we eat in the living room with *Jeopardy!* on in the background. We talked earlier when I was still at school. Then later she texted, offering to leave work and pick me up, but I told her she didn't have to come in from her job in the city because we'd have plenty of time to talk tonight. But Mom said she was still going to leave her office early because she was too upset to get any work done.

I press my feet into the floor and imagine I can feel the cool white tile through my sneakers. I'm still wearing Mike's old sweater. I wonder if I have to give it back now. Maybe I was supposed to give it back weeks ago but Mike was too polite to mention it. He can be really polite about things like that.

The weird thing is, I don't want to give the sweater back. Even now. I love this sweater. I love that it smells like Mike. I love that it feels like being held. I pull the sleeves down over my wrists and ball that material inside my fists.

"Of course there's something to explain," Mom insists.

"Like what?"

"Like, how often did this happen?"

I shrug, keeping my gaze focused on the kitchen counters, the stove, the sink—anywhere but Mom's face. It's weird that this kitchen can be so messy when no one who lives here cooks. My hands are sweating again, and I slide them under my thighs (again).

"I don't know. I mean, it's not like I was keeping track." That's not a lie.

"Well, when did it start?" Mom is staring at my eye. I looked at my reflection in the bathroom mirror before dinner. The bruise was even darker than it had been this morning. Magenta, maybe.

"I don't know. A couple months ago."

What would I have said if Principal Scott had asked the same question? She asked if it had happened before, but not exactly *when.* I don't think I could have lied to her the way I just lied to Mom. Because I know exactly when it started. Three months ago. The middle of January. I sat in the bleachers during his track practice—the spring season doesn't actually start until March—and I shivered in my too-light coat and the drizzling rain, and I cheered for him because I was a supportive girlfriend. We followed NCAA sports, and we'd decided that UCLA's track team would be a good fit if it turned out they didn't want him at Stanford.

He fell that day, rolling his ankle. He was so scared that it might cause real damage—bench him for a week or two—but by the next day it was good as new.

Sometime after that night—I don't remember exactly when—I began watching other couples. I'd stare at them walking down the halls at school hand in hand, just like Mike and I did. Sometimes I find myself gazing at them, wondering what it must be like, to be in love but not to be hit. It's not like I didn't know that people weren't supposed to do this. I knew it wasn't normal or okay.

I'd think about the fact that before the divorce (long after they'd stopped being in love), my parents fought to the point of shouting—well, mostly Mom had shouted—but my dad never hit my mom in all the years they were together.

And then I'd think: *That I know of.*

And then I realized all those guys I assumed didn't hit were just that—limited by *that I know of.*

And then I'd wonder if all boys hit, and all girls kept their secrets.

25

Until they didn't.

"A couple of months?" Mom echoes, covering her mouth with her hand. She looks like she's going to cry. "Why didn't you say something sooner?"

I open my fists and push the sweater sleeves up over my elbows. It's cold in our white kitchen, but I'm so hot.

"I don't know." Instead of looking at her, I concentrate on my fingernails, pressing the cuticles down.

I thought it wasn't that big a deal. I thought it would stop, eventually. I thought it was worth it if I still got to be with him. It seemed like a small price to pay for how good things were the rest of the time.

Things *were* good the rest of the time, right? I loved him. He loved me. That's good, isn't it?

"Was it always this bad?" Mom gestures to my eye.

I shake my head, and she looks relieved. She doesn't want to think that I stayed when it was this bad. She wants to think that the minute it crossed the line (what line? Who says where the line is?), I stood up for myself. That's what any self-respecting girl would do in this day and age. That's the kind of girl she wants to believe she raised me to be.

And she wants to think that if it had always been this bad, she would've seen it sooner.

Tuesday, April 11

six

THE BURNOUT

In the morning, I consider skipping school entirely, but I can't risk getting into more trouble. Of course they noticed that I wasn't there all afternoon yesterday. (*They* being Principal Scott and the guidance counselor, probably my classmates too.) Principal Scott said I wasn't in trouble this time—I'd never done it before and with everything that was going on, they knew it was a difficult time for the entire student body—but she encouraged me not to make a habit of it.

It wasn't like I did anything all that bad with my free afternoon. Hiram drove to the beach and parked. Neither of us made a move to get out of the car. It was April in Northern California, a sunny day after a rainy winter. The waves crashed on the beach. The water didn't look inviting, but I still kept my seat belt fastened because I was so tempted to dive in.

Hiram whistled. "Mike Parker, man," he said. "Never liked him."

I shook my head. "What are you talking about? *Everyone* likes him."

"Not me."

"You barely know him."

Hiram shrugged. "Guess no one knew him as well as they thought, huh?"

"Everyone loves him," I said reflexively. I gestured to the air in front of me as though we were looking not at a storm-tossed ocean but the school parking lot, just a stone's throw from Mike and his friends eating lunch at their usual table outside the school. I shuddered and the image disappeared. School—Mike, his friends, everyone but Hiram—suddenly seemed very far away, like a life I'd merely imagined, or a story I'd heard.

"Even his girlfriend," I added softly. "She still loves him."

Hiram looked at me sharply. For a second I thought he was going to take my hand, but he kept his limbs on his side of the car.

"Well, even if that's true," Hiram said finally, "he doesn't love *her*."

I shook my head. "Sure he does. *Everyone* knows he was so in love."

It was true. All of our classmates stepped aside when Mike walked through the halls, holding hands with the girl he loved so much. Other girls looked on wistfully. Even guys who talked a good game about not wanting to be tied down would occasionally concede that they'd give up their freedom for something as good as that.

Staring at the ocean from the passenger seat of Hiram's car,

I shook my head and swallowed, then slid off my sneakers and put my feet up on the dashboard so that I was curled into a ball. I bent my neck, letting my long hair fall forward so Hiram couldn't see my face.

"That's not love," Hiram said firmly.

"How do you know?" I asked softly.

Through my hair, I saw Hiram shrug. We watched the waves crash, one right after another. I remembered reading somewhere that waves come in sets, but these waves didn't look nearly so organized. The water looked messy. Falling on top of itself over and over again.

"Maybe it was love," I tried. My voice sounded small, far away somehow. I pulled my sleeves down over my wrists, but my skin felt suddenly itchy beneath the fabric. So I pushed the sleeves up again and leaned my head back, staring at the car's ceiling. "But maybe it wasn't *good* love."

"Maybe," Hiram agreed, then added, "but maybe that's just as bad as not being love at all."

We stayed at the beach until it got dark, and then he drove me home. Until then, I hadn't realized Hiram knew where I lived.

seven

THE POPULAR GIRL

I head toward our usual table outside for lunch the next day. I keep my eyes focused straight ahead so I won't have to see the Looks from all my classmates.

I got dressed carefully this morning. I know clothes can't actually *speak*, but when you're one of the most popular girls in school, people tend to look at you and now that *all this* is going on, I knew they'd be looking even more than usual. Besides, I like clothes. They let me express myself without saying a word.

So I'm wearing dark blue jeans with my favorite high-heeled clogs. A bright white T-shirt with the name of an old band (Led Zeppelin) scrawled across the front; I ordered it after I saw it in a picture from *Teen Vogue*. I leave my long brown hair down, but I'm wearing a pair of sunglasses as a headband even though the fog is thick today and the Weather Channel app on my phone said it might rain later. California cool. California casual. There's a chill in the air, but I didn't bring a jacket or sweater with me to school today. I didn't want to look like I was hiding anything, hiding from anyone.

Even though I keep my eyes focused straight ahead, it's impossible to avoid all of the sympathetic smiles, the raised eyebrows, occasionally even a hand on my arm followed by *How're you doing?* or sometimes *How's Mike doing?* I tell them I'd rather not talk about it.

Mike's already sitting at our usual lunch table, flanked on either side by his two best friends. I wonder if Anil and Kyle have been getting as many questions from our classmates as I have. Then again, they're a lot more intimidating than I am, so maybe not. In fact, maybe they're sitting beside Mike now expressly to stop people from asking questions.

They've always sat like that. We picked this table freshman year and haven't moved since. (We're juniors now.) Every so often an unknowing group of underclassmen will sit down, and all Mike has to do is throw them a look—he doesn't even have to say a word—and they move.

Mike always seemed so much more grown-up than the rest of us. Even in kindergarten, when most boys could barely keep still for more than a few minutes at a time, Mike sat at the same table for lunch every day, and he never tried to get up until the teacher clapped her hands and announced that it was time for recess. Then he sped off like a shot and won every game of tag, every relay race. I used to think he was so fast because, unlike the other boys, he held still the rest of the time, like he'd made the decision to store up his energy for when it mattered.

I linger near the school entrance, one hand against a stucco pillar. Our school is only one story tall, spread out so that it's long and curvy like a snake. On one side of the snake is the track where Mike runs almost every day, the parking lot beyond it. There are tables on either end of the school, but anyone worth anything sits at the tables on the south side like we do.

There aren't any girls sitting at our table. Maybe none of the female students will want to sit with Mike now. Or maybe they just haven't gotten here yet.

Someone grabs me from behind. I spin around.

"You scared me," I say. It's my best friend, Junie.

"Let's eat in the library today," she suggests. "I mean, who wants to deal with all that drama?" She gestures with her chin to the table where the boys are sitting. I see that a girl has sat down across from Mike and his friends. So much for female solidarity. It's a sophomore whose name I think is Eva Mercado. She's always had a crush on Mike. He never so much as smiled at her, though. I mean, he wasn't rude about it or anything, he was just a really faithful boyfriend.

I glance at the parking lot, where the losers and stoners slink off at lunchtime, then turn back to Junie. "The library sounds good to me."

◇◇◇◇

34

"I can't believe it. I just can't believe it." We're sitting at one of the five round tables set up in between the stacks of books, and Junie can't stop talking. "I mean, I'm not saying I *don't* believe it, of course I *do* believe it, I just *can't* believe it—you know what I mean?"

I shrug, wondering why my best friend seems so nervous. It's not as though she's the one accused of anything. Or the one doing the accusing. But Junie can be kind of intense—her parents raised her to care about *everything*, to try to see every side of every story. That must get overwhelming from time to time.

Especially at times like this.

Junie shifts in her seat, twisting a lock of her short dark hair around one finger, then dropping it to chew on her nails. Unlike me, Junie looks like she always has a tan, thanks to the rich complexion she inherited from her mom. Plus, she got green eyes from her dad's side of the family, and they're so light they make her skin look even darker. Also unlike me, Junie's wearing long sleeves that come down to her wrists and boots with her jeans. Junie's one of those girls who's so pretty, she doesn't need to show any skin or wear makeup or put product in her hair to get people to look at her. People will always look at her.

"Where were you yesterday?" she asks finally. "I didn't see you."

"I ate lunch in here," I explain. "I sort of just stayed after the bell rang."

"Right." Junie nods absently. "It was crazy out there." She gestures vaguely to the hallway beyond the library entrance.

"What are people saying?" I know they're saying more than

asking how everyone involved is doing, even if that's all they've been saying to me so far. I wonder how long until they start saying those other things to me.

Junie goes back to toying with her hair, trying to look nonchalant. (We've been best friends ever since her family moved here halfway through sixth grade—I know when she's lying.) "Oh, you know."

"No, I don't know. That's why I asked." Sometimes I wonder if Junie and I aren't really well-suited as best friends. Maybe the choices you made in sixth grade should expire before junior year.

"I mean, I think people believe it—'cause like, the evidence is hard to ignore." Junie points at her own face, as though she's the one with the bruised eye. "I think it's hard because everyone's always loved Mike."

"Right."

"Right!" Junie echoes enthusiastically. She starts chewing at her thumb again, her eyes darting around like she's worried someone might be watching us.

Finally, she says, "I heard the track coach said that this could ruin his chances for that college scholarship."

I know how much that scholarship means to Mike. Mike's told me that his parents are stretched pretty thin. His little brother, Ryan, goes to a private school too—not here at North Bay, but to another school that caters to children with special needs, because Ryan was born with a learning disability. I got the idea that Ryan's school is even more expensive than North Bay.

And college is even more expensive than that. So the

scholarship would be a big help. Plus, I think he just wants to win it.

"Why? It's not like any of this is going to affect his ability to run fast."

"Apparently there's, like, a morality clause to the scholarship that he'd be in violation of if it turns out he really did it."

"What do you mean *if he really did it*? You said people believe it. The evidence and all that." I point at my face like Junie pointed at hers.

"Yeah, but maybe it was an accident. Or just, you know, a misunderstanding?" Quickly, Junie adds, "I mean, that's what some people are saying." Junie always says *I mean* a lot, but I think she's saying it even more than usual today. "Some people are saying the opposite."

I wonder what the opposite is, but I don't ask.

Junie continues, "I heard some girls are planning a rally to call for his expulsion."

"A rally?"

Junie shrugs. "Yeah. You know, a protest. Some kind of demonstration."

"Will you go?"

"Will you?"

The truth is, I never actually considered that Mike could get expelled. I've only ever heard of one student being expelled from North Bay Academy, and that was for plagiarizing a paper.

I don't think I've heard of any student getting expelled for *this* from any high school. Because I don't think I've ever heard of *this* happening. I've read about sexual assault accusations at other schools, and of course, I believe that boys who commit sexual assault should be expelled. But Mike isn't accused of *that*.

"If he gets expelled, then he definitely wouldn't be eligible for the scholarship anymore," I say finally.

Mike must be freaking out about losing the scholarship, must be wondering how his girlfriend—the person who's supposed to love him the most—could jeopardize his future. Even if he did hurt her—bruises heal, but college debt can last a lifetime. I should know; I'm already looking into student loans even with college still a couple years away. I'm on scholarship here at North Bay, for academic excellence. I have to keep my grades up and even though no one ever said so, I think I'm also supposed to be generally well-liked, well-behaved. I try not to forget that I'm here out of the goodness of the administration's hearts.

"True." Junie nods. "But I'm not sure that *students* can call for expulsion. Even with a protest it's not, you know…" Junie pauses like she's searching for the right word. Finally she says, "It's not definite he'll get expelled. The school doesn't have a policy for something like this."

Junie looks like she's waiting for me to say something, but I don't know what to say. That I'm happy it's not definite? That I wish it were?

"What do you think will happen?" she asks finally.

I shake my head. "I don't know."

Suddenly, I feel very, very tired.

This all would be so much *easier* if everyone involved had just kept quiet.

Plenty of women never tell. They don't come forward and say their boyfriends are hitting them. They find thicker cover-up and better cover stories. They opened a cabinet and a mug fell on their faces. They walked into a doorknob in the middle of the night. Sure, it's completely implausible—why would anyone be eye level with a doorknob?—but that's what women in the movies say. They cover for the men in their lives, at least at first. Eventually the woman stands up for herself and says: *Enough*.

Couldn't this have waited until after Mike won the scholarship?

Anyway, Mike isn't like those guys in the movies—they're all bad guys. Their abuse escalates until it's actually dangerous, until those women get seriously hurt: rushed to the ER, emergency surgery, that sort of thing. Mike is a *good guy*. He didn't mean anything by it. Everyone knows he was the perfect boyfriend.

Everyone would tell you that.

eight

THE GIRLFRIEND

Okay, so yes, Mike asked me out to begin with, but I was the one who made things between us *official*.

I don't think anyone else knows that, because I was so embarrassed afterward that I begged him not to tell anyone, and he promised. Then again, now that we're broken up, I guess all bets are off in the promise department.

Although, we never technically broke up. I'm just *assuming* we're broken up. Under different circumstances that might even be funny because I was so unwilling to assume we were boyfriend/girlfriend in the beginning. Under different circumstances, it would make Mike laugh. (He always thought I was funny.)

We'd gone on three dates. Which isn't really that many. Two dates the two of us alone and one date that wasn't really a date since it was a party that I would've gone to anyway. But I would've gone with my best friend, and instead, I went with

Mike (he has his own car, he drove) and we walked in holding hands. At that point, I was still keeping track of how many times we'd held hands.

One: The end of our first date. Dinner at an Italian restaurant. He held my hand from the restaurant to the parking lot, and then from my driveway to my front door. I kind of wished he hadn't been holding my hand that second time because I knew my mom would be watching and she'd be so excited that at least one of us had a boyfriend, and I would've had to explain that Mike wasn't my *boyfriend*, someone doesn't become your boyfriend after just one date no matter how well it went or how much you already loved him.

Two: The beginning, middle, and end of our second date. From his car to the concession line at the movie theater; and then he took my hand halfway through the movie; and then after the movie we walked back to his car holding hands. That was the night of our first kiss, but kissing Mike for the first time didn't feel as important as getting to hold his hand. I'd seen him kiss girls in dark corners at house parties and even at school once or twice, but I'd never seen him holding those girls' hands. Then again, as of our second date, no one had seen us holding hands, unless you count my mother, which I didn't.

Three: This was actually between dates. He held my hand for about ten seconds during lunch one day. But it was under the table, so I'm not sure anyone saw it.

Four: The party. Our third date. It was a belated Halloween party. Costumes were optional, and Mike and I had both opted out, though we hadn't discussed it ahead of time. We were hand in hand practically the whole night. When Mike wasn't looking, our friends—most of whom had come in costume, unlike us—would shoot kissy faces or thumbs-up or pretend to swoon. They were happy for me. They were jealous. Until then, I didn't realize people could be both at the same time.

Mike and I left the party early. Anil and Kyle shouted that he was whipped, even though leaving hadn't been my idea. Mike shrugged off his friends' shouts. He never laughed when Anil and Kyle made jokes about the girls they'd hooked up with (or wanted to hook up with), about how Mike was pussy-whipped, about which celebrity had the best ass, about the latest free porn they found online. At least, he never laughed at that stuff in front of me. We held hands on the way to his car. (*You okay to drive?* I asked, and Mike said, *Of course.* I don't know why I asked. It's not like I would've suggested that I be the one to drive instead. I never drove Mike's car.) Mike drove toward my house but he parked down the block. He said he thought my mother might be watching, and I said, *Thank you so much.* I was touched that he'd picked up on how uncomfortable my mother's prying eyes made me.

We kissed for a long time. That was all, just kissing—I don't want to give the impression that Mike was aggressive that way. We never did anything I didn't want to do too.

After a while, he pulled away. "You'll miss curfew if you don't leave."

"Don't worry," I said, leaning in. "My mother doesn't actually

42

enforce curfew. It's more like she saw it in a TV show and thought it was something I should have without actually understanding what it was."

Mike laughed. I hadn't realized I'd been making a joke.

"So…" I began. "What happens on Monday?"

"On Monday?"

"At school."

"At school?"

"Stop repeating everything I say!" I gave him a shove. He pretended I was so strong that my touch left him leaning up against the driver's-side door. "I mean…" *Ugh,* I thought, *is he really going to make me say it?* I wasn't even sure whether I *should* say it at all. Part of me thought I should just keep my mouth shut and take what I got and be grateful because it was already more than Mike gave most other girls.

But I didn't want to be like my mother, who at fifty years old still didn't understand the difference between a declaration of love and a booty call. (She'd recently had some misadventures with online dating.)

So I screwed up my courage and asked point-blank: "Do you want to be my boyfriend?"

Now, I look back at that moment with wonder. Not because I was so brave to just ask the question. Almost exactly the opposite: I think of the way I worded it—like what we were was entirely up to him and not me. Was that when he realized that he was the one in charge?

Then again, perhaps it never occurred to him that he hadn't

been in charge all along. Not until I showed up in Principal Scott's office yesterday morning.

Mike laughed. Again, I hadn't meant to be funny, but like I said, he always thought I was funny. I was too embarrassed to even pretend-shove him again. But not embarrassed enough to open the door and walk away. I wanted to hear his answer. Even while he laughed at me, I was hoping he'd say yes.

And even if he said *No*, I still would've gone on kissing him if he let me.

But he said yes. Actually, he said *of course*, like it was something he'd already decided. Now, I wonder whether it was my idea or his that we make things official.

After that, we held hands all the time. In front of everyone. I was never so proud as when we were walking down the halls at school hand in hand.

nine

THE BULIMIC

Okay, so I throw up after dinner. It's no big deal.

I tried skipping every other meal first, but I could never keep it up for very long. I always got too hungry. Or too bored. Or too fed up with trying to starve myself, which is an ironic choice of words, I know, but what can you do? So eventually I stopped skipping meals and started throwing them up instead.

I'm not fat. I was never really fat. I'm just not that *thin*. But about six months ago, I started dieting. Over the years, I'd gotten good at disguising my fat bits with the right outfits—I had skinny legs but a bulge around my stomach, so I could stick with tight jeans or leggings or short shorts paired with long flowy tops. It had served me well, for the most part.

But it wouldn't work if I took my clothes off. And for the first time, it seemed like maybe someone might want to take my clothes off. And I wanted to look good. With my clothes off, that is. Even if I'd barely been so much as kissed before.

I never really understood why I was kissed so rarely. I went to the right parties and knew the right guys. I wasn't the prettiest (or obviously, the skinniest) girl, but there were plenty of girls who were less pretty—I know that's subjective, but I wasn't ugly anyhow—and even heavier—that's not subjective, that's math—who'd been kissed more than I had.

Finally, I decided it was probably a chemical thing. Like maybe those other girls gave off more pheromones than I did. Or maybe they were just more approachable—maybe guys were less intimidated by other girls *because* they weren't as pretty or thin. By which logic the super-pretty-fit girls would never get kissed, but I told myself that guys were willing to get shot down if it meant a chance at that level of hotness. Whereas I was somewhere in between—not pretty enough to be worth the risk and not plain enough to be a sure thing.

Ugh, guys are such pigs.

Anyway. I don't throw up, like, *every* night. And I never throw up during the day—never at school and never in a public restroom, because, gross. I do it in my own house, in the bathroom on the second floor next to my bedroom, and I always clean up afterward: flush the toilet, scrape away any detritus, wash my hands, brush my teeth. I haven't even lost that much weight since I started doing it. It's really just so I can go to bed most nights with a relatively flat (that is, empty) stomach. I know they say you don't sleep well when you're hungry, but I sleep better that way. When I'm hungry, that ache in my belly makes me believe I can actually *feel* my body metabolizing what's left inside. (I never succeed in throwing up every last bit that I've eaten.) It feels like it's hard at work. It feels *good*.

Throwing up does *not* feel good. The other day, I visited an online support group for recovering bulimics—I wasn't really sure if I was hoping to find advice that would help me stop throwing up, or tips from experts that would make throwing up easier. I felt like a total imposter just browsing through the website. Anyway, some of the girls talked about how much they missed throwing up. Like the actual physical act of it. They talked about it in practically fetishistic—is that a word?—terms: the sensation of their fingers in their mouth, their teeth rubbing the backs of their knuckles, the feeling of satisfaction when the food began to rise up through their bellies, the comforting scent of vomit.

I thought: *You've got to be kidding me.* You can't imagine how much I wish I didn't have to throw up. How much I wish I could just starve myself and be done with it. Or better yet, go back in time and be born one of those girls who can eat whatever she wants without gaining an ounce because it seems to me that one of life's great injustices is that some girls can eat what they want and still look great naked while the rest of us can't.

Isn't that what every girl—and probably every guy too—wants? I mean, I know we're not supposed to care, we're supposed to work out and watch what we eat to be *healthy*, not to be *thin*, but come on. That's another one of those things you have to pretend about, like how you have to pretend you don't

47

know if you're pretty, which is a ridiculous thing to have to be modest about, when you think about it, since it's not like you had anything to do with what you look like; it's just luck, a trick of genetics, a trick of timing. Girls who're considered unattractive now might have been the ideal in the nineteenth century, after all.

Anyway. So I throw up sometimes. Not enough to qualify as a *real* bulimic. An imposter, like I said.

I almost missed throwing up tonight because Mom wanted to linger after dinner, talk about what was going on at school. Apparently, all the parents know by now. I sat there quietly—engaging would've only prolonged the conversation and with each second that ticked by, more food was getting metabolized, which meant there'd be that much less left for me to vomit.

I finally ended the conversation by standing up and announcing, "Mike Parker's just an asshole. He had us all fooled, but there's no point in trying to make sense of it. Only an asshole would hit his girlfriend."

I walked away without adding what I was thinking, which was: *No self-respecting girl would stay with a guy who hit her.* I don't care how many times he apologizes or promises not to do it again or tells you he loves you. I may spend thirty minutes (twenty, fifteen, five—it varies) on my knees each night worshipping the porcelain god, so I'm not exactly an expert in self-respect, but even I know *that*.

ten

THE GIRLFRIEND

One of the few nice things about my parents having had a particularly contentious divorce is that they never want to talk to each other. Instead, they expect me to be the go-between.

Tell your mother…

Tell your father…

Your next visit…

Your last report card…

Actually, it isn't *usually* a nice thing. But now that there's something Mom knows that Dad doesn't know and I've decided I want to keep it that way, I'm newly grateful for their mutual animosity.

If my father knew about Mike, he might ask me why I didn't go to the police. I can practically hear his voice: *It's not a principal's job to deal with a criminal act.*

Then again, in the movies, principals are always breaking up fights between kids in the cafeteria, the gymnasium, the parking lot. Cut to the next scene and a couple of boys are on the bench outside the office; one has a bloody nose and the other a black eye. So maybe, it's exactly the sort of thing principals are used to.

Except maybe the principal gets involved because those sorts of incidents happened on the school grounds. That wouldn't apply here. Mike never hit me at school.

And in those situations, it's both kids fighting—I mean, maybe one of them started it and the other reacted—but me, I never fought back. Maybe I should have, but what would the point have been? Mike is nearly a foot taller than I am. He's an athlete. He can wrap his fingers around my upper arm like a very tight bracelet.

Plus, in those movie situations, it's usually two boys. Sometimes it's girls, but I've never seen a movie where it's a boy versus a girl. Unless the characters had superpowers or something.

My dad met Mike back when we were *just friends*, before the divorce, and Mike made enough of an impression that Dad remembered Mike when I said we were together. Not that I was all that excited to tell Dad I had a boyfriend, but he asked me over the phone once a couple months ago when we'd run out of things to talk about (grades, the weather, Mom's messiness) and there was an awkward silence: "What else is going on with you? Any beaux?" he said, like I was a Southern belle or something, and this was the 1930s, not the twenty-first century.

My dad isn't the kind of dad who would show up at Mike's

house with a baseball bat to break his car windows for hurting his daughter. You know, *If you ever lay another finger on my daughter, I'll kill you,* that kind of thing. He'd be mad, sure—he's not a terrible father or anything like that—but he'd probably be confused too. He'd wonder about how much Mike and I seem to love each other, how I light up whenever Mike's around. (We all went to dinner together when Dad visited last month, and that's what Dad said: "You light up around him.")

He'd ask me—like Mom asked me—how long it had been going on, and if I told him the truth, he'd ask why I waited so long to speak up. Don't people realize that question is a sort of accusation—*why didn't you speak up sooner? how could you keep quiet?*—like it's my fault for letting things go on as long as they did, go as far as they did.

Of course, Dad would support my decision to speak up, but he'd probably be sad for me too—not just that I'd been hurt, but that I was losing the boy who (he thought) made me happy. A boy I seemed to love. A boy I did love. Maybe Dad would be the one person who'd understand that was part of why I didn't say something sooner. Not because I was scared of what Mike might do—but because I wasn't ready to give Mike up.

Or maybe he'd think I was sick for wanting to keep a guy who hit me.

Anyway, Dad would ask why I didn't go to the police. Dad probably doesn't know how little the police can do, in circumstances like this. I looked it up last night and all they really do is issue a restraining order, but Mike and I go to the same school,

51

so how could that possibly work, like, mechanically? Anyway, that's not why I didn't go to the police. I didn't go to the police because going to the police seemed so much *bigger* than going to Principal Scott. Keeping matters within the school felt more manageable, more *contained*.

◇◇◇◇

When he hit me for the first time, I was startled but not surprised. Until that moment, I hadn't known it was possible to be startled but not surprised. *Startled* because being slapped is shocking, in and of itself; *unsurprised* because at the very moment it happened, I realized I knew it was coming.

We were in his room—his parents both worked, and we'd always felt lucky that we could be alone in his house after school each day. (My house was empty in the afternoons too, but Mike never wanted to go to my house.) His parents hadn't bothered to declare some rule like *No Girls in the House Unsupervised* because they knew they had no way of enforcing it. Mike's little brother, Ryan, has after-school activities scheduled every day of the week—Ryan goes to a series of occupational therapists and tutors—so Mike never even had to babysit.

Mike's room is on the second floor of his parents' house. He has an en suite bathroom, which meant a bathroom that was attached to his bedroom. Ryan's room is on the first floor, which means his bathroom is also the guest bathroom.

Mike and I were fully dressed, but we hadn't been a few

minutes earlier. The bag I'd filled with ice for his ankle was on the floor. Mike walked across the room normally. I guessed his ankle didn't hurt anymore, and I was relieved for him. He was getting ready to drive me home.

I remember all that, but I can't remember what I said, what he said, right before it happened. Did I ask about his ankle? Had we been arguing? Had I made him angry? I think there was a college basketball game on. Of course I rooted for Mike's favorite team.

I can't remember any of the details someone else would think was important: *What happened? Why did he get so upset?*

I hated that I couldn't remember. Maybe I could have stopped it from happening again, if only I'd remembered what made him do it.

It was a slap. It made my cheek burn, but it wasn't hard enough to leave a mark. (I wonder now: Did he do that on purpose? A slap is enough to shock you, even when it's not very hard. Did he think: *How can I make an impact without leaving a bruise?*)

I shook my head, not because I was trying to say *no* to Mike, but because I was saying *no* to what had happened: This couldn't happen to *me*, not with *Mike*, the perfect boy, the best boyfriend.

Should I have hit him back? It didn't occur to me to hit him back. Maybe if I hadn't been an only child—if I'd had a big sister or little brother that I'd grown up wrestling with—maybe then, my instinct would've been to fight back. Maybe that's what Mike used to do with Ryan—maybe that's what made him hit me, some muscle memory left over from horseplay with his little brother. But a slap isn't like wrestling and hair-pulling.

In my head, I narrated what happened next as though it were happening to someone else.

She started to cry.

He apologized before the first tear had time to fall as far as her chin.

He apologized but he didn't beg.

In movies and books, sometimes the man gets on his knees, pleads for forgiveness, promises it will never happen again—Mike didn't do that. Maybe if I'd been angrier—but I hadn't felt angry. All I felt at that moment was that I wanted to go home. And *Mike* was my ride home.

I could've called my best friend to come and get me, but then I'd have had to explain why Mike couldn't drive me, come up with some cover story: *Mike has to study, Mike's parents don't want him driving at this hour* (it wasn't even dinnertime yet). Nothing seemed like a good enough explanation. And a weak explanation would just invite more questions.

It never occurred to me to tell the truth. It would ruin Mike's reputation when it had only been a *fluke*, an *accident*, a *mistake*. Not that he said it was a *fluke*, an *accident*, a *mistake*. But what else could it be?

And, I knew that if I asked someone else for a ride home, I'd have to wait—first for that person to respond to my text, and then for that person to drive from wherever she was to Mike's house. There was no telling how long all that would take.

I remember wishing I had my own car, thinking how my mom said we couldn't afford it, but Dad had hinted he might give me one after graduation, and then wondering how Dad could afford it when Mom couldn't, and then wondering why I was thinking about any of that at all. Anyway, it wouldn't have mattered if I did have a car, because I wouldn't have driven myself to Mike's house. Ever since we had gotten together, Mike had driven me to school every morning in his gray hybrid SUV, he had driven me to his house after school was over or after track practice ended, and he had driven me home in time for dinner, before his parents got home.

She swallowed the lump in her throat and wiped away her tears.
She asked him to take her home.

He walked down the stairs two at a time. His steps were so heavy that the railing shook.

She followed behind slowly.

The stairs in Mike's house were carpeted with a plush, creamy rug. Mike's parents asked guests to take off their shoes before going upstairs, a request I always tried to remember even though Mike almost never did. I had to stop at the front door to put my shoes on. There was still a wreath on the front door, because Mike's mother hadn't taken down their Christmas decorations yet. I'd spent Christmas Day with Mike's family, and Mike gave me my first-ever Christmas present—a soft, warm scarf that I wound around my neck before stepping outside. My parents had always run out of presents by the fourth or fifth night of Hanukkah, and since the divorce, my mom didn't even bother lighting the candles.

The holidays with Mike's family were different: the scent of pine filled the house, and Mike's mother cooked a ham (I ate some to be polite; it was the first time I'd ever tasted pork), and he and his dad and Ryan tossed a football in the backyard. I felt like I was a guest star in an old black-and-white sitcom.

We were silent on the ride home. Mike turned on the radio, flipping until he found a song he liked the way he always did. It's a short drive, but it still gave me plenty of time to think. This was the first time he had hit me, but there'd been things before that—pinches and tugs and squeezes. That was all just playing, right?

But—then why hadn't I been surprised by the slap?

I didn't kiss him goodbye like I usually did when he dropped me off. I was proud of myself for that. Like I was teaching him a lesson.

But the next morning, he was waiting in the driveway to take me to school as usual and neither of us mentioned what had happened the day before. Maybe I'd imagined it. Everything was back to normal—Mike held my hand between classes, kissed my neck at the lunch table while everyone watched, ate half my sandwich off my plate. For a while, I managed to convince myself that it had just been a bad dream.

I know that's not what I was supposed to do. I was supposed to break up with him. To tell my parents. To at least not get in the car with him the next day. You're not supposed to love a guy who hit you. But it felt like it had been a dream. What if it had been a dream? You're not supposed to break up with a guy you love over a bad dream.

But then it happened again, and I never felt so wide awake.

Wednesday, April 12

eleven

THE BURNOUT

I let Hiram kiss me today. I'd like to say it was the first time, but it's been going on ever since I started knocking on his car window in January, even though I had a boyfriend, which I guess makes me a *slut* in some people's opinions.

Maybe even in my opinion, but I'm not going to think about that now.

Before that wet winter Thursday, I'd never actually spoken to Hiram. I knew who he was—it seemed like everyone knew who he was, like he'd been a fixture around the school forever even though he's only one year older than I am and he transferred to North Bay in his sophomore year. He showed up to class (sometimes) and to parties (all the time). He was the school loser, the school burnout, but he was always around for a good time.

It was raining that first time, not bright and clear like it is today. Knocking on his window was the sort of thing that would've scared me before. It was the sort of thing I would've asked my boyfriend to do for me, or at least I would've asked him to come with me while I did it. Or maybe it was actually the sort of thing I'd wait for my boyfriend to invite me to do with him. But this winter, things that used to scare me had started to seem a lot less frightening than they used to.

Now, with Hiram's arms around me on this bright sunny spring day, I know I *should* be worried that someone might see, someone walking to his or her own car, parked somewhere close by, even though Hiram's car is in the almost-empty far end of the parking lot. Someone could snap a photo, they could even live stream it for the whole world to see. What would my boyfriend do if he caught us together? Maybe he'd challenge Hiram to a fight, the way boys do sometimes, as though they were in prerevolutionary France and he was defending my honor in a duel.

But if I was worried about being caught, I wouldn't have ever gotten into Hiram's car to begin with. Just being there—here—at all is as scandalous as kissing him.

What kind of story could I come up with to explain what I'm doing here, kisses or no kisses? It's wrong to lie, but they'd believe me, if I told a good enough story.

Or anyway, they would've believed me *before*. With everything else going on, I'm not sure they'd believe me now. Maybe they'd think I was only saying it because of what was happening with Mike. Like that one accusation had started a snowball effect or something.

In between kisses, it occurs to me that the name Hiram is about as different a name from Mike as you can get.

Mike Parker.

Hiram—I almost stop kissing him when I realize that I don't know Hiram's last name.

Hiram is a good kisser. Better than you'd expect him to be. Or anyway, better than I'd expected him to be. Hiram isn't exactly traditionally handsome—another way he's different from a golden boy like Mike Parker—but I've always found him attractive, maybe because he doesn't seem to care about being traditionally handsome. He has a goatee—or is it a Vandyke, I can't remember what the difference is—but somehow it never tickles my chin. It's soft, silky, a few shades lighter than the almost black hair on top of his head. His lips are thin, but that makes his kisses gentle, tentative. With each kiss, it's like he's asking permission. Or maybe he's just trying to keep me interested by kissing me so that it feels as if I'm saying *yes, yes, yes,* over and over again.

In fact, when Hiram touches me, I can barely feel it. Not just because he's never, not once, been the one to slide my sweater off my shoulders or lift my shirt to my chest—come to think of it, was he the one who kissed me first or the other way around?—but because his touch on my skin is featherlight, cool and soft. I shiver.

"You cold?" Hiram asks. He keeps his lips so close that I can feel them move when he speaks.

"I'm okay."

"You sure?"

I nod, but he doesn't go back to kissing me until I say out loud, "I'm okay."

I hear the bell ring in the distance. Lunch is over. I have to get to class.

"I better go."

Hiram nods. "I'll be here," he says. He's never offered to drive me home after school, but I'm pretty sure he'd do it if I asked. I put on my jacket, and press my hands into the worn seat below me. It's upholstered in a gray fake-velvety material that must have been soft once, but is now spiky, as if someone spilled juice on it and never bothered to wash it properly, like I did once to one of my old stuffed animals. There's a burn mark below my left knee, maybe a remnant of some other girl who sat here. A girl who wasn't as careful as I am.

I get out of the car and close the door behind me. Before it slams shut, I hear Hiram say, "I would never hurt you, you know."

My back is to him so I'm not sure whether Hiram can see that I'm nodding in agreement.

Not all guys are like Mike Parker.

I know that.

Thursday, April 13

twelve

THE BULIMIC

At school today, I heard someone saying that maybe Mike's dad beat up his mom, like that would've explained everything, if Mike learned from example. They said of course that wouldn't excuse it (our student body prides itself on being sensitive and thoughtful, it's practically in the school catalog), but at least then we'd know *why* Mike did it. (*If* he did it. No one said it, but the words still hung in the air like a thought bubble in a cartoon.)

Then someone else chimed in, saying that in this day and age, if you don't know that you're not supposed to hit girls, "You're either an idiot or an asshole," and then the group laughed, as though being either an idiot or an asshole were a punch line.

Mike's not an idiot. When he took the SATs this fall, he practically announced his score at the next school assembly. He acted like he didn't mean to let it slip, and then he blushed and was all embarrassed about it, but come on—who lets something like that *slip*? I wanted to tell him that my score was higher. How would it have made him feel, being beaten (no pun intended) by a girl like me?

But I'm not the type of girl to pick a fight, to stir up drama, even when the people around me are saying idiotic things. Nobody likes a know-it-all.

But when someone hits you, you're not picking a fight. I know that much for sure. And if you hit back, that's self-defense, so it's not your fault, but it still might make things worse. Mike's so big and tall that if hitting him back made him angrier, a girl might find herself—or a guy might find himself, I don't want to be sexist—in even more trouble.

I read an article that said women should take pictures of every bruise and each red mark. That way when people ask how long it's been going on, how bad it was, how many times it happened—there's proof to back up the claims. Unless you don't want to get the guy in trouble, and what kind of girl doesn't want to get the guy in trouble?

Maybe the kind of girl who stays with a guy for three more months after the first time he hit her.

Anyway, I kept all these thoughts to myself. Like I said, I'm not the type of girl to pick a fight.

Now, I take out my earbuds and turn on my music as I walk through the school, so that I won't have to hear anyone else say something stupid. I still listen to breathy, moody folk songs like the ones my dad used to play when I was little and we went for long drives, just the two of us: Joni Mitchell, James Taylor,

Neil Young, Crosby Stills & Nash. (Right now Joni Mitchell is longing for a river to skate away on. She's not the only one.) I can still hear the chatter and hum from the kids around me, so I turn up the volume. I look at my feet, so no one has a chance to make eye contact.

Maybe I won't eat lunch today. I didn't eat breakfast, and it's already eleven and I'm not hungry. (The volume is loud enough now that I mostly only hear the sweet croon of Joni's voice.) Or, I could have a small lunch—if I can keep it under five hundred calories and then I don't eat until dinner, that'll be a good day. I mean, even if I eat a thousand calories at dinner, I'll throw up at least half of that, and then that'll be under one thousand calories for the whole day so I'll definitely lose weight.

Not that anyone is interested in seeing me naked anymore. If they ever really were. And no matter how much weight I lose, the area around my belly stays soft. Luckily it's cold enough today that I can layer a sweater over my T-shirt and call it fashion instead of camouflage.

A better feminist would say screw it. She'd bare her flabby belly for the world to see because love's not supposed to be about looks, and if a guy's only interested in a girl for her looks, then he's not worth her time. A better feminist would say that our bodies are meant to have soft spots, and a guy is lucky to see her naked no matter what her body looks like.

I mean, how can I claim to be such a good feminist when it comes to some jerk beating up his girlfriend when I'm such a bad feminist when it comes to body positivity?

I skip to another album. (One of Dad's favorite songs now, "Harvest Moon" by Neil Young.)

I'm sorry, but if there's a scale of what it takes to be a good feminist, I'm pretty sure that hating a guy for beating up his girlfriend counts for a whole lot more than embracing the circle of fat around your stomach.

No one would agree with me if I said this out loud, but: I think you could tell Mike was the kind of guy who'd hit a girl. When he talks to anyone shorter than he is—which is most people, and literally every girl in school—he always stands a little too close so that we have to crane our necks to look at his face, so it looks like we're asking him to kiss us, even when all we're asking for is to borrow a pencil. He's the kind of guy who has his hands all over his girlfriend when they're in public—sure, it looks like affection but maybe he just wants to make sure that everyone knows she belongs to him. And then there's the way he acts after every race he wins. He pretends to be modest, but you can tell that deep down he's thinking we should all personally thank him for deigning to be North Bay's best shot at finally winning a championship.

I heard some of the girls are planning a protest to call for Mike's expulsion. Maybe I'll go.

He hit a girl.

He's dangerous.

He shouldn't be at school with the rest of us.

Friday, April 14

thirteen

THE POPULAR GIRL

I did some research last night. Maybe I should have been curious about it sooner, but it didn't occur to me until last night to Google: *Why do men hit women?* Most of the data I found was about husbands who beat their wives, so it's not the same as what's going on here, but I read that most men who batter as adults were abused as children, or at least witnessed abuse when they were young. So they learn that violence is how to deal with strong emotions, even if those emotions are love and intimacy. In fact, men who beat their wives—according to one of the articles I read—are less likely to lash out at strangers. They beat their wives because, to them, it's part and parcel of a close relationship. They almost never admit that they've hit their partners, and they almost never see themselves as criminals.

Which means that maybe it's not Mike's fault. Like, maybe he wasn't doing it on purpose, and he wasn't doing it out of hate. I mean—I sound like Junie now—of course he has control over his actions, but maybe something happened to him that made him that way. Maybe he didn't want to do it, but he didn't know how to do anything else.

Like, maybe his dad beat his mom and *his* dad beat *his* mom and so on and so on and so on back to the very first male member of the Parker family, back when they still lived in the old country, which I think was Ireland, he told me once that his ancestors were Irish, even though Parker is technically an English last name (he told me that once too). But Mike's dad always seemed so nice. Then again, I heard his parents arguing when I was at Mike's house a few times, and even *my* parents didn't argue when we had guests.

Still, no matter how hard I try, I can't imagine Mr. Parker hitting Mike. I've seen him hugging Mike after a well-run race, praising him when he comes home with a good grade. (Then again, Mike always seemed like the perfect boyfriend, so maybe looks are deceiving.)

But if it's not a pattern Mike learned from his dad, then what explanation is left? Could Mike have been born this way—a little broken, a little bent, with some missing gene that made him a little more violent than most other people? Maybe he knew what he was doing was wrong, but he just couldn't stop himself because he didn't know how else to express himself.

Does that mean it wasn't his fault?

Can you be mad at someone for doing something awful when it isn't their fault?

Can you turn your back on them?

It's lunchtime on Friday afternoon, five days since Mike was accused. The rumors are swirling.

The protest's on Sunday.

Do you think he's still going to Big Night tomorrow? (Big Night is a North Bay tradition, the night before the track meet against our rival school, East Prep. Even the athletes who are running go, though they always leave early to get a good night's sleep before the races.)

Mike's going to be suspended.

He's going to be expelled.

He's definitely not eligible for that scholarship anymore.

His whole life is ruined.

Kids I've never spoken to come up to me in the hallways. They smile and try to look sensitive and sad, but inevitably they ask me to tell them what's really going on. Freshmen who would've been too intimidated to talk to me before ask all kinds of questions. It's hard not to think they're more interested in gossip than in expressing their concern. I wonder if people are peppering Mike (and Anil and Kyle) with questions too, but I haven't seen him, so I don't know. I know his schedule by heart, so it's easy to avoid being wherever he's most likely to be.

I've taken to listening to music in between classes to dissuade all the questions and drown out the chatter. Technically, we're not allowed to wear earbuds or headphones in the halls, but no one on the faculty is going to scold me, given the circumstances.

Every time anyone asks, I answer, "I'd rather not talk about it." They look so disappointed, like they're entitled to know what's going on. Some of the questioners are underclassmen who always showed up to cheer for Mike at his track meets even though he didn't know their names. I wonder if they're still rooting for Mike.

For what it's worth, *I'd rather not talk about it* happens to be the truth.

But I guess when you're caught up in this kind of scandal, you become public property, somehow, like how the paparazzi ask celebrities for details about their divorces because the rest of the world feels entitled to know.

I turn up the volume of my music a little louder.

Anil and Kyle are a few steps ahead of me in the hallway, headed for the south exit, for our lunch table. No one stops to ask them questions.

They don't know I'm behind them. Or if they do, they're ignoring me.

I keep my gaze focused on my steps, refusing to engage with any of the kids who want to shoot me smiles and ask me questions.

Junie comes up from behind me. I jump when she links her arm through mine. Gently, she pulls out my earbuds.

"It's just me," she whispers.

I look down at her arm against mine. Would it be easier or harder to hide a purple bruise on darker skin? I'm always pale. At best, I get a little bit freckly in the sun; at worst, bright pink.

"Come on." Junie tugs me toward the south exit. Our table is right on the other side of the door. Her eyes are open wide, and there's just a thin ring of green around her pupils. "I mean, we've been sitting there as long as they have, right?"

I realize that other than the one day we spent in the library together this week, I don't know where Junie's been eating lunch since Monday. Has she been sitting with the boys—with Mike? Mike was actually her first kiss back when we were in eighth grade, though she said it didn't count because it was only a dare, in front of everyone, and she didn't like him like *that* anyway. No one but me knew that she'd never kissed anyone before, not even Mike. Junie made me promise not to tell, so I never did.

When we step outside, the sun's so bright that I see spots.

"I mean," Junie adds, "we have just as much right to that table as the boys do, right?"

She makes it sound like Mike's going through a divorce, and the table is the child over which he's fighting for joint custody.

I disentangle my arm from hers. I don't care if I've already missed lunch every day this week. I'm not going anywhere near that table.

fourteen

THE GIRLFRIEND

For the record, he never punched me. The eye—faded now, almost a week later, to a sort of yellow-gray—makes it look like he did, but this bruise is the result of a slap. A harder slap than the first one.

And he rarely actually *hit* me. In fact, that only happened twice. It was more grabbing and pushing and pulling. Before that first slap, I didn't consider those sorts of touches *bad*, even when they hurt. Maybe he didn't know his own strength. Maybe it was passion. I didn't mind when it hurt like that (did I?) because he was pulling me closer, holding me tighter, kissing me harder.

It's funny now (is it?) because even back then, I wouldn't have described Mike as either passionate or careless. He's methodical, the most meticulous person I've ever met. Take running track: He didn't simply *burst* from his crouch into a sprint. I mean, he did during an actual race but prior to each meet, he'd practice, one step at a time.

Settling into his crouch, the tips of his fingers pressing into the track, just behind the starting line.

Lifting his hips into the air.

His first step—he'd tried it both left-footed and right-footed, and even though he was a righty, he clocked in faster (I was the one timing him after school, even on the days when the team didn't have practice scheduled) when he started with his left foot first.

Even when he won a race, his celebrations were thoughtful— he'd throw his arms overhead but almost immediately drop them. He'd turn around and shake the hands of the runners who came in second, third, fourth. The rest of the school would be cheering for him, but he didn't run around in circles relishing his triumph. When I'd run down from the stands to congratulate him, he wouldn't throw his arms around me in excitement. Instead, he gave me a quick hug, a peck on the cheek. He wasn't thinking about me. He wasn't even thinking about his win. He was already thinking about the next race.

Every move was intentional. Each step a decision he'd made.

The way he asked me out, *officially*, rather than waiting until we were at the same party and hoping that something might happen the way most other guys would.

The way he parked down the street from my house, so we could make out after our third date without my mother seeing it.

Maybe even the way he slapped me that first time, not hard enough to leave a bruise.

After that evening in January, like I said, I thought maybe it wouldn't happen again. And it didn't—at least, not like that—until the slap last Saturday. He went back to the other, smaller hurts: the pushes and pulls, the grip that was just a little too tight. Those hurts were gray, instead of black and white.

For a while, I was able to ignore (or pretend to ignore) those smaller hurts. But after Valentine's Day, it became impossible to pretend they weren't on purpose.

Mike does everything *on purpose*.

Of course, we spent Valentine's Day together. It was the very first time I'd had a real date on Valentine's Day, and I was so excited. I borrowed a red tank top from my best friend, but I had to wear a sweater over it because there were three bruises on my left upper arm, fingerprints from where Mike had grabbed me.

I told myself it didn't matter because it was cold outside. I would've worn a sweater anyway.

Later, when Mike undressed me, I figured he'd ignore the bruises. But instead, he kissed them methodically, one at a time, pressing his lips so hard against my skin the way another boy might kiss a tattoo you'd gotten, his name etched into your flesh.

"I love you." He went on kissing me. He even *kissed* carefully, as though he'd read a manual about where girls like to be kissed: beneath their earlobes, in the hollow of their throats, their eyelids.

"I love you too," I answered, and it was true. I loved the way it felt when he kissed me and when he held my hand. I loved how it felt to walk down the street with him, how it looked when I got into his car. I loved the way he drove: one hand on the wheel, one hand on my knee.

I'm supposed to hate him. I'm supposed to hate him because he hurt me. The problem is, I can hate him for hurting me and still love him for the way things were when he didn't hurt me.

It was nothing like it was in books or in the movies: the boyfriend who lost control in a fit of passion. He never asked me not to tell, never begged me to keep his dark secret.

I can't decide whether that would have been more or less frightening.

The thing is, I wasn't scared of him. Is that stupid? I didn't think he'd ever hurt me badly enough to do any real damage. He was too careful for that.

So methodical, so careful: Does that mean he intended to leave a bruise when he hit me on Saturday? Of course, he couldn't have been sure exactly how hard a slap would need to be, that depends on *me*, on whether or not I bruised easily (like a peach), on how much iron I'd eaten in the prior few days, on how much water I'd had to drink.

Not everything was in his control.

Maybe another girl would've hit him back. Maybe another girl would've told right away—after that very first hit, the day he rolled his ankle on the track. Maybe another girl would've told even sooner than that, would've recognized the tugs and pinches and pulls for what they really were, instead of excusing them as passionate affection. *That* girl wouldn't have fallen in

79

love with Mike. Or at least, she would've fallen out of love with him months ago. But *this* girl—me—I let it go on for months.

According to the rumor mill, a group of students is planning to call for Mike's expulsion before Sunday's track meet. He could lose his chance at a scholarship. He might never run competitively again.

Was that what I was hoping for when I went to Principal Scott on Monday?

Maybe I should have waited until after the season was over. Until after his scholarship had been awarded.

After all, I'd waited this long. Why couldn't I have waited a little bit longer?

But I wasn't thinking about any of that when I walked into Principal Scott's office.

I was only thinking one thing:

I wanted it to stop.

fifteen

THE BURNOUT

I walk straight past the table where the popular kids sit. I keep my gaze focused on Hiram's car at the far end of the lot, concentrating on the relief that lies waiting inside.

I've never smoked anywhere but inside his car. I guess that might look like it's a power thing, that *he* controls my access. But in fact, that's *my* way of controlling my access. I'm pretty sure Hiram would give me whatever I asked for. But I've *chosen* not to ask.

I walk as fast as I can without actually running. Everyone would look at me if I ran, and I need to blend into the crowd so no one will see where I'm headed. I feel like a little kid playing tag: *It* is right behind me and I have to hurry to make it to the safe zone where *it* can't get me.

I look at my feet, at the brand-new pair of sneakers I ordered on Monday night. I paid extra for two-day delivery even though that's the sort of thing my dad calls a waste of money.

But I needed the new shoes, and when they turned out to be a little too big, I wore them anyway. I'd already thrown my old sneakers away.

I feel *his* gaze on my back. No, that's ridiculous. A person can't feel another person's gaze. That's the sort of thing people say in romance novels and bad movies. But still, I can tell he's there, somewhere behind me. I look up—across the parking lot—and see Hiram getting out of his car. I can't remember the last time I saw him outside of his car, and he looks shorter than I remembered. Maybe only a few inches taller than I am.

There's a crowd, but I'm not blending into it. I'm at the center of it. I start to run. They're already looking at me, so what difference does it make?

Up ahead, Hiram opens his mouth, but no sound comes out. Or really, I'm too far away to hear him. Instead, I hear another voice, this one coming from behind me. I hear his footsteps hurrying to catch up with me: his enormous feet, his long strides, his fast pace. I stop running.

I could never outrun him.

There would be no point in trying.

sixteen

THE BURNOUT
THE BULIMIC
THE POPULAR GIRL
THE GIRLFRIEND

"Maya," he says. He doesn't raise his voice. He knows I can hear him.

I turn around.

the girls

PART TWO

Monday, April 10

one

THE ANXIOUS GIRL

She's going to end it.

I'm sure of it.

I can tell.

Okay, so yes, I think she's about to break up with me all the time. Especially at night. In bed. When I can't sleep. Like now. Maybe in the morning I'll feel fine.

Or maybe this time is different. Maybe this time it's not just my imagination, maybe this time she *really* didn't respond to my good-night text as quickly as she used to. And when she did respond, her answer was so short: *Good night.* No *baby*, no *love you*, no *sleep tight, don't let the bedbugs bite.*

And it's not just the latest text, I think as I roll over and adjust the covers (again), trying and failing to keep my eyes closed, to slow my breath, to drift closer to sleep. It's after midnight. I have to get up in six and a half hours. If I sleep through my alarm (again), I'll be late (again). Anyhow, I swear, Tess doesn't initiate the conversation as much as I do. Or our plans. It's always me:

Tess, how about dinner on Saturday?

Tess, I missed you at lunch today. (We never eat lunch together at school.)

(But maybe if I'd been the kind of girl who sat with her girlfriend at lunch Tess wouldn't be about to end it now.)

Tess, you looked so beautiful after your run this afternoon. (Tess is on the track team at school.)

Tess—

Tess—

Tess—

The minutes tick by, and now it's only six hours till my alarm goes off. I mean, who invented the notion that we *drift* off to sleep anyway? Falling asleep is hard work. It takes effort. It takes concentration.

And I *can't* concentrate on sleeping now because all I *can* think about is Tess.

I'd had a crush on her for ages before we finally kissed, at a party one night. She has this perfect skin (I don't think she's ever had a single zit), and an Afro that makes her look about three inches taller than she actually is, which, at five ten, is already much, much taller than I am. (I'm barely five feet tall. And my stick-straight brown hair, cut bluntly just below my chin, definitely doesn't add to my height.)

I can't stop imagining how she might end it. Where she'll do it. When. The words she'll use. No one's ever broken up with me before—no one's ever *been* with me before—so my imagination is limited to the phrases I've heard on TV shows and read in magazine articles.

Before track practice on a Monday afternoon. (*This* afternoon.) *It's not you, it's me.*

After school on Wednesday. *I need space.*

Before school on Friday. *I've fallen for someone else.*

Thinking about it makes my hands shake, so I try to think about anything else: our first kiss, our first real date (which came after the first kiss), the first time we held hands (which came after our first date), the first time she called me baby (which came after the hand-holding), the first time we said *I love you* (which came after calling me baby).

Maybe we did everything backward. I wish we could do it all over again, in order this time: first the date, and then the hand-holding, and then the kiss, and *then* the love, *then* the sweet nicknames.

But thinking about doing it over again makes me think about what went wrong, which makes me think about the inevitable breakup, which makes my hands shake all over again. There's only one thing that could make them keep still, and I'm not allowed to do *that* anymore.

That hadn't always been a problem—it only started a few months ago—but I've never been, let's say, easygoing. Never been the kind of girl who doesn't care what everyone else thinks.

Actually, I obsess (that's the right word, I have a diagnosis and everything) over what everyone else thinks. Every night—not just tonight—I lie awake, going over every single word I said that day (and lucky for me, I have a really good memory so I can usually remember exactly what was said), wondering whom I might have offended, what I might have done wrong, what terrible thing will come back to haunt me, ruin my reputation, or somehow get to the admissions officers at Stanford even though there are still nine months before I'm going to apply.

I'm the type of girl who sits at our table during lunch glancing carefully at every adjacent table to see if anyone is staring, wondering what they know that I don't, certain that they're talking about me, thinking about me, laughing at me, and sharing inside jokes and secret handshakes (the metaphorical kind, not the literal kind) that I'll never understand.

Dr. Kreiter told me that the way my hands tremble is a warning sign. Like how my mom sees spots when she has a migraine coming on. It's called the aura.

After our first session, Dr. Kreiter wanted to prescribe me antianxiety medication (diagnosis: *generalized anxiety and obsessive-compulsive disorders, self-harm*), but I begged my parents to let me try to handle my problems without pills. They agreed to a three-month trial: three months, no incidents, no need for meds.

Dr. Kreiter said I'd been hurting myself to help calm my anxiety, like a coping mechanism. To Dad, coping mechanisms are finding ways to take action when injustice makes you feel powerless, or practicing yoga each morning, and meditating each night. Dad's coping mechanisms are much more socially and medically acceptable than mine. But Dad doesn't have an anxiety *disorder*, so maybe that's why he doesn't have a disordered way of dealing with his stress.

Dr. Kreiter said we were lucky to have caught the self-harm—that's what she calls it, I call it cutting—early, to which Mom reasonably (that's Mom, always reasonable) pointed out that I'd hurt myself badly enough to need hospitalization, which didn't strike her as early. But Dr. Kreiter said that the behavior had gone on only for *months* before I began therapy. She said that some of her patients had been hurting themselves for *years* before they sought help. I was tempted to point out that I hadn't exactly sought help—I mean, I'd gone to the ER to get stitched up, which I guess is a kind of seeking help. But I hadn't asked to be put in therapy.

Dr. Kreiter didn't like the three-month deal I made with my parents. She pointed out that the incidents weren't the result of a lack of willpower. (My other symptoms included insomnia, increased heart rate, an inability to get places on time, biting my nails, and of course trembling like a Chihuahua.)

The doctor suggested that setting high standards and goals was part of what had gotten us into this situation in the first place.

I said that I found goals motivating, had all my life.

She said this wasn't a homework assignment, wasn't the sort of thing I should be rewarded or punished for. That an arrangement like this would keep us from delving deep into the reasons I'd started cutting in the first place.

I said, wasn't the point of therapy to get me to stop cutting?

She countered that the incidents had been going on for

months before my parents found out about them. What was to keep me from hiding them again?

I said: "If it happens again, I'll come clean right away."

I knew it would work because my dad's big on the honor code.

Dr. Kreiter said we'd caught the self-harm early, but she didn't say the same about my anxiety. I know my parents bristled at the implication that a doctor had recognized something almost the moment she met me that they might have missed for months or even years. I think it's part of what made them agree to my three-month deal, like if it worked, then they'd prove to the doctor that they knew me better than she did, knew I liked goals and wouldn't lie about whether or not I met them.

Anyway, I was confident the three-month deal would be effective. I'd had goals (though Dr. Kreiter called them *rituals*) when it came to cutting even before the doctor entered the picture: I wasn't allowed to cut anywhere but in the bathroom at night with my trusty razor blade, and only after I'd finished the day's homework, no matter how hard my hands might shake at school, no matter how hard they might shake sitting at the desk in my room as I struggled with the night's physics assignment. After each cut, I washed the blade with a cotton ball soaked in alcohol and blotted up the mess with tissues and toilet paper.

I made the rules, and I stuck to them. (Except for the occasional emergency.) It was part of how I knew that my problem wasn't really that serious, because I was able to contain it. (For the most part.) So I was certain I'd be able to stick to this new set of rules: No cutting for three months. I was confident I'd hit my goal and then even surpass it, because hitting goals and surpassing them was something I knew how to do. Or try to do.

After I was diagnosed, Dad told Dr. Kreiter that he'd raised me to care about the world, and the state of the world these days was enough to give anyone anxiety. He said he'd had sleepless nights too. He said he'd looked for unconventional ways to relieve the pressure too. (By which he meant new types of yoga and meditation.)

"It's only natural," he said. "It's a difficult time for so many of us."

I think Dr. Kreiter didn't expect my progressive, understanding parents to agree to a deal like the three-month trial, but I could've told her that my dad sees things in black and white. Good versus bad. A's versus F's. Acceptance versus rejection. Cutting versus not cutting.

Dad said: "You don't know my little girl like I do. She won't let me down."

It's been a month and a half.

I've made it halfway to my goal without an incident.

I've been okay, for the most part.

I mean, okay for *me*.

two

THE ACTIVIST

My parents are very supportive. They pride themselves on being allies. Once, when a colleague of Dad's came over for dinner and I mentioned my girlfriend, he said something about my sexuality being some kind of trend. It was so insulting. So *dismissive*. Like I'd grow out of who I am.

This led to one of my bigger speeches: about judging someone based on her age, based on how she looks, based on where she comes from. About foolish, cruel, and antiquated stereotypes.

Dad didn't stop me, didn't say anything about being rude to his important guest.

I literally stood up from my chair, my fork still in my hand.

The guy held up his hands, admitting defeat. "I didn't mean anything by it," he protested.

I shook my head. Of *course* he meant something by it. Everyone means something by everything they say. When you claim that you didn't "mean anything by it," you're really trying to free yourself from the responsibility of having said something rude. Like when people say "no offense" before saying something absurdly offensive.

"Don't say *sheesh* like I'm overreacting. I'm just reacting."

Across the table, I could see Dad trying not to smile. He was pleased with my outburst. He's the one who taught me to argue. He's always liked picking fights with me—he likes having a sparring partner. He takes credit for how strong my opinions are because he's the one who instilled them to begin with. He wants me to be a human rights attorney one day, just like him. He started training me to argue when I was a little kid, using the sort of stuff that little kids believe but are totally wrong about because they can't yet conceive of the real explanations. One of my earliest memories is the time he held a flashlight and told me that I wasn't fast enough to beat the beam of light from one end of the room to the other.

"Ready," he began. "Set." He held up the light, his finger over the button that would turn it on. I screwed up my face, ready to run as fast as I could. How could that silly little flashlight be faster than I was? I was so sure I'd win.

"Go!"

Of course, I lost. And he used the opportunity to teach me about the speed of light.

Dad likes to turn everything into a Lesson with a capital *L*.

three

THE COOL GIRL

Tess finds me in the hallway at school on Monday. (I'm late to homeroom. A few weeks ago my parents had a long conversation with my homeroom teacher—apparently I was one *tardy* away from detention—but now Mrs. Frosch doesn't mark me as late anymore. She understands that I'm *trying* to get to school on time. A for effort and all that. It's not like I *want* to be late. I always end up with the crappiest spot in the student parking lot. Well, second-crappiest. Hiram Bingham's spot is even worse.)

At the time, Tess was amazed that I avoided detention. "You can get away with murder!" she'd shouted, impressed.

I shrugged like it was no big deal, like cool things happened to me all the time. I wasn't about to tell her the real reason: my obsessive-compulsive disorder.

"That's ridiculous," I protested when Dr. Kreiter insisted that

OCD was part of my diagnosis. "OCD would make me get to places *early*, not late."

Dr. Kreiter explained that OCD can manifest in different ways, and while it's come to mean one thing in the pop-culture lexicon—being organized and neat and prompt, none of which I was—it can also make a person habitually late and unable to manage her time or responsibilities.

Lucky for me, those symptoms make me look cool and carefree. Tess has never suspected a thing.

Now, Tess runs down the hall toward me as the bell rings for first period. (Apparently, I missed homeroom entirely.) I watch her hair bounce with each step. "I can't believe you didn't tell me. Of course, I understand, but we said no secrets. Though maybe you didn't think it was *your* secret to keep?"

"What are you talking about?"

Tess rolls her eyes. "Don't play dumb. There's no use trying to keep it quiet anymore."

Oh, god. Someone must've found out about my cutting and my multiple diagnoses. And of course, that someone told Tess. And now Tess is furious at me for keeping such a huge secret from her. By the end of the day, the whole school will know.

I ball my hands into fists. Dr. Kreiter would say I'm *spiraling*, making assumptions without actual evidence.

I wish I could simply ask Tess what she's talking about, but that would sound needy, and I want to sound aloof. So I unclench my fists, fold my arms across my chest, and say, "If I'm dumb, believe me I'm not doing it on purpose."

Tess responds by folding her arms across *her* chest. She's flat-chested (unlike me) and her arms are so long she can twist them over each other and still fit them around her neck. (It's hard to explain, but it's a cool party trick.) She's wearing a black sleeveless shirt with a high crewneck (the sort of shirt that would look terrible on my shorter, curvier frame). She blinks her big brown eyes. She never leaves the house without a coat of mascara.

"You really don't know?" I watch her long lashes when she blinks.

"Don't know what?"

She shakes her head. "I guess she kept it a secret from everyone."

The bell rings again. Last call for first period. I can't miss homeroom and also be late to first period. My parents' deal with Mrs. Frosch doesn't extend to me missing class.

"I gotta go," I say, pretending I don't want to stay here and talk to her. "Text me."

Tess shakes her head again. "It's not the kind of thing you text about."

I stand on my tiptoes to kiss her on the cheek (so carefree, so easygoing). Some guy wolf whistles, and I roll my eyes (immature idiots like him don't bother cool girls like me), and book it to chem lab before Tess can say another word.

The first time Tess told me she loved me, it was via text, so whatever Tess is talking about, it must be bad—breakup bad, I mean—if Tess thinks it's *not the kind of thing you text about*. If I were actually cool instead of just pretending to be, I'd break up with Tess before she has the chance to break up with me. But I won't, because I'm not.

In physics class, Mr. Chapnick surprises us with a pop quiz. (Hooray.) The classroom is so silent that everyone hears it when my phone vibrates with one text message, then another, then another.

"What is that racket?" Mr. Chapnick finally explodes.

I lean down to pull my phone out of my backpack. "I'll turn it to silent," I offer. Mr. Chapnick grabs my phone out of my hands before I can even glance at the screen. "Off until the end of class," he says, powering my phone down. My classmates giggle. A few of the boys wink at me, like they're impressed with my nerve—texting during class is strictly against the rules.

I wink back. Can't let them see I'm mortified.

◇◇◇◇

When I finally get my phone back after class, I'm surprised to discover that in addition to two *Call me, we have to talk* texts from Tess (is this her way of building up to the breakup?), there's also a message from my mother.

Call me when you have a minute, sweetie.

Crap. Mrs. Frosch must have called when I wasn't just late but completely absent from homeroom this morning. Even OCD can't get me out of detention now.

I wonder what detention will be like. (I've never actually been in detention before.) Maybe it'll be like it is in the movies, and

I'll bond with kids I barely know and we'll dance and get high (surely Hiram Bingham will be there, he must have a permanent place in detention), and fall in love and learn something about ourselves.

Or maybe we'll just sit there without our phones or laptops, bored out of our minds, getting a head start on the next day's homework because we don't have anything better to do.

I don't call Mom. Mr. Chapnick made me stay late so he could lecture me about phone etiquette, and if I don't hurry, I'm going to be late (again) to my next class, European history. I actually like European history (unlike physics) and Ms. Smit actually likes me (unlike Mr. Chapnick), so I don't want to get on her bad side.

I need all the allies I can get, especially if I'm about to lose Mrs. Frosch.

The bell rings. Last call for second period. I'll have to call Mom during lunch.

four

THE ANXIOUS GIRL

After fourth period, I gather my books and head toward our usual lunch table.

I've been sitting with the same group of friends since freshman year. We probably don't have that much in common anymore, but no one ever suggested a change in our routine.

And that routine makes it easier to avoid Tess and the terrible news she has to share with me.

Seriously, what else but a breakup would be *not the kind of thing you text about*?

But… she wouldn't just squeeze it in between classes, would she?

After school makes more sense. It would give us time to talk it out.

But maybe not, because it's only Monday and she might not want to start the week off badly. Maybe she'll wait until

Friday, and I'll have the weekend to wallow over it. She can't do it on Saturday because she wouldn't do it before Big Night (our school's annual blowout), and anyway she has a track meet Sunday and she wouldn't want the distraction. Which brings us to next Monday, and if she was going to do it *next* Monday, she may as well do it *today*.

My hands are shaking. I ball them into fists like I did this morning, but that only makes them itch.

Everyone stares at me as I walk down the hall. (Dr. Kreiter says that's my imagination. She says no one is staring at me. She says, *People are never thinking about you as much as you think they do.*) But what about the boys who make kissy noises at Tess and me when we walk down the halls holding hands, or the jerk who whistled at us earlier?

Every time it happens, I roll my eyes like it's no big deal. Sometimes, I even call the gross boys out. But later, at night, in bed, trying and failing to sleep… It's like I can still hear them. And sometimes it makes me wonder what it would be like to be straight, because maybe then those boys wouldn't look at me.

Then again, maybe they'd find another reason to stare. Even before I came out, I was sure people were looking at me. (Dr. Kreiter would say that was my imagination too.)

And my dad's colleague. I stood up to him with aplomb—I really did!—and Dad was so proud. But that didn't keep me from worrying that I might have gotten my father into trouble. Of course, Dad would say he didn't care because I'd been right to stand up for myself—but what if he lost his job? Dad would say it was more important to be right than employed. He'd say he wouldn't want to work for a man who fired him over something like that anyhow. But what if he couldn't afford to pay my tuition, or our mortgage, or to put food on the table?

I pull my phone from my back pocket to text my best friend— **hey wanna ditch lunch and chat?**—even though I know she only skips lunch to study. Maybe I can convince her to make an exception, just this once. But I hear Tess's voice calling my name before I can type a word. I tuck my phone back into my pocket.

"Eat lunch with me today," she says.

We agreed weeks ago that we were *not* going to be the kind of girls who blow off their friends the instant they're in a relationship. My best friend started canceling our plans literally the day after she and her boyfriend got together. (She didn't even always cancel them, sometimes she simply didn't show up.) So no matter how much I might have wanted to spend every spare second with Tess, I forced myself to eat lunch with the same crowd as always. Why would Tess suggest making a change now?

Unless she really is planning to fit the breakup in between classes.

I shake my head, shove my hands in my pockets, and tell her, "I can't."

I expect her to tell me that of course I can, there's no rule that says I can't sit at another table just this once, but much to my surprise, she nods and says, "I understand."

She must feel sorry for me. She says, "I never know what the right thing to say is at times like this."

The words come out before I can stop them. "So don't say anything. Please." I hate that I sound like I'm begging. Was it really just this morning that I managed to play it cool?

Tess shakes her head. "I have to say something. I have to *do* something. *We* have to do something, you know?"

I nod. Maybe that's the kind of thing people say to make a breakup sound less one-sided.

Tess says, "Could you just tell her—I don't know. Tell her I'm thinking about her, I guess."

Tell who? Tell *me*? Is she talking about me in the third person? Will that make it easier to dump me?

Tess leans in to kiss me. I'm so startled that I pull away before our lips touch. Who kisses the girl she's breaking up with?

"I've gotta go," I say, setting off down the hall. "The guys are waiting at our table."

Tess follows me, the look on her face shifting from sympathetic to angry. "You're going to sit with them?"

I shrug. "I always sit with them."

"But I thought *today*—" She shakes her head. "I can't believe this." She looks so disgusted that I freeze in my tracks.

"Believe what?"

"You're not actually taking *his* side, are you?"

"What are you talking about?" I ask, utterly confused.

"Oh, I get it." She folds her long arms across her chest. "You're going to play it like, *Innocent until proven guilty, it's her word against his, there's no evidence*—as if *she* isn't evidence! How can you do that to her?"

106

"How can I do what to whom?" I stuff my hands even deeper into my pockets, hoping she can't see them shaking through my jeans. I want this moment to end. I want to make it outside and to our table, where I can sit down and let the guys do the talking. They're loud enough that no one will hear how hard my heart is pounding.

"I heard it had been going on for a while," Tess spits. "You know, if you were any kind of a friend, you'd have figured it out months ago. There *must* have been signs."

Everyone in the hallway has stopped to look at us. At *me*. I'm not just being paranoid like Dr. Kreiter says. This isn't me spiraling—they really are staring now.

"I've gotta go," I manage. My voice sounds small. Thin. Weak.

"I don't even feel like I know you anymore." Tess shakes her head. "It's over."

Oh, god, I can't believe it's actually happening here. Now. In the middle of school. With everyone staring at us. In the made-up scenarios that dance around my imagination, I never pictured anything this awful.

"You're not going to say anything?" Tess asks. She doesn't know how hard I'm working to keep my jaw still, trying to keep my teeth from chattering.

So I stand there silently while Tess turns around and walks away.

◇◇◇◇

My pulse is so fast, it doesn't feel like a beat at all. It's more like an endless, deafening hum.

Count backward from one hundred, I tell myself. (That's what Dr. Kreiter suggested once. She also suggested squeezing an ice cube to mimic the discomfort of cutting, using a marker to doodle on the part of my body I want to cut, ripping up paper into tiny pieces, or eating sour food. But the only one of her ideas I've tried is the counting backward one because it's the only one that doesn't require a prop.)

I dig my fingers deep into the pockets of my jeans. Through the material, I can feel my nails against my skin. I've only ever cut on my upper thighs, where no one will see. With Tess, I undressed in the dark, dove under the covers immediately, so my scars would stay as invisible as possible.

At least I don't have to worry about that anymore.

I'm supposed to go to the nurse's office if I feel the urge, that was part of the deal. But the nurse would call my mom, and Mom would call Dr. Kreiter, and Dr. Kreiter would insist on scheduling an emergency session. She'd bring up medication again, group therapy. Dad would be disappointed that I wasn't able to hold up my end of the deal after all. I'd let him down, just like I did when I got an eighty-nine on my physics test last semester. (Eighty-nine is the cut off between an A-minus and a B-plus, and people who get B-pluses do not get into Stanford.)

I run across the parking lot until I get to my car. I manage to open the door and slam it shut behind me.

My trembling hands reach toward the glove compartment of

their own volition. I feel—as I always did (do?) before cutting—like an outsider floating above my body, watching what's happening. Dr. Kreiter calls it a trance.

I used to keep an extra razor blade in the car for emergencies, but I threw it away because my parents asked me to get rid of anything I used to cut, and I promised I would. (That was part of the deal.)

I open the glove compartment. The instructions that came with the car when my parents leased it for me are stuffed in there, along with some tissues, a granola bar, my registration, and god knows what else. I dig through it all until I find the mirror. It's tucked into a bright yellow compact with blush on one side, even though I never wear blush.

When Mom first found out about the cutting, she acted like she wanted to get rid of every sharp object in the house: every razor blade, every steak knife and butter knife, and each pair of scissors. She said she didn't want anything to trigger me. I considered suggesting that she redecorate the bathroom, since I'd (mostly) only cut in there, and the familiar surroundings might trigger me even more than knives and scissors (which I'd never used for cutting), but in the end I kept the thought to myself.

Eventually, Dad pointed out the impracticality of getting rid of everything sharp. Plus, I'd never cut myself with anything but an old-fashioned razor blade, and I'd tossed those like I promised. So I'm allowed to cut my own food and (after a few weeks) to shave my legs. Honor code and all that.

The very first time was in December. End-of-semester finals.

And the SATs were only months away. I needed to study all weekend. Dad was planning a demonstration (immigrants' rights) in the city, and he was disappointed that I couldn't come. Home alone while he and Mom were out protesting, I was full of nervous energy. I felt guilty that I hadn't gone with my parents. After hours of studying, the words were swimming on the pages and screens in front of me, but I had to keep going, to justify staying home. But I couldn't concentrate on *anything*. I even tried to take a break, but I couldn't sit still long enough to read or watch TV. My heart beat so fast, it felt like a bird in a cage that thought if it beat its wings hard enough, it would take flight, cage and all. My hands shook so hard that it felt like I was bursting with energy waiting to be set free.

So I walked into the bathroom off my parents' bedroom. I took one of Dad's old-fashioned razor blades from the medicine cabinet. He inserts a fresh blade into a shiny chrome safety razor each month. He says it's the only way to get a properly close shave. I brought the razor blade back to my room. I'd seen characters on TV do this, read about it in books. Even though I was home alone, I shut the door. I pulled down my pants and made a tiny cut on my inner thigh.

And I felt better.

It was a relief, like all that energy finally had a way to escape. My heart stopped racing, my hands stilled. I had one thing—the pain—to focus on, and suddenly it was easy to concentrate on that, and only that.

That makes it sound so much simpler than it was. The truth is, it wasn't that easy to cut myself. At least, not the first time. I was surprised by how hard I had to press, by how my skin resisted. I thought of all the times I'd cut myself accidentally: paper cuts and slipped knives and poorly shaved legs. It had never seemed difficult. If anything, it had been all too easy before. But I was patient, and eventually I pressed hard enough that my skin gave way. I thought about surgeons—surely they don't hesitate before making a cut.

I wasn't scared when I saw the blood. It didn't even startle me, the dark red against my skin. You know in the movies when some character is freaking out, and another character slaps them across the face, and then the first character feels better? It was like that. The cutting calmed me down.

Later, I rubbed Neosporin over the cut and covered it with a Band-Aid. I cleaned the blade with rubbing alcohol and slid it beneath my mattress. The cut was so shallow that it had already stopped bleeding, and probably wouldn't leave a scar, but better safe than sorry. The next day, I bought myself a fresh tube of Neosporin at the pharmacy, a bottle of rubbing alcohol, and a bag full of cotton balls. I used each item every time I cut. I even bought a second set of supplies, including an extra blade, to keep in my car's glove compartment.

Now, I open the car door and drop the compact on the ground, hard. I can hear the glass shatter. Mom once told me that a cracked mirror means seven years of bad luck.

I'm not sure my luck can get any worse.

I've never cut with anything but a blade, never gazed longingly at sharp objects, wondering what would be able to pierce my skin.

But desperate times call for desperate measures.

Just knowing what's coming makes me calmer. I stop trembling, and my heartbeat slows. I bend down to pick up the mirror.

Where will I cut? I could unbutton my pants and nick my upper thigh, but in the car it would be easier to lift my shirt and cut my belly, maybe just below my waistband. But then the band might rub against the cut all afternoon, which might become a problem if it bled into my shirt (my tee is white today) and someone saw.

Hiram Bingham's ugly brown car is behind me. He's the only person with a less desirable parking spot than mine. It's not like he needs to be particularly close to school since he barely bothers to go to class.

I've heard that Hiram can get *stuff*. Something to calm you down, something to perk you up. Something to help you sleep at night, something to help you stay awake and study.

But I have no idea how it works. Are there secret code words, some way of asking without actually saying what it is you're asking for? And anyway, what if someone saw me approach his car, knock on his window? What if they figured out I was crazy?

I shake my head. Dr. Kreiter told me she doesn't like the word *crazy*, but that hasn't stopped me from using it.

At the end of our first session, Dr. Kreiter recommended antianxiety medication. She's a psychiatrist, not a psychologist, which means she can prescribe medication alongside advice and talk therapy. I think the hospital recommended her on purpose—clearly the doctors in the ER thought I needed to be medicated. So from day one, I worried that just because she *could* prescribe drugs, Dr. Kreiter probably suggested them for all of her patients, like how surgeons see surgical solutions to whatever is wrong with you because that's what they know.

To be fair, medication wasn't the only thing Dr. Kreiter recommended. In addition to weekly talk therapy, she suggested I attend a support group for teens suffering from anxiety, OCD, self-harm. Mom thought it was a good idea, but I convinced her—or rather, I convinced Dad—that we should revisit it at the end of our three-month deal. (Sitting in a circle with a bunch of other cutters definitely isn't the kind of extracurricular activity that looks good on a college application, and it would take time away from things that would.) But I promised that if I failed to live up to my end of the bargain, then drugs and support groups would be back on the table.

I was so certain I could meet the three-month goal. I believed that the possibility of meds and extra support would be enough to motivate me, like how getting into Stanford was motivation enough to take dozens of SAT practice tests. I truly thought that setting a goal would be enough, because it always had been before. (I mean, mostly.)

But that was before Tess broke up with me in front of everyone.

Before Dad said he knew his little girl wouldn't let him down.

I'm still counting backward. Negative two hundred and seventy-six.

I leave the compact on the ground beside the car and rifle through my backpack on the passenger seat, digging until I find my wallet buried somewhere beneath my books and sunglasses.

It'll be temporary, just until I get over Tess. Nothing like the pills the doctor would put me on for the rest of my life. (True, she said they might not be for the rest of my life, but I didn't believe her. I thought she sounded like a drug dealer, enticing me by promising that it might not last forever when she knew full well I could get hooked.)

When I get out of the car, I step on the compact, grinding whatever glass is left into shards too tiny to be useful. But when I turn around to face the back of the parking lot, Hiram's car is gone.

I'm alone.

five

THE ACTIVIST

Over dinner, Mom says, "We need to talk." Crap. I completely forgot about Mom's text message this morning.

"I'm sorry I didn't call. It was a really busy day."

I made it back to class after lunch, but I refused to talk to anyone. I knew they were all staring at me, whispering about how Tess dumped me in the hallway, the most embarrassing breakup in North Bay Academy history. Luckily Mrs. Frosch (she's my English teacher in addition to homeroom) assigned us an in-class essay this afternoon, so the classroom was quiet and I could keep my eyes on my paper. And then I had computer science, where we're all stuck in front of our own little portals, learning how to code, which half of us already know how to do. And in the little breaks between classes, I hid in the nearest bathroom. After the final bell, I rushed to my car and drove straight home. I used to wait for my best friend so I could give her a lift home—she doesn't have a car of her own—but she's been riding with her boyfriend for months. (One of those plans she canceled without telling me.) It was so easy to keep to myself all afternoon that it made me wonder whether I should do it more often.

The three of us—Mom, Dad, and me—are eating at the small table in the kitchen. Dinner at our house is rarely just *dinner*. Sometimes it's a strategy session for Mom's latest cause for concern or for Dad's next opening or closing statement. I was eight years old when Dad took me to my first protest. (Women's rights.) Or, at least, that's the first protest I remember. We have pictures of me at two years old attending a protest for marriage equality, but I don't remember that one. In the pictures, I'm sitting on Dad's shoulders. He's grinning from ear to ear.

Sometimes dinner is a chance to review my current course load and discuss whether there's any room for additional extracurricular activities. Dad and I argue over whether my membership in the school's LGBTQIA+ Alliance counts. Dad's convinced that's more socially oriented than cause-oriented.

Sometimes dinner is a chance to talk about my GPA or the SATs and compare my grades and scores to the grades and scores of whichever North Bay senior just found out he or she got into Stanford. (It's April, so the seniors are getting their acceptances and rejections. Though in the fall there were two students who applied early action, which led to a long discussion at our dinner table about whether I should do the same next year. Dad says yes, but Mom wants me to keep my options open.)

I'm not sure what tonight's dinner is about to turn into. Maybe they found out Tess dumped me. Maybe they heard I ran into the parking lot and locked myself in my car during lunch. Maybe they know I was late to fifth-period English because I was still in my car, counting backward. All the way up to—or rather, down to—negative 8,002.

No, it can't be any of that. Mom texted me before any of that happened.

"How's Maya?" Mom asks. Sometimes Mom likes to engage in small talk before Dad digs into the heavier topics. Asking how my best friend is doing is one of her go-to topics.

I shrug. "I didn't see her all day." At some point this afternoon, I noticed a text from her saying that she was studying through lunch, but I never got around to writing back. It's not all that unusual for us to go a full day without talking lately. Sometimes I think I call her my best friend out of habit.

Mom nods. "I suppose she was in the principal's office. Or did they send her home?"

"Why would they send her home?" And why would Maya be in the principal's office, for that matter? She's not exactly a troublemaker.

Mom's eyes crinkle with concern. "Sweetheart, haven't you heard? I just assumed—"

"Assumed what?"

"I mean, Maya's mother—Mrs. Alpert—called me, and I promised to do everything I could to help—"

"To help with what?"

Mom lifts her napkin from her lap and puts it on the table. She's done eating, but she doesn't move to get up.

"You didn't hear?"

"Hear what?"

Mom pauses. "I thought for sure the rumors at school would be swirling, but maybe Principal Scott managed to keep this quiet after all."

"As though Maya has anything to be ashamed of," Dad breaks in.

Mom takes a deep breath. "I hate to be the one to have to tell you this, but maybe it's best coming from me. Maya says that Mike has been hitting her."

I squeeze my fork. "What?"

"Apparently she came to school with a black eye this morning."

Generally speaking, I hate sentences like *rage boiled up in my stomach* because ugh, clichés—but I swear I actually feel something hot and angry shift in my belly. I glance at Dad. He looks like he's sitting on some barely contained rage too.

Mom leans across the table and puts her hand over mine. When she speaks, she keeps her voice low and reasonable, like I'm a horse she doesn't want to startle. Mom has a gift for sounding calm during stressful moments. "I don't know all the details. But when Maya's mother called to ask for my support, of course I said yes. She knows I'm experienced with this sort of thing. Community organizing, I mean, not domestic abuse." Mom adds, "I'm going to plan a meeting for the parents. Advise them on how to talk to their children about this. Not all parents are as open as your father and I when it comes to discussing difficult topics."

I nod. "That's a good idea," I say. The words come slowly. I have to concentrate to keep from hearing *Maya says Mike has been hitting her* over and over again.

Dad pounds his fork against the table. "It's a good *start*," he corrects. "But really, we need to think bigger than talking about our feelings." His voice isn't calm like Mom's.

"Aaron, I believe there's value in teaching the kids how to express their emotions in times like this." Mom has a master's degree in social work.

"And there's even more value in teaching the kids how to take *action* in times like this. You know, they didn't even send that boy home today?" Dad's voice gets louder with each syllable. "He just went to class like nothing had happened. He even had his usual track practice after school."

I don't bother asking Dad how he knows so much about Mike's comings and goings. Like Mom, Dad's the kind of person who gets *involved*.

Mom cocks her head the side. "Maybe I should reach out to the Parkers," she muses.

"Mike's parents?" I ask.

"This must be difficult for their family," Mom continues. "They probably don't know how to talk to their son about his behavior—"

"Mom, do you actually think the Parkers believe Mike did what he's accused of? Mike's parents *worship* him. They'd never believe their son was capable of hitting Maya."

To be fair, they're not the only ones. *Everyone* likes him. If

North Bay were the type of school that had a homecoming king or a prom king, Mike would've won every time. Even I'd have voted for him. Last year, when I organized a protest on behalf of the school's maintenance staff to have their wages increased, he came to every meeting and got the entire track team to participate.

But of course, I believe my friend.

Mom says, "If Maya has a visible bruise—how could Mike's parents possibly deny what happened?"

I don't answer right away. Dad says Mom's an idealist, while he's a realist, and the combination helps make their marriage work. I try to picture what dinner at Mike's house must look like right about now: Mike and his little brother seated across from each other, his parents on either end. I imagine they're sitting in a real dining room—they're not eating at a tiny kitchen table, and they're definitely not digging into the pot with their own forks instead of using a serving spoon.

Maybe Mike says it was an accident.

Or maybe not, because that would require admitting he did it in the first place.

Maybe he says some other guy did it. (But who? And why? Everyone knows Mike and Maya are together.)

Then again, maybe his parents don't even ask for an explanation. They're probably calling Maya *confused, troubled, attention-seeking*. They're probably saying she needs help—a doctor, a therapist, to be checked into the hospital.

Maybe even medication.

Even if Mike admitted what he'd done, I bet his mom would tie herself in knots trying to come up with a reason to justify it.

It wasn't his fault.

He didn't realize his own strength.

He's been under so much pressure lately.

He's really such a good boy.

I shake my head. Why am I thinking about what's going on at *Mike's* house? I should be thinking about *Maya*. She must be having dinner with her mom right now. Mrs. Alpert is probably peppering her with questions.

How long has this been going on?

Why didn't you tell me sooner?

Are you sure it wasn't an accident?

(Like everyone else, Mrs. Alpert loves Mike.)

To be honest, I have all the same questions. But I'd never ask Maya the way her mother would. Maya's mom drives her nuts.

"Apparently the abuse had been going on for months," Dad growls. I slide my hands beneath my legs so Dad won't see them shaking. "*And*," he continues, "they might not expel him. The school doesn't have a policy in place for something like this."

"How can they not have a policy in place?" Mom shakes her head like she's disgusted. "There are three full pages in the student handbook outlining the cyberbullying policy and nothing for this?"

The first day of freshman year, in addition to the student handbook, they distributed the North Bay Academy code of conduct. It was peppered with words like *respect* and *community*. It said violence among students wouldn't be tolerated.

They were probably thinking of boys punching other boys or an occasional heated argument among girls.

What Mike did to Maya probably isn't what they had in mind.

"You know how these things work, Fee," Dad answers. (Fee is Dad's nickname for my mom.) "They didn't see the need to create a policy to address something that had never happened before."

"Never happened before *that we know of*," Mom counters.

Our school may pride itself on being a respectful community, but it's also a private institution that relies on tuition and donations so it needs to retain a pristine reputation in order to appeal to more students and earn more tuition. I try to imagine the next North Bay board of trustees meeting, where they'll decide whether it would be better for the school's reputation to expel Mike, or to cover this up entirely.

I can't believe I was upset about my breakup with Tess. That's *nothing* compared to this. (I mean, it doesn't actually *feel* unimportant, but I *know* it is.)

Oh, god, Tess.

This is what she was talking about in the hallway.

When she said *we have to do something*, she wasn't talking about *us*, she was talking about *Mike* and *Maya*.

About the fact that the school doesn't have a policy for something like this.

She *wasn't* going to break up with me. Not until I let her down so completely by telling her I was going to sit at my usual table. With Mike.

I press my thighs into my seat so hard that my hands start to go numb. I glance at my dad. He looks like he's waiting for something.

"I'll organize a meeting too," I say. "For the students. To express ourselves—how we feel about what happened, about how the administration is handling it."

Mom nods. "I think a discussion would be very healthy. Maybe we could ask the guidance counselor to lead it."

"Maybe," I echo, but I glance at Dad. He wouldn't be impressed by a group of students gathered in the cafeteria, sharing their fears and worries. Neither would Tess.

We have to do something.

"Just take it easy," Mom adds. "Don't be ashamed to take a step back if it gets to be too much."

"She can handle it," Dad says proudly. "After all, we didn't raise her to sit on the sidelines, did we, Frida?" He uses his knife to point at me. He's the only one who's still eating.

He grins, and I smile back. "That's my girl."

Tuesday, April 11

six

THE COOL GIRL

I spot Tess in the hallway on her way to lunch on Tuesday. She and her friends usually sit in the grass beyond the lunch tables, happy to welcome whoever might join them. Sometimes Tess sits out there all by herself, not the least bit embarrassed to be alone. I hold out my arm but stop short of touching her to get her attention.

"You were right," I begin. I have to concentrate to keep my voice even. I memorized this speech before I fell asleep last night and practiced it before leaving for school this morning.

"About what?"

"When you said you didn't know me."

"Oh yeah?" Tess folds her long arms across her chest.

I nod. "Because if you knew me, you'd know that I never would've gone to sit with those boys if I knew what had happened between Maya and Mike."

I pause to let the words sink in, just like I rehearsed. The expression on Tess's face twists. Her eyebrows go from knitted together to raised.

"I just assumed—"

I don't give her a chance to finish. "Yeah, well." I take a step back because she's so much taller than I am. I have to tilt my neck to look her in the eyes. She's wearing another sleeveless shirt, and I can see the goose bumps on her skin. It's cold out for a tank top, but Tess likes to show off her arms.

She reaches out like she's going to take my hand, but I stuff my hands in my pockets. "I'm sorry," she says. "I shouldn't have snapped the way I did. I was just so upset."

I pause. I prepared several possible responses to meet each of Tess's potential reactions: anger, disgust, pity. But I didn't expect an apology, so I don't have a response ready.

I decide it's too risky to wing it, so I stick to my script.

"You know, this isn't about you. Mike didn't hurt *you*. This isn't happening to *you*."

"Look, I know you're closer to this than I am, but if someone hurts one of us—"

"One of *us*? You wouldn't even know Maya if I hadn't introduced you." It's not entirely true—Maya is nice to everyone—but I don't know what to do other than keep up my indignant act. Out of the corner of my eye, I see Maya walking past us in her favorite tight blue jeans and a faux-vintage band T-shirt tied into a knot at her waist. The door at the end of the hallway is open, our usual table right on the other side of it. She's not thinking of sitting there, is she? Mike and his friends are already in place.

"I gotta go," I say to Tess, pushing past her to head for the door.

"I really think we should talk—"

"There's nothing to talk about, Tess." If we talk any more, I might start to cry, or break down and beg her to take me back. I can't risk her seeing me like that.

I have to keep my cool, stick to my script, no matter how much I might want to get back together. So I swallow, prepared to walk away with the words I rehearsed. My voice refuses to stay even, no matter how hard I try, but hopefully Tess won't notice. "Like you said, it's over. Now I have to go be with my best friend."

seven

THE BEST FRIEND

Maya's leaning against a pillar up ahead of me. I want to put my arms around her, but I don't want to startle her, so instead of hugging her, I reach out and tap her shoulder. She still spins around like I burned her.

"You scared me," she says.

This is my first time seeing her black eye. It's not really black, or even purple—more of a dark pink. I wonder if I'd be able to see Mike's fingerprints if I looked closely enough—I heard it was a slap, not a punch, that caused the bruise. I'm tempted to reach for Maya's face, but just touching her shoulder was enough to make her jump, so maybe I should keep my distance.

Of course, it makes sense that she'd be on edge. Mike is only a stone's throw away.

"Let's eat in the library today," I suggest. Maya looks surprised. Maybe she thought I'd insist on sitting with the boys to prove that they can't drive us away. It's what my dad would want us to do. He'd argue that by walking away, we're letting them win without putting up a fight. But he's not here to see how pale Maya looks. I mean, she's always pale, but right now, she looks like she's about to faint.

I should've texted her last night. I should've said that I was thinking about her, that I loved her, that it was going to be okay. But how could I? I have no idea whether it's going to be okay or not. I don't even know what would qualify as *okay* in this situation. I told myself she was probably getting plenty of calls and texts, and maybe as her best friend, the best thing I could do for her was not to add to the noise.

I stuff my hands in my pockets and try to make it sound like where we sit for lunch isn't a big deal. "I mean, who wants to deal with all that drama?"

Maya stares past me, to the table where the boys are sitting. A sophomore named Eva Mercado sits down across from Mike, leaning forward so he can probably see her bra.

Finally, Maya nods. "The library sounds good to me."

◇◇◇◇

We settle at a table in the corner and spread out our lunches, but neither of us eat. I want to ask why she didn't tell me what was going on sooner, but I don't want her to feel like I'm accusing her of doing something wrong. Maybe Mike threatened to make things worse if she told. I try to imagine going into Principal

Scott's office to say that Tess beat me up, and just thinking about it is enough to make me sit on my hands.

But I have to say *something*.

"I just can't believe it," I begin. Crap, does that sound like I don't believe *her*? Quickly, I add, "I mean, I'm not saying I *don't* believe it, of course I *do* believe it."

Maya doesn't say anything, so I keep on talking. "I just *can't* believe it—you know what I mean?" I'm rambling, but it's better than silence. (Isn't it?) "Where were you yesterday? I didn't see you all day."

Not that it's actually unusual for us to go a day without seeing each other anymore. For months, Maya has spent her free time with Mike. The first few mornings after their first date, I showed up at her house to drive her to school, but each day Mike had already picked her up. With Mike, she didn't have to worry about being late to homeroom.

"I ate lunch in here." She looks down, and I realize I've been staring at her eye. "I sort of just stayed after the bell rang."

I nod, remembering that she texted me she was going to eat lunch here. After everything that happened, I forgot. "Right." Yesterday at this time, Tess was breaking up with me in the hallway outside. "It was crazy out there." Or anyway, *I* was crazy out there, trying desperately to keep it together in front of everyone. I scratch at my jeans. My bitten nails are too short to rip the denim, so the skin beneath it is safe.

"What are people saying?" For a split second, I think Maya's asking about Tess and me—any other week, our very public

132

breakup would've been hot gossip—but then I realize she wants to know what people are saying about *her*.

Our classmates have been coming up to me all morning. They think I know something they don't. They wait for me to tell them something, but I don't know what to say. Should I thank the ones who express support? Say she's fine to the ones who ask how Maya's doing?

"Oh, you know." I pause.

"No, I *don't* know. That's why I asked."

Some of our classmates think *they* know something *I* don't—that Mike, track star and all-around good guy, could never have done what Maya's accused him of. In between first and second period, Mike's best friend Kyle grabbed me and hissed in my ear: *Tell your girl to stop making so much trouble.* At first, I thought he meant Tess, but then I remembered she isn't my girl anymore. He was talking about Maya.

I'm not about to tell her that.

"I mean, I think people believe it—'cause like, the evidence is hard to ignore." I slide my hands out from under my lap. I don't want to point at her eye—I have to concentrate to keep from staring—so I point at my own instead. I try to think of the gentlest way to let her know the different things people are saying. Carefully, I start, "I think it's hard because everyone's always loved Mike."

She shrugs. "Right."

"Right," I agree.

I wonder if Maya remembers that Mike was my first kiss,

during a game of Truth or Dare in eighth grade. He tried to stick his tongue in my mouth. I don't think he ever forgave me for giggling at him.

I continue, "I heard the track coach said that this could ruin his chances for that college scholarship." Actually, I heard that the coach was ranting that some silly girl was going to ruin the poor boy's life, but I'm not about to tell Maya that either.

"Why?" Maya asks. "It's not like any of this is going to affect his ability to run fast." Maya's the one who clocked his running time, race after race, practice heat after practice heat.

"Apparently there's, like, a morality clause to the scholarship that he'd be in violation of if it turns out he really did it."

"What do you mean *if he really did it*? You said people believe it. The evidence and all that."

"Yeah, but—" I pause. I remember the conversation I imagined his parents having at the dinner table last night, the slightly less offensive things I've heard in the halls. "Maybe it was an accident. Or, you know, a misunderstanding?"

Maya's face falls.

"I mean, that's just what *some* people are saying." Crap. "Some people are saying the opposite. I heard some girls are planning a rally to call for his expulsion."

Okay, so technically that's not true yet, but it could be. It *will* be. I'll make sure of it. I'm my father's daughter.

That's my girl.

"A rally?" Maya asks.

"Yeah. You know, a protest. Some kind of demonstration."

"Will you go?"

Mom wouldn't want me to. She'd be worried it would lead to an incident. That's what she calls the cutting—*incidents*. Dad doesn't believe in euphemisms, but he hasn't stopped Mom from using that one.

"Will you?" I ask.

Maya pauses. "If he gets expelled, then he definitely wouldn't be eligible for the scholarship anymore."

"True," I agree carefully. I don't want to get her hopes up. "But even with a protest, it's not, you know… It's not definite he'll get expelled." I remember what my parents said last night. "The school doesn't have a policy for something like this."

My father would say that's the whole point of demonstrating. To demand the change—the *justice*—that's missing from the status quo. I open my mouth to explain this to Maya—a protest is just the first step—but she doesn't look like she's in the mood for a lecture on social justice. Actually, it looks like she's about to cry.

I beg my brain to think of the right thing to say. How can I be so comfortable and confident debating hypotheticals with Dad at the kitchen table, but not out here in the world, where it really matters, where saying the right thing might actually help someone I care about?

"What do you think will happen?" I ask finally.

Maya shakes her head. "I don't know."

I can't read the look on her face. Is she sad? Maybe she's angry. *I'm* angry. Angry because it's entirely possible that *nothing* will happen. The board of trustees might decide it's better to keep

135

this quiet. Mike might get nothing more than a slap on the wrist. Maybe they'll make us sit through a special assembly about respecting our peers, and then we'll all be expected to have learned our lesson and life will go on as if none of this matters.

My father would point out that there's nothing quiet about a protest. The school can't hush it up if the students make enough noise.

But I don't think Maya wants to hear that either. I try to think of what I *should* say.

It's going to be okay. But I can't say that, because it might not be.

I'm here for you. Except, I'm not, because if I were a better friend, I would've figured out what was going on sooner.

I'm so sorry. Sorry that I don't know what to say.

I can't even put my arm around Maya and hug her, because if I touch her, she'll feel the way my hands are shaking. So I slide my hands beneath my thighs again, and we sit in silence while all the wrong things to say go round and round in my head.

eight

THE ANXIOUS GIRL

I have a fifty-minute hour with Dr. Kreiter on Tuesdays after school. (That's what Dad calls it, a "fifty-minute hour," because the appointment is fifty minutes long even though Dr. Kreiter refers to it as an hour.) Weekly therapy sessions were part of the three-month deal I made with my parents. In the beginning, I thought the doctor would make me undress at the start of every session so she could check my body for new cuts and scrapes. I imagined all the reasons I'd list to explain away any innocent wounds: I cut myself shaving, my hand slipped when I was helping Mom with dinner, I fell off the bed and landed on a sharp edge of the metal frame. (That actually happened to me when I was six years old.)

It turned out my hypothetical excuses weren't necessary because Dr. Kreiter never inspects me. (Plus, I've kept up my end of the three-month deal, so there haven't been any cuts to explain away.) She told me that since I made a deal to be honest about cutting with my parents, she'd trust me to make the same deal with her. I thought that was odd because she didn't exactly seem like a fan of the deal we'd made in the first place, but maybe she was trying to prove something to me about trust between a therapist and her patient (and the patient's parents).

The hospital recommended Dr. Kreiter. She wanted to see me multiple times a week, but my father agreed when I said that wasn't necessary.

Of course, my father didn't know how long this had been going on.

He didn't know how many times I'd cut myself, because the earliest cuts weren't deep enough to leave scars.

The thing about cutting is that it isn't an accident. I read an article about a girl who slid into anorexia—she started with a diet and then restricted herself further and further until she descended into illness. Cutting isn't like that. I mean, I guess there's probably someone out there who cut herself (or himself) by accident, found it a relief, and then began doing it intentionally—but once you do begin doing it intentionally, there's no pretending it's an accident. It's a choice, each and every time.

I only ever cut myself on the upper part of my thighs, where no one would see. I did it in my bathroom at night with the door closed. Mom thought I was taking long, soothing baths. It was the sort of thing she'd normally admonish—wasting water in an often drought-ridden state—but much to my surprise, she told me she was glad I was taking time for self-care.

I ran the water while I cut myself. (Even more wasteful than taking actual baths.) The first few cuts were shallow, just enough to relieve the pressure, like opening a window to let in a breeze. I barely even bled.

In bed at night, I'd lightly run my fingers over my scabs. I didn't pick at them because I didn't want to bleed on my sheets and I didn't want to scar.

On New Year's Eve, Mom and Dad went out to a party at their friends' house, and I stayed home alone.

Maya went out with Mike, of course.

School was off for the holidays; technically I had no reason to be stressed.

Maybe I was just bored.

But my hands started shaking, and that was that.

Even though I was alone, I went into the bathroom and locked the door behind me like always, though this time I didn't bother running a bath. I pressed the blade—my special razor blade just for this, which I cleaned with rubbing alcohol in between uses, possibly the only thing I'd ever managed to keep neat and tidy—into my leg.

Before that night, I'd never cut myself all that deeply. But that night, I wanted to know how it would feel if I did. I told myself I was being scientific about it, like it was an experiment.

There was so much blood, it should have scared me. Instead of dripping like it usually did, it ran out in a stream. As always, I'd moved the bath mat aside so it wouldn't get stained, but that night the blood was running too fast. It got all over everything.

As the clock ticked down to midnight, I was on my hands and knees, scrubbing as best I could, washing my bloody handprints off the wall, off the shower curtain, off the mat. I'd taped the wound shut with a row of Band-Aids but all my moving around made it reopen, and I had to start cleaning all over again.

Eventually, the bleeding stopped, but that was the first cut that left a scar behind.

It might have gone on like that forever if it hadn't been for Valentine's Day. By then, Tess and I had kissed, but we weren't an official couple yet, so we weren't spending the holiday together—she'd already had plans with another girl, someone she'd dated on and off sophomore year. Maya was with Mike again, of course. My parents were out on a date.

And so, once again, I was home alone.

Once again, my hands started shaking, full of energy that needed to find a way out.

It's not as though I was planning to go so deep. I'd read about cutting online—some cutters liked to look closely, to stare at the layers of flesh beneath their skin. I wasn't like that. I usually only wanted to cut enough to relieve the pressure, and then I'd stop.

But that night—home alone, the entire evening stretching out in front of me—a little cut wasn't enough. Every time I came close to stopping, I thought about Tess, out with another girl. Or Maya, out with Mike. Or even my parents, out together. (Dad says Valentine's Day is nothing more than crass commercialism, but he does it for Mom.) Every time I eased up, loosened my grip on the blade, all I could think was that I was all alone, while everyone else was out together.

So I went deeper again, like I thought maybe I could cut out the bad parts, the lonely parts, the needy parts. The parts that were sad about being alone. The parts that explained why I was alone in the first place.

There was so much blood. More than there had been on New Year's. More than a row of Band-Aids could contain. I tied a towel around my leg, got into my car, and drove to the nearest ER. I didn't hesitate, even though I knew this meant my secret would come out—the doctors would call my parents, my parents would worry, et cetera. Maybe it was my survival instinct kicking in, but it wasn't until later that I berated myself for cutting so deep, being so foolish, exposing my secret.

Luckily (or was it intentional?), I'd cut my left leg, so my right was free for driving. The blood didn't scare me, not even as it soaked my pajama pants (the only pants loose enough to fit over the towel) and dripped onto the driver's seat. Until that night, it never occurred to me that I could do any serious damage with my trusty razor blade. After all, cutting had always made me feel better, not worse.

The doctors admitted me, and I lay in a narrow bed waiting for my parents to arrive. "You could've killed yourself," one doctor said—I don't remember which one. I didn't bother learning their names.

"I'm not suicidal," I explained when the staff psychologist came to see me. Dad stood by the bed, while Mom filled out

141

forms down the hall. "If I were, would I have driven myself here?"

Dad nodded, as if even then, he was pleased with me for making such a rational and clear argument. He didn't know—I knew because I read it online—that the suicide rate for cutters is kind of sketchy because doctors can't know who accidentally cut too deep versus who actually intended to kill themselves. But of course, that wouldn't apply in my case because I drove myself to the hospital. Even the doctors had to admit that it was a sign I wasn't suicidal, but they still wanted to keep me there for a few days' observation.

"That won't be necessary," Dad said. There were no chairs next to the bed, though I don't think he would've sat down anyhow. A nurse had dressed my leg with a tourniquet, but we were waiting for a doctor to stitch me up. Apparently, Valentine's Day is a busy night in the ER.

The staff psychologist explained that it was protocol to admit patients like me for observation and therapy, followed by an outpatient program. I saw Dad bristle at the words *protocol* and *patients like your daughter*. Getting around protocol is practically his job.

Dad insisted that I be released to my parents' care. He offered to sign papers stating that the hospital wouldn't be held responsible.

So after they stitched my leg, I got to go home. Mom drove me in her car, and Dad followed us in mine.

But I also got Dr. Kreiter.

In our first session, I sat stiffly on the couch across the room from Dr. Kreiter. No way was I lying down like they did in the movies.

She introduced herself, then said she'd worked with kids like me before. I bristled just like my dad had. We'd barely exchanged pleasantries and she'd already reduced me to a *type*.

"Cutters, you mean?" I asked. I'd Googled cutting and self-harm months earlier. Apparently, the urge can manifest in more socially acceptable ways, like people who have lots of tattoos. And some cultures have ritualistic scars, and no one accuses them of being mentally ill.

I mean, it's not like I thought what I was doing was *okay*. I'm not an idiot. I kept the cutting secret for a reason, careful to use tissues or sometimes toilet paper to blot my wounds, flushing them down the toilet to hide the evidence. I knew it wasn't normal, but maybe *I'm* not normal.

Then again, according to what I read, it's not that *weird* either. One website said that one in fifty teens cut themselves. If that statistic is right, then (given the size of North Bay Academy), at least seven of my classmates were also doing this to themselves. Even Princess Diana was a cutter at some point.

Plus, plenty of people bite their nails, cut their cuticles until they bleed, pick at scabs that haven't healed. Isn't that just a (socially acceptable) kind of cutting? Mom never suggested I see a therapist for nail-biting. (And okay, yes, I read once that some people develop obsessive disorders that take nail-biting and scab-picking too far, so those habits can become problematic too.)

But what I did wasn't nearly as bad as what some other people do. I read about teens who burned themselves, or used thicker, dirtier devices like nails and screwdrivers to cut themselves, not clean razor blades like I did. I even read one story about a girl who broke her own arm, another who broke her kneecap.

In fact, people have been hurting themselves for hundreds of years. In Victorian times, doctors bled sick patients, cutting into people's skin to make them well. The science behind it had long since been debunked, but maybe it offered patients relief nonetheless, even if it was just a placebo effect. And even before that, people cut themselves for religious reasons, like self-flagellation.

The truth is, I'm not sure anxiety and OCD are particularly good reasons for what I did. Some of the case studies I read online were about teens who'd been sexually assaulted, physically abused, seriously neglected. And here I was worrying about my SAT scores and not having plans on a Saturday night.

But Dr. Kreiter said, "There's so much pressure on teens today. It's not enough to get good grades, you also need the best extracurriculars, the best friends, to wear the best clothes, and drive the best car. It's a lot to take on."

I looked past her to the framed degree from Duke University that hung on the wall behind her desk. Was I supposed to believe she'd gotten into the college and graduate school of her choice without a perfect GPA and extracurriculars?

I slid my hands beneath my thighs, hoping it looked like

an absent gesture, just an awkward teenager trying to get comfortable.

She said, "The endorphin rush that comes with cutting can be incredibly powerful."

I nodded, because I'm a good student, and that's what you're supposed to do when a teacher makes a point, but the truth was, I didn't think the doctor's endorphin-rush theory applied to me. I cut to calm down, not to get high.

Then Dr. Kreiter asked me if I had people to lean on.

"Of course," I answered. "My parents. My best friend. My girlfriend." *Almost*-girlfriend, at the time, but Dr. Kreiter didn't need to know that.

She nodded. "Do you go to them when you need help?" I didn't answer. Dr. Kreiter rephrased, like she thought maybe I didn't understand what she was asking. "Do you trust them enough to let them see your weaknesses?"

I tried to imagine telling my father that I worried about getting into Stanford, that I didn't know if I wanted to be a lawyer. I thought about Maya, so busy with Mike that I hardly ever saw her anymore. I thought about Tess, who thought I was cool because I never bothered getting to class on time. If she knew it was a symptom of OCD, she'd never look at me the same way. And if she knew about the cutting—well, then she might never look at me again at all.

"Juniper?" Dr. Kreiter prompted. I shrugged. "It sounds like you don't trust any of them enough to let them see when you need help."

I wanted to say that it didn't *sound like* anything because I hadn't answered her question, but she kept talking.

"I'd like to help you develop that trust with some of the people in your life."

I nodded, but really I wanted to roll my eyes. Tess wouldn't fall in love with a crazy person. My parents were already disappointed enough about the cutting and my diagnoses—letting them see any more of me would only make things worse. And everything came so easily to Maya. She would never understand.

"And," Dr. Kreiter added, "we'll work together to help you find healthier ways to reduce and manage your stress."

I didn't like the sound of *reducing* my stress. Did she mean she wanted me to drop some of my extracurriculars, move from advanced classes to regular ones? Had she already decided I wasn't strong enough to do the things I had to do to get into Stanford like Dad?

"For now," Dr. Kreiter continued, "I want you to know you can trust *me*. You can ask me for help, and I promise I won't judge you."

I nodded again, but I mean, what did it matter if I could trust Dr. Kreiter? I didn't care whether or not *she* loved me.

Today, Dr. Kreiter tells me she's already spoken to my mother, so she knows about the *situation* at school. For a second, I think she means how Tess broke up with me in front of everyone, but then I remember that Mom doesn't know about that, so she can't have told Dr. Kreiter, and anyway it's not nearly as important as the real situation—the one between Maya and Mike.

"This must be difficult for you," the doctor says.

I shake my head. "It's difficult for *Maya*," I correct her.

She nods. "Of course it is. But these things don't happen in a vacuum."

"That's true," I acknowledge. "My mom wants to get the parents together to talk about it. I mean, something about our school created an environment where Mike thought he could get away with hurting his girlfriend."

"Perhaps," Dr. Kreiter concedes, "but that's not what I meant."

She wants me to ask her what she did mean, but I know if I wait in silence for a few seconds (letting the clock on our hour tick down), she'll explain.

"I meant that the things that happen in the world around us affect us. Maya is your friend, and she's in pain."

I don't say anything. Dr. Kreiter continues, "When things happen to our close friends, we tend to absorb them, especially at your age."

I hate when Dr. Kreiter says things like *at your age*. It's reducing me to a type again. They really should've taught her not to do that in medical school.

I never told Maya that I'm in therapy. I never told her about the cutting. When I missed school in February, I said I had strep throat. She and Mike came over after school with flowers and soup. (And my homework assignments, since I didn't want to fall behind.) She returned the tank top I'd lent her to wear on their V-Day date. I didn't really want Mike to see me sick in bed like that (I kept my legs under the covers, afraid they'd be able to see the bandages through my pajama pants), but Maya hadn't called to check first, and it's not like I didn't know that a visit from Maya would probably mean a visit from Mike too since they were always together. Anyway, Mike would have been her ride, and it's not like I could have asked him to wait in the driveway while Maya and I talked.

I asked how her Valentine's Day had been, and she shrugged like it was no big deal because she knew I'd been alone, and she was always thoughtful about things like that.

"It was awesome," Mike interjected. "Did she show you the bracelet I got her?" He'd been standing in the room with us the whole time, so obviously he knew that she hadn't. Maya held out her pale arm to show me the slim silver bangle around her wrist. "She promised never to take it off," Mike said.

Now, when I think about it, the bracelet reminds me of a handcuff. But at the time, I thought it was pretty, and I wondered if Tess and I would ever have the kind of relationship where we exchanged gifts, where everyone knew that if you invited one of us somewhere, the other was likely to come along.

Now, I can't remember if Maya was still wearing the bracelet when I saw her earlier. I should've looked.

"This must be very unsettling for you," Dr. Kreiter says. "After all, Mike is your friend too."

I shake my head. "He's definitely not my friend anymore."

Dr. Kreiter nods. "Okay. So that's at least one way in which your world has changed since Maya's confession."

I don't like her choice of the word *confession*. Like Maya's the one who did something wrong.

"Can you think of any other things that have changed?"

I have nowhere to sit at lunchtime. I'm determined to plan a protest that my mother won't want me to attend.

Oh, and my girlfriend broke up with me in front of the entire school.

"Juniper?" Dr. Kreiter prompts.

My parents unintentionally named me after a Franciscan priest named Junipero Serra who set up missions along the California coast. They saw the name on a sign and liked the sound of it for a girl born in June, so I'm Juniper Serra Mesa-Stern—my parents hyphenated my last name so both of their heritages (Mexican Catholic and Eastern European Jewish) would be represented.

Because I have a June birthday, my parents could have waited a year before having me start kindergarten, so that I'd be one of the oldest kids in the class instead of one of the youngest. Apparently, my pediatrician suggested waiting, because in addition to being young, I was also (I still am) small for my age, and he was worried I might be intimidated by bigger kids.

But my dad said he wasn't worried. He said I was big on the inside.

Of course, I was young enough that no one asked what I thought about it. Young enough that I didn't even know these conversations were happening at all. I only know now because my dad loves telling that story.

Dr. Kreiter is still waiting for an answer. I shrug. "I don't know," I say finally. Then I glance at the clock and add, "Time's up."

Wednesday, April 12

nine

THE ACTIVIST

The thing is, I actually think Tess was right the other day when she said that if Mike hurt *one of us*, he hurt all of us.

Well, actually, she didn't say that, because I cut her off before she could finish her sentence, but I think that's where she was headed.

It *is* about us: about the girls, the *women*, of North Bay Academy. We deserve a school where we feel safe.

And how can we possibly feel safe with Mike walking the halls?

How can any of us feel safe coming forward in the future if this time, the first time (that we know of), the administration takes the side of the abuser rather than the abused?

I send a text message to almost every female classmate whose number I have in my phone. (After a pause, I decide to include Tess, though a wave of butterflies crosses my stomach when I type her name.) I invite them to a meeting, but I ask them to keep it quiet, explaining that I don't want the administration to get wind of it. I say boys are welcome too. I say we're meeting on Wednesday after school. That's when the LGBTQIA+ Alliance meets, so I already have a classroom reserved.

I don't include Maya. She doesn't need this on her plate. I'll loop her in after all the details are ironed out.

About thirty girls show up. Maybe ten guys. Some of them look like boyfriends who've been dragged along. "Is this everyone?" I ask, standing on a chair in the center of the room. That's something my dad taught me—be in the center of the room, not the front. It promotes a feeling of equality, plus you don't have to shout as loud. I suppose my standing on a chair mitigates the equality part of things, but I'm so short that no one would see me otherwise.

I shake my head. "This is pathetic." There are around two hundred girls at North Bay Academy, about fifty girls per grade.

"It's just the first meeting." I turn and see Tess standing behind me. *She* wouldn't have to stand on a chair to be seen. We must have looked ridiculously lopsided walking down the hallways hand in hand. "Word will spread."

I jump off my chair, pretending not to see it when Tess offers her hand to help me down. "We don't have time for word to spread."

"What do you mean?" There's so much chatter in the room that Tess has to raise her voice.

"We have to act fast. The school's board of trustees is meeting

154

on Monday to decide how to handle this. We have to show a united front before then."

Someone shouts out, "How is Maya?" The room goes quiet. I get back up on the chair.

"If you're here because you think I'm going to give you some details that haven't been included in the rumors floating around school, then you're gonna be disappointed. We're here to help, not to gossip."

I reach into my backpack and pull out a wrinkled piece of paper. I hold it up over my head.

"Do you guys remember receiving the North Bay Academy code of conduct freshman year?"

Most of the girls shrug. Lucky for me, I'm a pack rat; this page was tucked into a folder beside my freshman schedule. (One of the benefits of my particular form of OCD: I don't throw anything away.)

I practiced this speech last night. I wrote it down and read it over and over until I memorized it. I watched myself recite it in the bathroom mirror. I didn't want to risk not knowing the right thing to say.

"I'm sure you guys gave the code of conduct as much thought as I did on the first day of school—barely any at all." A few of my classmates laugh, and I continue, "But Mike is clearly in violation of it. It says that physical violence among students is unacceptable." The crowd murmurs and I keep talking. "We have a precedent. A few years ago, two sophomore boys were expelled for fighting on campus."

"Yeah, but Mike didn't do anything on campus."

"As far as we know," someone else adds.

"But it doesn't matter whether it was on campus or not, if there weren't any witnesses. It would be her word against his."

"What about her black eye? Doesn't that count as proof?"

"That happened over the weekend. Not during school hours."

I hold up my hands to try to quiet the conversation, but it's taking on a life of its own. I glance at Tess, and she puts her fingers in her mouth and lets out a deafening whistle. Everyone shuts up. I try to ignore the butterflies that have returned to my belly. I'm here to work, not to flirt with my ex-girlfriend. And definitely not to think about the fact that I've never called her my *ex-girlfriend* before.

"The code of conduct doesn't say it has to be on campus. It just says violence." I figured someone might ask this question, so I practiced this response too.

Someone shouts, "Yeah, but fights break out at parties all the time, and no one gets kicked out."

I nod. "That's because no one turns anyone in." I pause, then resume my speech. "The truth is, North Bay doesn't have a policy in place for this sort of thing. And whatever the code of conduct says, I know *this* probably isn't what they had in mind." I practiced that too, deciding which words to emphasize. "But that means what happens next—what happens with *Mike*—is going to turn into the rule that applies the next time this happens, and the next time, and the next. We have to set an example. If Mike gets away with it, what's to stop the next guy from doing what Mike did? From doing something even worse?"

The crowd rustles with agreement.

"We have to show a united front. Let the administration know what we want. Insist they do the right thing."

"What *is* the right thing?" someone calls.

I take a deep breath and say, "Mike Parker should be expelled." The murmur softens. "I know it's harsh," I say carefully, "and the code of conduct says that punishment is at the school's discretion. But we can—we have to—organize and *insist* that North Bay's policy is one of zero tolerance."

"I thought maybe suspended for the rest of the year."

"Kicked off the track team."

"Sent to summer school and like, anger-management classes or something."

I nod. "Look, all that would be a good start, but even if he gets suspended, eventually Maya will have to walk onto a campus that welcomes her abuser. It's bad enough she has to do that now, while we wait for Monday's board meeting. Bad enough she's had to do that for the past few months."

Someone shouts out, "We're sure she's telling the truth, right?"

Tess answers before I can. "What are you suggesting, Erica?"

"I mean, like Juniper said, it's been months—Mike and Maya have been together since last semester, right?"

"Right," I answer. The last time I drove her to school was the first week of November.

"So," Erica continues, "I just think we have to be sure—we don't want to stand behind her if there's a chance she's lying."

"Lying?" Tess echoes.

Erica shrugs. "Exaggerating, maybe. Or confused. I mean, remember what happened when that magazine article about campus rape was debunked? It hurt the whole movement."

My hands are shaking so hard, I can't even manage to shove them into my pockets. I swallow a gasp of surprise when Tess reaches up to take one of my hands in hers. Her palm is cool against my clammy one.

"We're not here for a movement," Tess says calmly. She probably thinks my hands are shaking because I'm angry at Erica. She squeezes tight. "We're here for *Maya*. And Maya wouldn't lie about this."

Tess says it as though she knows Maya a lot better than she actually does. But it's enough to shut Erica up.

Someone else says, "Maybe we should let the administration deal with this, not the students?"

Tess says exactly what I'm thinking: "If that's how you feel, then why did you bother coming to this meeting?"

My dad taught me not to let these kinds of meetings get contentious, so I break in. "Did you guys hear what happened over at Highlands High?" Only a few people nod, so I explain, "A sophomore accused her boyfriend of sexual assault."

I pause like I practiced, letting my words sink in. "But she didn't have any proof, so the administration didn't do anything. Eventually, the girl changed schools to get away from him." I look around gauging the levels of disgust on the faces around me. A few of my classmates are holding their hands over their mouths, and I notice one girl blink back tears. Dad would say I'm doing a good job—he always said it's key to get your audience emotionally invested. "We can't let that happen at *our* school."

"But Highlands *couldn't* do anything," Erica interjects. "I mean without proof, it's her word against his, right?"

"Legally, that's true," I agree. "But this isn't a *legal* issue. According to the code of conduct, North Bay can suspend or expel a student at its discretion for violations. If this were a legal case, Maya would've gone to the police, but she didn't. She went to *our* principal. At *our* school." I say it as if I know why she chose to go to Principal Scott instead of anyone else. As if she confided in me.

"So, what do we do?" someone calls out.

"We need to make an impact," I say. "I think a protest, showing our solidarity, could be really effective. But we have to pick the right moment. We need all eyes on us."

Tess speaks up. "The track meet," she says. "On Sunday."

I look down at my ex in disbelief. The meet on Sunday isn't a championship meet, but it may as well be. It's against our rival school, East Prep. They crushed us last year—Mike was out with an injury, Tess hadn't yet started attending our school—but between Tess on the girls' team and Mike on the boys', we're favored to win this year.

"What do you mean?" I ask softly.

"We'll walk off. The girls' team. We'll refuse to run. And the rest of us"—she gestures at the students around us—"can march onto the track. It'll keep the races from even starting. We'll hold up signs and demand justice. We'll block the track. We won't let Mike run."

Tess drops my hand and folds her arms across her chest like it's settled.

"What if the rest of the team doesn't agree to it?" I ask softly. Only a couple of Tess's teammates are here today.

"I'll talk to them." She makes it sound simple.

"But you might have to forfeit the match."

Tess's dark eyes look fiery when she says, "This is more important."

I look back at the crowd, my heart beating fast. For a few seconds there, I managed to forget that everyone was watching us. "Okay," I shout. "So now we have a time and place. Let's get organized."

I jump down off my chair and start splitting the group up into teams. The most important thing is to spread the word, get more people on our side. We agree to wear pink. We agree on a few phrases for our signs. We agree to arrive an hour before the races are set to start. We promise up and down to keep our plans quiet because we'll make a bigger impact with the element of surprise.

At the end of the meeting, I pull Tess aside. Her wrists are so thin, I can wrap my fingers all the way around them, just like the bracelet Mike gave to Maya.

"Thanks," I say. "That was a great idea—the track meet, I mean."

Tess shrugs. "Organizing a protest in the first place was a great idea."

I'll never tell Tess how much time I spent rehearsing. I need her—and everyone else—to believe I'm good at this, that it comes naturally to me. Dad says activism is in my blood.

Tess dips her head, curling her shoulders so she's closer to my level. She lowers her voice. "I know you didn't want to say anything in front of everyone, but how is she?"

I pause. "I mean, how well can she be doing?" It's an honest answer. I haven't seen her since lunch yesterday.

"Well, hopefully this will help."

I nod. Tess would never guess that Maya doesn't know I'm planning the protest. "I hope it'll help too."

Tess kisses my cheek before she leaves. Her scent is familiar against my skin. I wish I could kiss her back, but then she might guess that I want her back, and cool girls don't want the girls who dumped them to take them back, even if it was all a misunderstanding. I stuff my hands in the pockets of my jeans as I watch her walk away.

ten

THE BEST FRIEND

I need to talk to you.

    Delete.

    Do you have a few minutes to chat?

    Delete.

    Remember I mentioned that rally?

    Delete.

    Are you okay?

    Delete.

    Tess dumped me.

    Delete.

    How can I tell if Tess wants to get back together?

    Delete.

I don't know what to say. I never know what to say when things are tough or serious—like last year, when one of our classmates passed away from cystic fibrosis and our whole grade went to the funeral. After the service, everyone lined up to say something to Sophie Lowry's parents. I watched while everyone I knew hugged them, said how sorry they were, told an anecdote about Sophie. When it was my turn, I just sort of nodded. I'd never met them before. They didn't even know my name.

Beside me, Maya enveloped Sophie's mother in a hug. "I'm so sorry," she said. "Sophie was such a special girl." Mrs. Lowry's eyes filled with tears, and her father patted Maya's shoulder and said, "Thank you."

Later, I asked Maya why she said that. We'd barely ever talked to Sophie, let alone known her well enough to know she was special.

"That's just the right thing to say at a time like this, you know?"

I nodded, but I didn't know.

Maya knows. She's the kind of person that people always *like*: well-dressed, poised, pretty, smiling, smart, funny. Popularity comes easily to her; she doesn't have to work for it, it's simply who she is.

And now, when Maya's got *real* problems, problems I should be helping her through, all I want is to tell her about Tess because she would know exactly what to say to make me feel better.

I look at my phone like I expect a text message from her to pop up like magic:

You're better off without her.

Her loss.

That kiss on the cheek was definitely code for: Take me back, please!

163

But of course, my screen remains blank.

Besides, Maya wouldn't say any of those things. She'd say something else, something perfect, something I could never think of myself.

Dr. Kreiter says when I get into a negative loop like this, I should make a list of all the reasons why my thoughts aren't true. She calls it a *thought exercise*. Like, I should tell myself that Maya wouldn't be my best friend if she didn't *want* to be. Or, that she'd forgive me if I said the wrong thing. But I think that's a useless exercise because how can anyone ever know *which* thoughts are the *true* thoughts? Sure, Maya's my best friend, so I could try to convince myself that she'd forgive me, but maybe she wouldn't. Maybe she'd see my text and roll her eyes and hate me. I already wonder sometimes if she ever really liked me. Maybe I just sort of attached myself to her in sixth grade, and she was too nice to tell me to go away.

Maya's the one who showed me that popular girls usually aren't mean girls—*cool* girls can be mean girls, but that's not the same thing as being *popular*. Popular girls are friends with everyone. I mean, that's literally the definition of popular. The popularity x-factor is that you have to be so likeable that everyone wants to be friends with you, which describes Maya exactly.

I lie back on my bed and close my eyes. I can *see* Mike hitting her—his hand open as he brings it down hard, against her face. His mouth is twisted in an ugly grimace, his is brow furrowed with concentration the same way it is at the start of a race.

Over the past couple months, since I've been with Tess, I hardly missed a track practice and never missed a meet once the season started in March. I sat next to Maya, and we rooted for Tess and then for Mike. It was one of the only times I got to be alone with Maya since she and Mike got together, though I guess it wasn't really alone since half the school came to the meets too. It's not like we could've talked about anything.

I never liked watching Mike run. You know how they say that experts make hard things look easy? Well, Mike made running look hard.

Nothing like Tess. When she runs, it looks like she's floating. She lands on the balls of her feet—not hard on her ankles like Mike—so that each step sort of flows into the next. I didn't cheer when she ran like Maya did for Mike. Instead, I got quiet. Watching her made me feel so calm, every time. It was almost as good as cutting.

Maybe I can ask Tess to run circles around me during the protest. (Except watching her probably won't be so soothing now that we're broken up.) I look at our recent texts on my phone, rereading my attempts to sound relaxed and aloof, grateful that Tess couldn't know how much time I spent staring at that little *dot dot dot*, wondering what she was writing back to me, how long I should wait before writing back to her, how carefully I considered each word before sending it.

I drop my phone on my bed like it's hot. There's nothing cool about texting the girl who just dumped you, no matter how much you want to. No matter how much time you spend crafting the perfect message in an effort to sound cool when you're anything but.

And I shouldn't be thinking about Tess anyway. I should be thinking about *Maya*.

I take a deep breath.

I open my eyes and grab my phone, type a message, and hit send before I can second-guess myself.

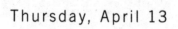
Thursday, April 13

eleven

THE ANXIOUS GIRL

For once, I get to school early. (Apparently I can overcome my OCD with the right motivation, this time at least.) The fog is low in the sky, and it's so cold I can see my breath. I always check the weather on my phone before I leave the house in the morning, which is how I know that the temperature is below normal for this time of year and that even after the fog burns off later, it's not going to get warmer than sixty degrees today. I ease my car into park and glance around. The lot is almost empty, but I park in the back like I usually do. There's only one car parked even farther away from the school than mine. I drop my keys in my backpack and start walking toward it.

"Thanks for meeting me at this hour," I begin, though I'm starting to worry this wasn't such a good time to meet. Won't people be *more* suspicious if they see me here so early? It would've been better to do it in the middle of the day, when I'd have a chance of getting lost in the crowd. Except that I always feel like everyone's staring at me.

Hiram shrugs. "Happy to help."

I think about Dr. Kreiter, asking me if I had anyone I could lean on for help when I was struggling. I don't think *this* is what she had in mind.

Anyway, *this* is only temporary. I mean, between Tess and Maya and Mike and the protest, this is a seriously stressful week. If I told Dr. Kreiter that, she wouldn't understand. She wouldn't believe I won't need chemical help once this week is over. And all it takes is one slipup for me to fail the three-month plan.

I don't ask (though I wonder) how Hiram knows what to give me. I don't ask (though I wonder) where these pills came from. I don't say (though I think it), how relieved I am that it turns out there's no secret handshake, no special password. Last night, I got Hiram's number from the student handbook and texted him like it was no big deal, like we talked all the time, like I was only asking him to return a textbook he borrowed. Hiram hands me a ziplock bag, a tiny row of pills across the bottom. "Take a blue one about twenty minutes before bedtime tonight," he says.

"Well, thanks," I say, putting the Ziploc into my bag and zipping it shut. "How much?"

Hiram shakes his head. "Don't worry about it." Before I can argue, he asks, "How's Maya?"

Hiram leans against his car, one foot propped up on the fender. There's a familiarity in his tone, as though he's not asking just because he wants the good gossip.

I'm so surprised that I answer almost honestly. (Total honesty would be admitting I've barely spoken to her since Monday.) "She's okay, I guess."

"I'm worried about her, you know."

I shake my head because I didn't know. "You hardly even know her."

Hiram nods, looking at the ground. "Right," he agrees, like it's a fact he forgot. "I heard you were planning some kind of demonstration."

Crap. What if Maya finds out before I get a chance to tell her myself? "It's supposed to be a secret," I explain, feeling (surprise, surprise), shaky all over again.

"How are you gonna get people to show up if it's a secret?"

"I mean, the only people who are supposed to know are the people who are going to be there."

Hiram nods. "Well," he says, and I realize that he wants to join us. "How does Maya feel about it?" he asks suddenly.

"She thinks it's great," I lie. "I mean, of course she wants Mike expelled."

"Does she?" I must look irritated because Hiram holds up his hands and explains, "I'm not saying he doesn't deserve to be expelled, I'm just saying I'm not sure that's what she wants."

How would Hiram know what Maya wants?

He continues, "It just seems like in spite of everything, she still really cares about that creep."

I nod, thinking about our conversation in the library.

She didn't exactly say *yes* when I asked her if she'd go.

If he gets expelled, then he definitely wouldn't be eligible for the scholarship anymore.

I can't remember now if her voice sounded hopeful or worried.

I thought it was hopeful.

Or maybe I just *decided* it was hopeful.

Maybe I should have made sure this was *exactly* what Maya wanted before I set things in motion. My heart starts to pound. To keep my hands from shaking, I grip my backpack tightly, picturing the plastic bag Hiram gave me rattling around inside.

I lean against Hiram's car beside him. "It's too late to stop it," I say softly. "I mean, even *you* know about the protest." I mean for it to be a joke, but it comes out cruel.

"Do you think she'll go?"

Hiram is the only person who's asked me that. Everyone else assumes she'll be there.

"I don't know," I admit. I feel like crying. "I haven't really talked to her about it."

"You should."

"I should," I agree.

Friday, April 14

twelve

THE ACTIVIST

I didn't hesitate before taking the blue pill last night. I took it twenty minutes before bed—just like Hiram suggested—and when I lay down and turned off the lights, for once I wasn't reviewing every conversation I'd had that day, weighing every decision I made that might have been wrong. Instead, I fell asleep almost immediately. It was the first good night's sleep I'd had all week. And maybe for a long time before that too.

I take my morning dose (the daytime pills are red, it's easy to tell one from the other) as soon as I wake up. I feel something kick in after breakfast when I'm in the shower—a slight buzz radiates through my body, then disappears, like I absorbed it. Hiram said these pills were first prescribed as diet pills but were taken off the market once doctors realized their side effects included "a false sense of well-being," which raised concerns that it might be addictive. I wanted to ask how he had them, since they'd been taken off the market, but then I figured that wasn't the kind of question you're supposed to ask.

When I look at my reflection in the mirror, I can see that my pupils look bigger than usual, but I don't think anyone will notice.

Wait. I don't think anyone will notice? I *always* think *everyone* will notice.

And that's not all. As I get dressed, I'm not wondering what Tess will be wearing if I see her in the halls today, not imagining the awkward conversation we might have, word for word, not trying to come up with things to say that could make it less awkward somehow.

And, I'm not dreading telling Maya about the protest. I'm not searching my vocabulary for the right words to say while all the wrong words go round and round in my head like my own private soundtrack. I don't wonder which words will let her know that of course I understand if she doesn't want to come, but really she should because it will add weight to our cause if she's there. I'm not mentally rehearsing telling her that of course she doesn't have to speak out, although it would be really impactful if she did, but if not, then that's fine too. I literally don't think about any of those words, don't come up with a speech or a few phrases to memorize.

Instead, I simply *know* that I'll tell her about the protest clearly and plainly whenever I get the chance to talk to her.

Just like that.

We'll probably have time to talk over lunch, so I'll tell her then. But not in the library, screw that, we're going to sit at our usual table because why should we let those boys scare us away? It's time for us to fight back, and Maya *must* feel that way too because why would she have told Principal Scott about it if she didn't? I mean, she *must* want him expelled because she went to the school administration—not to her parents, or to his parents, or to the police.

In between classes, I imagine Hiram's pills rattling around in my backpack—I wasn't about to leave them at home where Mom might come across them—but I don't worry that any of my classmates suspect what's in there. Hiram gave me twice as many red ones as blue so I can take a second red one this afternoon if the one I took this morning wears off. In physics, Mr. Chapnick isn't mad, and my hands are still—I don't drum them against my thighs or shove them into my pockets or *anything*.

When the bell rings for lunch, I practically march down the hallway. One foot in front of the other. Left, right, left. Those boys may be a foot taller than me and twice my weight, but I don't care. I'm going to sit at that table and *they're* going to be the ones to leave, and if anyone stares, it'll be to cheer me on.

"Hey, Juniper," Tess calls my name from somewhere behind me. I have to concentrate on slowing my pace so she can catch up, but I don't stop walking. (That must be another side effect, along with a false sense of well-being—an urge to move quickly.) Who the heck designed our single-story school anyway? It's stretched out like a snake, and it takes forever to get from one end to the other.

177

"Hey," I say when Tess falls into step behind me.

"I thought we might work through lunch. Iron out some of the details for Sunday."

"I can't right now." I pick up the pace again because it feels more natural to walk fast. Even with her long legs, Tess has to rush to keep up with me. "After school?"

Tess slides her fingers up my arm, gently grabbing hold and tugging me to stop walking. "I just wanted to make sure—it's just, I know I already told you how sorry I am, but—"

I shake my head. "Don't worry about it." A false sense of well-being makes it easy to let these things go.

"It wasn't right of me to end things like that. Out here, in front of everyone." She gestures at the crowd around us.

"Don't worry about it," I repeat. I lean in, standing on my tiptoes to kiss her. I don't hesitate to consider all the different ways she might interpret the kiss before I do it. I don't worry that I won't seem cool and aloof kissing her after she dumped me. After all, she only dumped me because of a misunderstanding, right? She looks surprised—even when we were together, I always waited for her to initiate affection, but right now, I'm not scared she's going to reject me. Across the hall, some idiot boy calls out *whoo-hoo*. I don't flinch. I don't even roll my eyes. I don't wonder how that sound will make me feel later, in bed, unable to sleep, because now I have blue pills for that.

"I gotta go," I say, pulling away. "I'll see you later."

I notice Anil and Kyle up ahead. They're so tall and athletic, it's like they take up the entire hallway. Or maybe they spread themselves out on purpose, silently communicating that they think they deserve more space than the rest of us.

But I'm going to get ahead of them, going to get to our table before they do.

Just then, Maya walks into the hallway from a classroom in front of me. She falls into step behind the boys. I rush toward her and link my arm with hers, pulling out her earbuds.

"It's just me," I say, excited. I tug her toward the south exit, trying to get her to walk faster. "Come on. I mean, we've been sitting there as long as they have, right?"

The boys make it out the door before we do, but they aren't sitting down yet. They look up at the sunlight, and I think they look like lions, basking in the sun's glow, as though god (or whoever) put the light there expressly for their enjoyment. I wonder how I've been sitting beside them all this time without noticing what jerks they were.

I pull Maya toward our table. "I mean, we have just as much right to that table as they do, right?"

Maya pulls her arm from mine and starts walking away.

I pause, then follow.

thirteen

THE COOL GIRL

Okay, maybe I made too big of a deal about the table.

The table doesn't have to be the symbol of the fight between Mike and Maya. It's not like he wins the instant Maya decides to sit somewhere else.

Either I'm slowing down—when did that happen?—or Maya's moving faster, blending into the crowd ahead of us. She heads away from the school and toward the track where the protest is supposed to take place in a couple days, not that Maya knows that.

I pick up my pace.

fourteen

THE ANXIOUS GIRL

Oh my god, what was I thinking kissing Tess like that before? She probably thinks I want to get back together. Maybe she's sitting with her friends and laughing as she tells them all about her pathetic little ex right now. Maybe she's trying to figure out how to confront me about kissing her without messing up the march on Sunday. She's probably figured out I'm too much of a basket case to handle a (second) breakup and plan a demonstration at the same time.

My hands are starting to shake. I stuff them into my pockets and follow Maya across the track and toward the parking lot. I'm not the only one following her. Or is that my imagination, thinking that everyone's watching me, watching her, watching us?

Apparently, the red pills don't wear off gradually. This feels more like a switch has been flipped, and my usual endless inner monologue of questions and concerns are back and every bit as loud and distracting as they ever were.

Okay, so that means now I know about how long the false sense of well-being lasts. Which means I need to do some math to make sure Hiram gave me enough to make it through the weekend. I need enough to sleep tonight, study tomorrow, and rally hard on Sunday.

But then maybe I'll need some for Monday too. It'll be stressful while we wait for the board to make its decision about Mike. And then I'll need to talk to Tess once all this is over, to tell her I'm sorry and I understand and I'm fine and it's okay and I apologize for kissing her like that. I shake my head. I definitely don't have enough to get me through next week.

I'll need more.

Across the parking lot, Hiram gets out of his car, like he knows I'm headed straight for him.

I shake my head. *Not now*, I think, as if he might be able to read my mind. *Not in front of everyone.*

Heavy footsteps come up behind me. A hand lands on my shoulder, like someone wants to move me out of the way. I look up and see Mike rushing past me.

"Maya," he says. He doesn't raise his voice. He sounds exactly the same as he does when he speaks up in class, makes a joke at lunch, says *hey* when you bump into him at the movies on a Friday night. Like all of this is normal, no big deal. Or at least, like he wants it to sound that way.

fifteen
THE BEST FRIEND

I drop my bag to rush up ahead of Mike and take Maya's hand in mine. "She doesn't want to talk to you," I say.

"This isn't really any of your business, Juniper." His voice stays low and even. But I've watched enough of his races to know the look on his face before he takes off.

At once, I realize that Mike never actually liked me. He only tolerated my presence because I was Maya's best friend.

I turn to Maya. "Do you want to talk to him?" I ask. She shakes her head. Or maybe she's just shaking.

"Let's get out of here." I pull her toward my car, then freeze as I remember my keys are in my locker.

But there's Hiram, still standing beside his ugly brown car. He waves, inviting me to come closer.

I look around. It's not my imagination, everyone is definitely watching us. I'll play this moment over and over in my head next time I can't sleep, wondering if I made the right decision, cursing myself for not having my keys with me at all times. But I really think the right thing to do right now is to get my best friend out of here. I hope I'm right.

So I take Maya's hand and lead her toward the back of the parking lot. I don't break into a run. I know enough to know we couldn't outrun Mike if we tried.

I glance sideways at Maya's face. Her eyes are focused like lasers on Hiram's car ahead of us. I know she can hear Mike's footfalls following us as clearly as I can.

the girls

PART THREE

Friday, April 14

one

MAYA

The hand that takes mine isn't cool and calloused but smooth and warm. I turn and see Junie standing beside me.

"Maya doesn't want to talk to you," she says. She sounds so calm. Can she feel my heart racing?

"This isn't really any of your business, Juniper."

I try to remember if Mike has ever called Junie *Junie* or if it's always been *Juniper*. Maybe it's only me—and her parents—who call her *Junie*. Maybe she'd prefer if we called her Juniper because it sounds more grown-up than Junie, and right now she seems so grown-up, standing calmly beside me, even though she barely comes up to Mike's chest. Her mom has that ability too. I've seen her during school meetings—she sounds calm even when talking about stressful topics. Nothing like my mother, who can get stressed even when talking about something relatively harmless.

Then again, Junie doesn't know Mike's voice as well as I do. Maybe she doesn't realize there's any reason not to be calm. She doesn't know that when his voice gets all quiet and even, it means he's angry. I imagine I can see the blood moving in his veins as his pulse quickens. Sometimes, when he talked like that, he was close enough to me that I could actually feel his heartbeat change. I wonder if he's the only boy in the world whose voice gets calmer and softer when he's upset or even when he's turned on—that's when I first noticed it, when we were messing around. He didn't whisper sweet nothings like men in the movies, and he didn't moan with pleasure either. He was always quiet, even, controlled. Except for his heartbeat. I loved—love?—that about him. I loved—love?—that I knew something about him that maybe no one else did.

Junie says something to me, but I'm too busy imagining the sound of Mike's heartbeat to hear her. Then, she squeezes my hand and tugs at it gently. It's enough to make me look at her and listen.

"Let's get out of here," she says.

Junie starts toward her car, a little blue hybrid, then turns abruptly toward Hiram instead. He's still standing outside his brown car, but now he's waving us closer.

I hear the rhythm of Mike's steps behind us. Mike's legs are so long that he doesn't have to rush to catch up. His fingers wrap around my upper arm. Sometimes he held me there instead of holding hands, and I'd see extra flesh in between his fingers. I don't remember if I noticed that before or after I started throwing up.

"This is all a misunderstanding," he says. Junie and I don't stop walking. Mike's fingers are on my other arm, not the one attached to the hand that Junie's still holding.

"Don't you remember it was an accident?" he asks. Junie tightens her grip as if to say she's not going to let him trick me into remembering things differently.

"I just want to talk to you, My," Mike adds.

Then, "We can work this out."

I stop then, dropping Junie's hand. She stuffs her hands into the pockets of her jeans. Mike wants to work this out? Isn't he furious with me for getting him into trouble? Or at least, *potentially* getting him into trouble, since the board of trustees isn't meeting to discuss us until Monday. I turn to face him.

He looks calm. He loosens his grip on my upper arm. He moves his thumb up and down, rubbing the soft spot on my inner arm the way he knows I like.

And finally, softly as though he's embarrassed Junie will hear—but loud enough to be sure Junie will hear—"I love you."

I feel the words *I love you too* building up in my throat. I've always said it back. It's like muscle memory, a reflex like when the doctor taps your knee with a hammer and your leg kicks out. It would be so easy to say the words, so easy to lean into his touch.

And yet, I also want him to let go of my arm. Maybe if he doesn't let go, he'll start to squeeze, and if he squeezes, it will start to hurt. I know he'd never hit me—not here, in front of all these people. He'd never be that careless. But he could still *hurt* me.

A crowd has gathered around us. Someone calls a teacher's

191

name—they think the adults will intervene, break this up. And of course, if any authority figure showed up now, Mike would do whatever he was told. Maybe both of us would be led to Principal Scott's office with everyone watching.

I glance at Hiram. A few more steps and I could be inside his car. He could make me numb so I won't feel anything: not the part of me that wants to stay, or the part of me that wants to hide, or the part of me who can't stop feeling her flesh between Mike's fingers.

I don't know what to do. I don't know which part is right.

Hiram moves so quickly that I wonder if he might actually be faster than Mike. He slides his fingers up my arm and beneath Mike's until Mike has no choice but to let go. Hiram plants himself between Mike and me. He's nearly a head shorter than Mike, but his body looks so solid, like a wall between us. He puts his hands flat on Mike's chest and shoves. Mike stumbles backward. I see a flash of something on Mike's face—rage? frustration? surprise?— but then his features reset, as though he'd been wearing a mask that slipped, and now it's back in place. It reminds me of the expression on his face at the start of a race; every meet is a chance for him to show the school, his coach, his parents, the opposing team, college scouts just how fast he can be.

And right now, here in the parking lot, Hiram has given Mike a chance to show everyone how *good* he can be.

Hiram pulls back his left hand and balls it into a fist. I never noticed he was left-handed before. He has to reach upward to hit Mike's jaw.

Mike falls backward to the ground, but he has the where-withal to bend his knees and put his hands down carefully so he doesn't hurt himself when he lands. I don't think Hiram punched Mike hard enough to make him fall. But I'm not sure anyone else realizes that.

The student calling the teacher's name gets louder. I look up and see Eva Mercado with her hands over her mouth. Kyle and Anil stand at the edge of the crowd like they're awaiting instructions. Hiram's hand is still balled into a fist. He wants to hit Mike again, but he's not going to do it while Mike is on the ground. Mike doesn't get up. Why should he? He has more to gain by staying down.

"Let's get out of here," I say to Hiram, repeating the words that Junie said to me. I reach for him. I feel his muscles unclenching.

"You sure?" he asks, and I realize that if I wanted him to, he'd go on punching Mike, even with everyone watching, even with Mike down on the ground. He'd do it for me.

I shake my head and tug Hiram toward his car. He's breathing hard, but he lets me push him into the driver's seat. I walk around to the passenger side. Now, Kyle and Anil come forward. They help Mike off the ground. He stands with his hands on his knees like he's winded. Hiram didn't even punch him in the stomach.

"I'll take you home," Hiram offers, but I shake my head. I don't want to go home.

"Just drive," I say.

He drives.

two

JUNIE

We drive in silence for so long that I don't think Maya and Hiram even realize I'm in the back seat. But I wasn't about to wait for an invitation. I mean, I couldn't let Maya just drive off with the (apparently) violent class burnout, even if the only violence I'd see him actually commit was against the guy who hurt Maya.

"You okay?" Hiram asks finally. He takes his eyes off the road to look at Maya.

"You didn't have to do that," Maya says.

"Yeah, I really did." Hiram pauses. "Anyhow, I wanted to."

Maya smiles. "I could tell." She leans across the seat and takes Hiram's left hand off the wheel. His knuckles are still pink.

Hiram takes his hand back. "You didn't answer my question."

"What question?"

"Are you okay?"

They're talking like old friends. I can't remember the last

time Maya and I talked so easily. I tuck my hair behind my ears. It fell out of its ponytail when we were rushing across the school parking lot.

"I'm fine."

"I'll take you home."

Maya shakes her head. "I don't want to go home."

"You want to go back to the beach?"

Back to the beach? That makes it sound like they've been to the beach. Together, I mean. But since when does Maya hang out with Hiram? I only pulled her toward his car because I didn't have my keys, which made his car the closest available getaway.

I remember the way he asked how she was doing when he gave me the pills. He sounded so concerned, but I didn't think much of it because everyone cares about Maya. I mean, even before all this happened. She's the kind of person people care about even when they don't know her well because she's the kind of person everyone wants to know well.

I slide my hand into my pocket before remembering my phone isn't there. It's in my bag, which is in the school parking lot because I dropped it when I ran after Maya. Someone will pick it up for me, but what if that person looks inside and sees the pills? At least you can't tell what they are and how I got them just from looking at them. I mean, we're not supposed to bring medicine to school, but for all anyone knows they could be for allergies, or maybe my therapist did prescribe me real antianxiety pills. Not that I'd want anyone to guess that I have problems with anxiety. Crap. I really wish I had my bag because

195

then I could take another pill so I wouldn't be scared to be sitting in Hiram's back seat. Better yet, I wish I had my bag and my car keys had been inside it instead of back in my locker, because then I wouldn't be sitting in Hiram's back seat at all.

What beach is Hiram taking us to? I mean, sure, we live in California, but it's not like the beach is our backyard. I think Hiram is driving toward Sausalito, toward Marin Headlands. There are beaches there, but it's more than thirty minutes from school. Which means we probably won't be back in time for fifth period, which means we'll be cutting class, which I have literally never done unless you count being late so many times that it probably all adds up to missing a class or two. But everyone saw what happened, and no one would blame me for leaving with Maya. How could I really get into trouble for helping my best friend at a time like this? I mean, *Mike* isn't even in trouble, not really, not yet. But even if I'm *not* in trouble, the school will probably call my mom to let her know I left, and then she'll call me but she won't be able to reach me because my phone is back in the school parking lot.

I shake my head. I shouldn't be worried about getting into trouble for cutting class or forgetting my phone. I should be worried about *Maya*. *I* should be the one asking if she's okay. *I* should've been a good enough friend to get Mike to let go of her. I should've been a better ally, prepared with my phone so I could have recorded the way Mike held her arm, so that everyone would see what only I (and eventually, Hiram) was close enough to see, that Mike was holding on too tightly. Or maybe I should've kept my cool and yelled for a teacher to come help us, instead of just standing there holding Maya's hand.

Oh crap, I really wish I hadn't left Hiram's pills behind. He might have more, but I'm not about to ask in front of Maya, who's never broken a rule in her life. (Until now, I guess, since we're cutting class.) But she's definitely never done *drugs*. Anyway, I'm still not sure Hiram and Maya even realize I'm here. They're talking to each other as though they're the only ones in the car. I slide my hands beneath my thighs.

Actually, they're not talking at all anymore, but sitting in comfortable silence. Maya never does say whether she's okay or not, which I guess means she isn't okay, because really, who would be? *I'm* not okay, and I'm not the one whose boyfriend (ex-boyfriend?) grabbed her in front of the whole school. Since I don't have my phone, and I don't wear a watch (and the dashboard on Hiram's old car doesn't have a working clock from what I can tell), I have no idea what time it is, or how long we drive, but eventually Hiram pulls into a sandy parking lot and shifts into park. He turns back to look at me and smiles. "How about a swim, Juniper?" he asks with a grin.

I guess they did know I was back here after all.

◇◇◇◇

It's only April, but it's sunny and warm today. Unseasonably warm, my dad would say, and then he'd launch into a lecture about weather patterns and climate change. It's not that I don't care about climate change (it's literally the greatest crisis facing mankind, of course I care), but right now I'm happy it feels like summer. It feels less like cutting class that way.

Of course, if it were summer, the beach wouldn't be empty.

Hiram sits on the hood of his car and squints in the sunlight, but Maya grabs my hand and pulls me toward the water. She takes off her pants, right there in the sunshine. She doesn't seem to care that Hiram might see her half-dressed.

"Come on," she shouts. She sounds like a little kid. I glance back. It doesn't look like Hiram's really watching. Slowly, I slide off my pants and follow her toward the water. If I get underwater fast enough, they won't have time to see my scars. It's going to be freezing. Even in summertime, the water doesn't really get warm here, just slightly less cold. I read once that apathy is a side effect of hypothermia. Maybe the cold water could freeze me into feeling calm.

Maya shouts when she hits the water. It's so cold that it hurts, but I don't so much as whimper when I cut myself, so why should this be any different? I don't see Hiram strip down to his boxers, but in a flash he's splashing around beside us, rubbing Maya's shoulders to keep her warm. Maya leans against him, then dives beneath the waves. She comes up gasping.

The water's so cold that we can't stay in long. I'm not sure we're actually in the water for more than thirty seconds. Maybe a minute or two total. Hiram leaves the water first, then Maya. She collapses onto the sand and lies down with her eyes closed and Hiram follows suit. I leave the water last. Eventually, I follow them to the spot on the sand where they're lying flat on their backs in the sunshine. I ball my hands into fists to try to stop their shaking, but then I see that Hiram and Maya are shivering too. It's just the cold.

Maya opens her eyes before I have a chance to put my pants back on. "How'd you get that?" she asks, reaching up and touching the scar on my left inner thigh with her fingertips. The doctors had to close it with nine stitches.

I shrug.

"You didn't have that the last time I saw you in a bathing suit." She squints in the sunlight, which makes her bruise even more noticeable. "Last summer."

"I know."

I glance at Hiram. His eyes are still closed and his breathing's steady. There's no way he fell asleep so fast. It's not like he doesn't know I have issues, given our recent interaction. I wonder if he told anyone. He's not exactly bound by doctor/patient confidentiality. Even Dr. Kreiter isn't entirely—since I'm underage, she has to report back to my parents on my progress.

I sit beside Maya. Sand has sharp edges. Isn't it technically, or at least partly, tiny pieces of glass?

Maya asks, "So, how'd you get it?"

Before Valentine's Day, my cuts were mine and mine alone. No one saw them. Before our three-month deal, there were no expectations attached to whether I was going to cut or not. It was entirely up to me. Afterward, it was like having something taken away from me—not just getting to cut, but getting to cut *in secret.* Now, it's something I have to share. Something I have to talk about. (Or anyway, something I'm *supposed* to talk about. Usually Dr. Kreiter does the actual talking.)

But Maya is the first person to simply, plainly *ask.* For some reason, that makes it easier to talk about.

"I cut myself," I say softly. I slide my hands beneath my hips. I've never *told* anyone about the cutting before. The people who know—Mom, Dad, Dr. Kreiter, the doctors in the ER—didn't find out because I actually *told* them.

Maya doesn't ask if it was an accident. Instead, she says, "Why?"

"Feels better." I've never said that out loud either. Dr. Kreiter didn't need me to tell her that. Like she said, she'd worked with other patients like me. She knows—or anyway, she thinks she knows—why we do what we do. Why I did what I did.

Maya doesn't ask better than what (which Dr. Kreiter did), or say that's insane (like my father did). Instead, she says, "It feels better after I throw up too."

I don't ask whether she means she *makes* herself throw up. I slide my hands out from beneath my legs.

"Other people don't get it," I say.

Maya nods. "Nope."

"I mean, it's not like I think it's good for me or anything."

"Of course not," Maya agrees.

"But other people don't understand how hurting yourself could possibly feel more *right* than not. Even though I know it shouldn't."

"I understand," Maya says.

"I didn't know you would."

"You didn't have to keep it a secret from me."

"You didn't have to keep it a secret from me either."

"Which part?"

"Huh?"

"The throwing up or Mike?" Maya surprises me by laughing, as though she's made a joke. After a beat, I join in. It probably shouldn't be funny, but we can't stop laughing. We laugh until our stomachs hurt. We laugh until we're not cold anymore.

"If I were a better friend, I would've known what was going on," I say finally. Maybe she knew I'd say the wrong thing. Maybe she tried to tell me, but I wasn't listening. Or maybe I was too busy talking and thinking about my own stuff to notice she had something to say too. Not that we've talked that much lately.

Maya shakes her head. "No, you wouldn't. I hid it. The same way you hid it."

I nod. Maya's right. We both know how to hide what we don't want others to see. "Why did we do that?"

Maya shrugs.

I glance at Hiram, still politely feigning sleep, then say, "I didn't see you as much once you were with him. You didn't even let me drive you to school anymore."

"I know." She sits up and wraps her arms around her knees. Her long hair falls across her face, partially hiding her bruise. "He wanted us to be together. All the time. As much as we could."

She sighs. I think of the way I wanted to be with Tess. The way I waited for her to respond to my text messages. When she didn't answer right away, I was so scared she didn't care about me.

Maya's eyes are very bright. "He was always so nice to me."

"How can you say that?" The words come out before I can stop them. I always say the wrong thing.

Maya shrugs. "I don't know," she answers.

"Can I ask you something else?" Maya nods. "Do you want him expelled?"

"I don't know," she says again.

Quickly—again, so fast I can't stop myself from saying the wrong thing—I ask, "But you *must*, right? Otherwise, why would you have gone to the principal instead of anyone else?"

"Habit?" Maya suggests. "You know, some leftover thing from elementary school, when they taught us to tell the teacher if something was wrong."

I nod. "Makes sense."

Maya smiles. "No, it doesn't."

"It does a little bit," I insist.

"You're just trying to make me feel better."

"Hey, I'm the one who feels better when she's bleeding. I'm in no position to judge."

Maya laughs, not a deep long-lasting laugh like before, but a real laugh nonetheless. "You always know just what to say," she says.

"Are you kidding?" Now I laugh. "I *never* know the right thing to say."

Maya's wavy hair is even wavier in the salty beach air, and she tucks a few strands behind her ears, then rests her chin on her knees. I try not to stare at the dark pink skin around her eye.

"You've heard about the protest on Sunday, right?" Of course, I know she has. I told her about it at lunch. "They—we—are going to ask them to expel Mike." Maya doesn't respond. I rush to add, "I can stop it if you want me to. I could try."

Maya looks out at the water and takes a deep breath. Finally, she says, "You remember how they used to tell us not to tattle? Like, in kindergarten. *No one likes a tattletale*," she singsongs. "No matter what the grown-ups said, we knew that kids weren't supposed to get other kids in trouble."

"You didn't *tattle* on Mike. You…" I'm not sure what the word is. Eventually I say, "You *reported* on him," like Maya's a journalist and her relationship with him was research for her latest exposé.

No; that makes it sound like she did this on purpose.

Maya watches the waves, one after the other, as if she's hypnotized. I adjust so I'm sitting the same way, but instead of looking at the waves, I look at her.

"You're still wearing the bracelet he gave you," I notice out loud.

Maya nods. "I know."

"Do you think you'll ever take it off?"

Maya's gaze moves up and down, in time with the waves. "I don't know."

three

MAYA

By the time we got to the beach, I could still feel Mike's touch on my upper arm. I knew he wasn't still holding me, but it was like my *skin* didn't know. I used to love that—how I could feel Mike after we'd been together. Now, I wanted it to stop. So I ran into the water like I thought I could wash him off. I knew Hiram and Junie would see my upper thighs, my stomach, the spots that are thicker and softer than I want them to be, parts that I usually camouflage with clothing, but I needed to wash off Mike's touch.

I guess it worked. Or at least, the water was so cold that I couldn't feel anything else.

I still don't want to go home, but we've been here so long that the fog is rolling in, and it's getting cold. Junie doesn't invite us over to her house. Maybe she doesn't want her parents to see her with Hiram. Her mom might know about him, since (unlike my mother) Frida is one of those moms who's involved

in everything and seems to know about everything and everyone. She asked about Mike's and my first date a few nights after
it happened, when I was at Junie's house for dinner. That was
before I stopped coming over for dinner. Junie's mom is a great
cook (unlike mine).

"Let's go somewhere without parents," I say finally. "Or teachers. Or guidance counselors."

"Got it," Hiram says. We get back into his car, and he starts
driving again.

"Does your hand still hurt?" I ask after a while.

Hiram grins. "Not as much as his face does."

I twist back around to look at Junie and see that she's covering
her mouth like she's trying not to laugh. We're finding strange
things funny today.

Hiram drives up into the hills above school, where the nicest
houses have views of the San Francisco Bay and the Golden Gate
Bridge. Kyle—Mike's best friend—lives up here. I've been to his
house with Mike a few times.

Hiram keeps driving, up past Kyle's street. The streets are
lined with hedges so thick that you can't even see the houses
behind them. Finally, Hiram pulls into a driveway. There's a
gate blocking the way, but Hiram leans out and punches some
numbers into a keypad. The gate swings open.

In front of us is a house that looks like it's entirely made of glass.
It's all windows, floor to ceiling. Hiram puts the car into park.

"Whose house is this?" Junie asks from the back seat.

"Worried about getting into trouble for breaking and

entering?" Hiram asks. Junie doesn't know him well enough to hear the joke in his voice. He twists around in his seat and sees how nervous Junie looks. "Don't worry," he adds gently. "This is my house."

"It is?"

"Yup. How else did you think I knew the code for the gate?"

Junie shrugs.

"Believe me, I'm not nearly as much of a criminal as the North Bay student body seems to think I am."

He opens his door, and after a beat, Junie and I each open ours. At the front door—also made of glass—there's no keyhole, but another keypad. Hiram punches in a few more numbers, maybe the same numbers as the numbers at the gate. I wasn't paying close enough attention to know.

The lock unclicks, and Hiram says, "You wanted a place without parents."

"What about *your* parents?" I ask.

Hiram opens the door, and Junie and I follow him down a flight of stairs into the fanciest living room I've ever seen. The furniture is all white, and the wall of windows looks out onto the bay. "Mom's at a retreat in Big Sur," Hiram says. "Dad's at work in the city."

Hiram's phone dings with a message. He reaches into his pocket and pulls it out. He makes a face, then hands the phone to me. I read the message and pass the phone to Junie.

"Are you kidding?" she practically shouts. "*You* violated school policy?" She shakes her head. "They haven't even officially ruled that *Mike* violated school policy, and you're practically expelled on the spot."

"It doesn't say I'm expelled," Hiram corrects. "Just that they'll discuss it at next week's board meeting."

"When they should be discussing Mike," Junie scoffs.

"There were at least a dozen people watching this afternoon," I interject. "Unlike what happened between Mike and me."

"So, Hiram will be punished while Mike gets off with a slap on the wrist, if that?"

I shake my head. "Everyone saw what happened—Hiram was provoked, he thought he was protecting me. The board of trustees will understand, and they'll do the right thing."

Junie shakes her head. Her parents raised her to believe that the right things don't come without a fight. But unlike Junie, I'm not sure what the right thing is in this case. Because Hiram *did* punch Mike, and even if it was provoked, it's still against the rules. And if they're going to expel Mike for breaking the rules with me, then they'd have to treat Hiram the same way, right? Otherwise it wouldn't be fair.

Not that I want Hiram to get expelled.

Or Mike.

Maybe.

I'm not sure.

If Mike gets expelled, he'll lose any chance at that track scholarship.

Which could impact the rest of his life.

"You can't really turn this into one of your social justice

crusades, Juniper," Hiram says as he leads us into the kitchen. The counters and cabinets are gleaming white. Hiram opens a fridge that's camouflaged to look like just another white cabinet. He pulls out several containers of food and offers us each a soda. Junie and I perch on cold steel stools surrounding the kitchen island across from him. "It's not exactly like I'm an underdog," he adds, waving at the absurdly nice house around us.

"It still wouldn't be right if you get expelled and Mike doesn't."

"You could both be expelled," I say. "I might have screwed up both of your entire futures."

Junie shakes her head. "What are you talking about?"

"Hiram never would've punched Mike if I'd kept quiet. And Mike—no one would've known if I hadn't said anything. If they get expelled, it will be my fault."

"If we get expelled, it will be *our* fault," Hiram says. "You didn't make me punch Mike."

"Yeah, but you never would've if—"

Hiram cuts me off. "And you definitely didn't make Mike hurt you. That was *his* choice, not yours. If he got expelled for cheating on a science test, you wouldn't blame Mr. Chapnick for making the test too hard, would you?"

But coming forward was *my* choice. I put my elbows on the counter and rest my head in my hands. How can I simultaneously feel bad about keeping everything with Mike a secret and feel bad for telling on him?

"Anyway." Hiram shrugs. "I haven't gotten expelled so far."

"How is that?" I ask suddenly, looking up and feeling

grateful for a new subject to focus on. "I mean, you hardly ever go to class."

Hiram shrugs again. "Doesn't seem to matter much," he says. "I still got into my first-choice college."

"You did?"

Hiram leans back against the refrigerator and runs his hands over his dark hair. He keeps it cut short, almost a buzz cut. I always liked the way it felt under my fingers. "Columbia."

"In New York?"

I didn't think he'd be going someplace so far away. Then again, I didn't think he was going to college at all. It's not that I don't think he's smart. I just didn't think he cared about those kinds of things.

"That's the one." He winks at me. "My sister's already there."

"You have a sister?"

All this time sitting in his ugly brown car, and I really don't know that much about him. I never asked. I don't mean that he asked about my life, and I never returned the questions. I mean, we never spoke much. Not about anything important. Not from the very first time I knocked on his window that Thursday in January.

It was two weeks after Mike slapped me. We were still together, and he hadn't hit me again, though the little hurts had continued. I didn't know whether or not they *counted* the same way the slap had, and I was sick and tired of thinking about it. I was sick and tired of thinking about much of anything. At lunch, it was too rainy to sit at our usual table, so we'd gathered in the hall near Mike's locker. Mike put his arm around me, squeezed me tightly (did that count?), and took a bite of my sandwich. I stood up suddenly.

"I gotta study," I explained quickly and rushed off in the direction of the library. I left my lunch for Mike to pick at, telling myself I'd rather he eat it anyway. Fewer calories for me that way.

But before I got to the library, I turned and headed for the parking lot. There weren't as many cars as usual, since some of our classmates drove off campus at lunchtime, but Hiram's car was in its usual spot. I could see him sitting in the front seat, his eyes closed. I wondered if he ever got bored, sitting out here like that.

I knocked on his window before I could stop myself. Hiram opened his eyes—he hadn't really been sleeping—and I opened the passenger door and ducked inside. I'd walked here so fast, sat down so fast, that I didn't think anyone had seen me. After all, this was the last place any of my classmates would have expected me to be.

Hiram seemed to know what I came for without my having to explain. And he didn't ask why, though he didn't seem disinterested either. Instead, he gestured at the school and said, "Sometimes you just need a break from all *that*, huh?"

It was my first time, and Hiram patiently explained the mechanics of when to inhale and exhale. He didn't make fun of me when I coughed, didn't scold me when I did it wrong. I leaned back against my seat. I'd only been there a few minutes, and already I thought of it as mine. I wondered if I'd ever been so comfortable sitting anywhere else, beside anyone else.

"Yeah." I nodded in agreement. "Just taking a break."

Now, Hiram grins at me from across the kitchen island as Junie's mouth drops open. "How'd you get into Columbia? I mean, I don't want to be rude or anything, but like you said, you hardly ever go to class."

For the first time, I realize that maybe Junie says *I mean* before half her sentences because she's worried that whoever she's talking to will be mad about what she has to say.

"Attendance isn't necessarily a prerequisite for good grades," Hiram answers with another shrug.

Junie looks positively awestruck. She gets straight A's—I know—but I also know that she studies harder than anyone else. She reaches for some of the food on the kitchen counter, and I realize I'm starving. But if I eat dinner here, I might not be able to throw up afterward. I've never thrown up anywhere but home.

I guess it's okay if I eat something, right? I threw up last night, and the night before that. I won't get fat from one meal.

Will I?

Hiram continues, "My parents both went there. My sister's there. And I actually have some pretty good extracurriculars."

"You do?" Junie can't hide her surprise.

"I volunteer at my dad's hospital every weekend. One of my letters of rec came from the parent of a patient I used to help out."

"Wow," Junie says. "Okay, but then," Junie continues in between bites of chips, "why do you drive that crappy car? Can't your parents afford something nicer?"

"My parents could," Hiram concedes. "*I* can't."

"You paid for your car yourself?"

Hiram nods. "They pay for school. But that's it."

"Other than the roof over your head."

Hiram laughs. "Fair enough."

"So that's why you sell—" Junie stops herself.

Hiram shakes his head. "I don't sell. What I gave you was a onetime thing."

"It was?" Junie sounds incredulous.

"My dad's a doctor. He gets all kinds of free samples, so there are pills stashed in every bathroom in this house. I don't mean he abuses them or anything," Hiram adds quickly, "but that's how we end up with pills that have been discontinued. My dad empties his pockets in one bathroom or another, then forgets which pills went where." He leans across the countertop like he's sharing a secret. "And this house has a lot of bathrooms."

"What are you two talking about?" I ask. What exactly did Hiram give to Junie?

Hiram leans back again. "Nothing important," he says. "Just that my parents are too checked out to notice much about me."

Before I can ask anything more, I feel my phone vibrating in my pocket. I can guess who's calling—my mom is pretty much the only person who still actually *calls* anymore, except for rare calls from my dad—but I still take a deep breath when I see her number on the screen. "A checked-out parent sounds good right about now." I sigh. At least talking to her will keep me from eating.

"Hi, Mom."

"Where are you? I've been worried sick." This isn't the first time my phone had rung since I had left school this afternoon. It's just the first time I've answered.

"I'm fine," I say, even though that doesn't answer her question.

"You have no idea how upset I've been. After everything you kept from me, how was I supposed to know whether or not you were safe?"

"I'm sorry," I offer, though I think it's kind of ridiculous that I'm apologizing. Sure, I've been out of touch for a few hours, but as usual, she making everything about *her*—how worried *she* is, how much all of this upsets *her*, how much it hurts *her* to know her daughter was hurt, could be hurt again. I shake my head. Shouldn't she be the one comforting me?

"I'm sorry," I repeat. "I'm fine. I'm with Junie. I'll be home later."

I hang up before she can ask *when*, before she can try to play mom by assigning a real curfew for the very first time in my life. She never minded when I was out late with Mike.

"Your mom still bugging the crap out of you?" Junie asks, nodding at my phone. I slide it across the kitchen counter absently. Before Mike and I were together, I complained about my mother to Junie almost daily.

"Of course," I answer.

"Thank goodness I left my phone at school." Junie sighs. "I mean, I can only imagine what I'd be hearing from my parents right about now. Especially my dad."

213

"Are you kidding?" I ask. "Your parents are the best." If Junie's mom was here, she'd put her arms around me and ask what she could do to make me feel better. At Junie's house, dinner is a homemade affair, eaten at the kitchen table instead of in front of the TV. And Aaron—Junie's dad—is her biggest fan. He encourages every cause she takes up, and I swear he doesn't think there's a person out there good enough for Junie to date.

"I'm not sure whether my dad would be more disappointed that I cut class, or that I wasn't the one who punched Mike in front of the whole school," Junie says finally.

I nod, remembering the scar I saw on her leg this afternoon. I'm not the only one who has secrets. "I actually think my dad will be sad when he hears I'm not with Mike anymore."

"When he hears?" Junie echoes. "You didn't tell him about—"

I bite my lip. "I didn't know how to."

"I haven't told my parents about Tess and me either."

"You and Tess?" I ask.

"We broke up." Junie says it fast, but I hear her voice catch.

I shake my head. "Wow, I'm a terrible friend, aren't I? We've spent the whole day together, and I didn't even ask about her."

"It's okay." Junie shrugs. "There was plenty of other stuff to talk about."

"But I don't want to be that kind of friend," I insist.

"It's not like we've spent all that much time together over the past six months." Quickly, Junie adds, "I mean, I know it's not your fault."

"It *is* my fault," I counter. "Partly, at least. He never said I couldn't spend time with other people."

The truth is, Mike isn't the only one who wanted to be together all the time. I wait for Junie to reproach me, to point out all the ways I failed as a woman, as a feminist, as a human being. But she keeps quiet.

"Aren't you disappointed in me?" I ask, a lump in my throat.

"For what?"

For missing him, even now. For staying with him after he hit me. "*You* never would've stayed with someone who hurt you."

"I hurt myself," Junie points out, too thoughtful to contradict me.

Hiram keeps quiet. He's good at blending into the background. Maybe that's how he lasted so long at North Bay without getting into trouble despite cutting class. Maybe the teachers don't even notice whether he's there or not. But he didn't blend this afternoon, when Mike came after me.

Hiram said that bad love isn't any better than not being loved at all.

I reach out and take a chip, dip it in a bowl of guacamole.

"I guess it doesn't matter what I eat anymore." I stuff the food in my mouth. I barely chew, and the chip's jagged edges scratch my throat as I swallow. "It's not like Mike will ever want to see me naked again." Again, I feel like crying. What's *wrong* with me?

"I think you look great," Hiram says, at the same time that Junie says, "Who cares what Mike thinks?"

Junie doesn't notice that I'm blushing under Hiram's gaze.

What would Junie think if I told her about Hiram? Maybe she'd think that Mike had every right to hit me since I was cheating on him. I know she'd never say that, but maybe deep down, she'd *think* it. Nobody's going to feel sorry—or at least, not *as* sorry—for the girl who was cheating on her boyfriend.

Maybe not even Junie.

Maybe not even me.

"Kyle lives around here, doesn't he?" Junie asks suddenly.

"Yeah." Hiram nods. "We passed his house on the way up."

"He's hosting Big Night tomorrow, right?"

Hiram shrugs. "Yeah."

Junie turns to me. "Let's go."

"Go where?" I don't want to leave yet. I like it in this big glass house that's so clean, it doesn't look like anyone actually lives here.

"Tomorrow. To Big Night."

"Are you kidding?"

Junie shakes her head. "Nope. I'll show Tess that I'm not embarrassed to be in the same room as her, even when she dumped me in front of the whole school."

I blink. "She dumped you in front of the whole school?"

"Yeah, but don't change the subject."

"What's the subject?"

"You're going to walk into Kyle's house like you own the place. Because Hiram's right. *You* didn't do anything wrong. *Mike* did."

It doesn't feel like I didn't do anything wrong. I cheated on Mike. I got Mike into trouble. I'm still keeping secrets.

"*Everyone* will be there," Junie adds. "We'll be able to spread the word about the protest. Even more people will be on our side after what they saw in the parking lot, right? The way he grabbed you, I mean."

But his touch was slow and deliberate. He did that on purpose, making it look gentle, so that people would see a nice guy. I spin Mike's bracelet around and around on my wrist. He gave it to me, but I've always thought of the slim silver bangle as his, not mine.

"We have to go," Junie says. "Isn't this what we're marching for on Sunday? The right for you to be wherever you want without worrying about him?"

I notice that Junie doesn't say *I mean* nearly as often when she's excited about a cause. Maybe she needs to work herself up enough that she doesn't care whether or not she offends anyone. Maybe it's because she sounds so confident and sure that I don't feel like crying anymore.

I say, "Okay, you're right. We'll go."

four

JUNIE

I'm not saying I didn't consider going through the medicine cabinets in one of Hiram's many bathrooms in search of the same kind of pills I left in the school parking lot. I could've used a false sense of well-being, because even though Hiram said it was his house, it sure felt like we were breaking and entering. As far as I could tell—at least in the living room and kitchen, where we spent most of our evening—there was no evidence that Hiram actually *lived* there. No leftovers from breakfast in the sink. No embarrassing baby photos on the mantel. Instead of a pile of wood inside the fireplace, there was a row of big, perfectly round black rocks. (I guess it was more of a decorative fireplace. Or fireplace as art. Or maybe architecture as art.) There weren't any pictures on the walls, just all those floor-to-ceiling windows looking out over the bay, like whoever designed the house said hanging pictures on the walls would distract from the view. It's the sort of thing Mom would read about in one of her design magazines, which are her guilty pleasure. She reads them the way other people read tabloid magazines because she knows Dad thinks they're frivolous.

Looking around the empty house, I wonder whether Hiram answered my text and showed up early to school because he was lonely. Why else would he cover for me? We'd never even had a real conversation before yesterday. People don't usually help you just because you ask, do they? (Or in the case of covering for me with Maya, without my even having to ask.)

Anyhow. I'm not saying I wouldn't have enjoyed feeling the way I felt this morning. I probably could've asked Hiram to give me more pills, but then Maya would've definitely known what was going on.

Telling Maya about Tess made me so nervous. I bet that Maya was thinking Tess was right to break up with a basket case like me (now that she knows about the cutting, she knows I'm a basket case), but then I remembered that Maya had confided in me about the bulimia too. And then I remembered what Dr. Kreiter said about how people aren't thinking about you nearly as much as you think they are, and that made me realize that Maya was probably thinking about her own relationship, about *Mike*, which made me feel really bad for assuming she would've been thinking about my relationship with Tess in the first place, which was a normal (if humiliating) breakup, but *nothing* compared to what Maya's going through. And that made me feel bad and anxious all over again, so Dr. Kreiter's advice totally backfired. Anyway, as tempting as it was, I wasn't about to go rifling through Hiram's bathrooms. What if I took the wrong pill and ended up *more* nervous instead of less nervous?

But then I had the idea about crashing Big Night, and I felt better. Technically it's not crashing, since the whole school's invited, but it's not like Kyle will want Maya there. Kyle is one of Mike's best friends. Plus, the whole track team will be there. They can't drink or stay out late—they're supposed to get a good night's rest before the meet—but they always at least make an appearance at Big Night. Which means Tess will be there too, but I'm not going to see Tess. I'm going to support my best friend. What better way to show Mike he doesn't get to decide where Maya goes and who she goes with than showing up at his best friend's house like we own the place?

On the ride home from Hiram's, Maya tinkers with the radio, landing on one classic rock station after another. I never knew she liked that kind of music, but she sings along as though she's heard every song a million times before. Meanwhile, I'm trying to remember whether I still have that gray-green T-shirt with the rips in the sleeve or whether I gave it away last time Mom was collecting donations. But maybe I should wear pink tomorrow night, since that's the color we're wearing for the protest on Sunday. No! I should wear the tank top that Maya borrowed for Valentine's Day with Mike this year, or maybe Maya should wear it, actually. I'm about to ask her whether she wants to borrow it again when Hiram puts the car into park in front of my house.

"Door-to-door service," he announces. I'm surprised he

dropped me off first since technically Maya's house is in between his house and mine, but maybe he didn't realize that because it's not like he knows where Maya lives any more than he knows where I live. (I had to give him my address before we got in the car tonight.) Then again, he offered to drive Maya home before we went to the beach this afternoon, so maybe he knows exactly where she lives.

◇◇◇◇

My parents are sitting at the kitchen table when I walk in the door, which isn't a good sign. It's late enough that normally they'd be in bed by now, or at least getting ready for bed, but they're still dressed and the lights are still on.

"First things first," Mom begins. "Are you okay?"

"I'm fine," I answer quickly.

"And Maya's okay?"

Mom must've seen Maya in the car with me just now. "Yes," I answer.

"Who was that driving?"

"A friend from school." I add, "Hiram," so that she doesn't think I'm trying to keep anything from her. Mom likes to think she knows everyone at North Bay Academy, but she's never met Hiram, and I've never mentioned his name before. "A new friend. You don't know him." Maybe that's too much information, but it's hard not to talk when I'm nervous.

"Okay, then." Mom takes a deep breath. "Do you have any idea how worried we've been?"

"I'm sorry," I begin, but Mom holds up her hand.

"Not only did you cut class—"

"I couldn't leave Maya—"

"Not only did you ignore my calls and texts—"

"I didn't have my phone with me."

"Oh, and I suppose Maya and Hiram didn't have one you could borrow? You couldn't have sent us a message so we'd know you were okay?"

I don't have an answer to that. I thrust my hands into my pockets.

"You're grounded," Mom says finally. Her voice is perfectly calm. At the hospital on Valentine's Day, talking to the doctors about my cutting, she kept her voice reasonable even though she was blinking between sentences, which I knew meant she was fighting a migraine. She was in pain, but she was still able to keep her voice even and clear. Why couldn't I have inherited that ability?

Instead, my voice is shaking when I say, "But tomorrow night, Maya and I—"

Mom shakes her head. "Don't use Maya as an excuse. I happen to know that Mrs. Alpert and Maya spoke hours ago."

I bite my lip. "Oh." Mom and Dad told Maya to call them by their first names from the day they met her, but Mom likes me to call adults Mr. and Mrs. because it's more polite. Dad used to argue against it, but he gave in eventually. (*Gotta choose your battles*, he told me later with a wink.)

Mom softens. "I know you want to be a good friend. This is a

222

difficult time for Maya. But it's a difficult time for you too. Let's not forget everything that's happened."

"I've kept up my side of the deal." I haven't cut. I've gone to therapy every week.

"I know you have," Mom says. "And we're proud of you. But you can't imagine how worried we were today."

"I'm sorry," I say again. "What about the protest?" I ask. "On Sunday."

"Grounded is grounded," Mom begins, but Dad interjects.

"We'll talk about that tomorrow." Dad's trying to sound as strict as Mom, but he can't keep the excitement out of his voice. He's proud of me for planning a demonstration. "For now, why don't you head to your room? We asked your teachers to email your assignments so you won't fall behind after missing this afternoon's classes."

I nod. I'm pretty sure if Dad has anything to say about it, I'm not missing anything on Sunday. He thinks my participation will look as good on my college applications as the straight A's I'll keep by making up today's schoolwork.

"Tess brought your backpack home," Mom adds as I head up the stairs.

My heart starts to pound. Mom obviously didn't go through my backpack. If she'd seen the pills, we'd have been having a different conversation. But what if *Tess* saw them? Well, it's none of Tess's business. We're not together anymore. What would she care?

Well, maybe she'd care a little bit, since she's the one who picked up my bag and brought it home for me. I feel myself smiling and try to set my mouth back into a straight line. *Happy* isn't the appropriate way to feel right now.

With my bedroom door closed behind me, I open my bag and sort through the contents. I take out the Ziploc and shake the pills into my hand, counting out the reds and the blues to make sure they're all still there. I'm not going to take one to sleep tonight. I don't think I deserve any help, not after the way I made my parents worry. Grounded or not, Dad will drive me to school in the morning so I can bring my car back home. He won't want me leaving the car in the parking lot all weekend. I shove the Ziploc back into my bag.

I take my phone out of the side pocket and the screen lights up, showing all the missed calls and texts from Mom and Dad.

I jump when my phone buzzes in my hand, alerting me to a new message from Maya.

Thanks for today.

Before I can write back, she adds, **Were Aaron and Frida freaking out?**

Yeah, I type. **I'm grounded. How about your mom?**

She was okay. Mostly I had to apologize for making her worry so much. You know how she gets.

I know.

If you're grounded, does that mean we can't go to Big Night?

Before Maya and Mike got together, she and I always texted before we went to sleep. Sometimes we talked about the test we were studying for or my latest crush or Maya's mother's latest date with some loser. Sometimes we talked about TV or which celebrity feud seemed faked, but we always talked. This feels familiar.

I picture Mom blinking in between sentences. I worried her so much today that it made her sick.

That just means I'll have to do a good job sneaking out tomorrow. Mom can't know I'm gone. As long as she doesn't know, she won't have to worry.

Of course we're still going to Big Night, I type. **Wouldn't miss it!**

Saturday, April 15

five

MAYA

"I'm so glad you're going tonight. It'll be good for you."

Junie has to sneak out tonight, but not me. My mom is practically pushing me out the door. After all, I've never missed Big Night before, not even my freshman year, and not that many ninth graders go to Big Night. I think Mom feels better, seeing me getting dressed for an evening out, like it means maybe what happened with Mike isn't such a big deal after all—things are going back to normal, and her daughter's going to be okay.

She doesn't realize that Mike will be there tonight. She probably thinks Mike's parents are making him stay home as punishment for what he did. But I know Mike's family well enough to know his parents would never do that.

Mom lingers in my room while I get dressed, commenting on my potential outfits, even though I never listen to her opinion when it comes to fashion. I still have half an hour before I have to leave. Big Night starts at nine, but Junie said we shouldn't arrive too early, so we're planning to get there at nine forty-five. Late enough that Kyle's house will be full of our classmates, but early enough that the students who are running tomorrow will still be there. Junie didn't mention it, but I think she knows—the track team never stays at Big Night late. Mike and his teammates will leave by ten thirty, eleven at the latest. This way, I won't have to be there with him for too long. And Junie won't have to be there with Tess for too long either.

Not that either of us will be *with* either of them. I can't imagine Mike will want to talk to me, and I can't imagine Junie wants to talk to Tess.

I hate the way Mom's lingering. Not only because I'm not interested in her never-ending commentary, but because I don't like changing my clothes in front of her.

I threw up after dinner tonight. I thought I wouldn't, now that there's no Mike to impress, but I did anyhow. And I skipped lunch, to make up for not throwing up after dinner last night. As I reach for another T-shirt, I wonder whether Mom notices that my stomach is flat, empty, even though we had dinner together an hour ago.

Yesterday, Hiram said I looked good the way I am, but the way I am is a result of making myself throw up, so how can I be sure he'd like me any other way? Not that I threw up for Hiram. But I'm not throwing up for Mike anymore either—am I?

I start to shake my head, then stop myself before Mom can ask what I'm thinking about. Maybe I threw up because I knew she'd watch me get dressed tonight and I wanted to at least look good in front of her.

I didn't used to be like this. As a little kid, when we had to change into our bathing suits in the communal locker rooms at camp, I really didn't care who saw, even as some of the other girls engaged in some serious acrobatics to change under their T-shirts.

Clothes are like armor, when you think about it. Those girls in the camp locker room hid beneath their clothes because it made them feel, safer, more secure. Clothes allow you to choose what the rest of the world gets to see—literally, clothes determine how much of your body is exposed to the world. And figuratively—the clothes you wear let you decide who they'll see: Cool-girl casual in jeans and a T-shirt? Unafraid-to-be-overdressed in skirt and button-down? Trendy girl in tight black pants and cool boots?

I thought about dressing up tonight—a dress, a skirt—but I never wore anything but jeans to Big Night before. So, jeans and a T-shirt. But which T-shirt? Which jeans? I've tried on three different options so far and none of them feel right.

Everyone's going to be looking at me tonight. (Not the way they look at Junie, who's hard not to stare at because she's so beautiful.) I never minded when they looked at me before. They looked because I was popular and stylish, because I was lucky to have landed Mike, because we were so in love. But tonight, they'll be looking at me because I'm the girl who accused Mike of hitting her, the girl who stayed for months after the first time it happened, the girl who drove off with the school burnout after lunch yesterday, the girl who might get Mike expelled.

Just thinking about walking through Kyle's door makes my palms all sweaty. I'm scared to see Mike, but I'm also curious to know how he'll react to my being there. Will he look at me with anger? With hatred? With love? And maybe a part of me is excited to see him, the same way I've been excited to see him every day for the last six months.

Junie would say I'm entitled to feel however I want. But she wouldn't understand that my feelings are completely at odds with one another.

No one else could possibly feel such different things at the same time.

Finally, I decide on my Led Zeppelin T-shirt, even though I already wore it this week. I pair it with my favorite dark blue jeans, just a little bit ripped over one knee, and black boots with a short heel. I turn to face the mirror over my dresser and pull my hair into a loose ponytail. I put on earrings that make my neck look long.

"Those are so pretty," Mom says from her perch on the edge of my bed. She's picking up my discarded shirts and putting them down, but she doesn't bother folding them because she knows I'll do it better than she will.

Unlike Mom, I make my bed every day. I fold my clothes, and my closet isn't overflowing, and the books on my shelves are arranged by color, not stacked haphazardly, because I like the way it looks. I once arranged the books in Mike's room in ROYGBIV order while he was studying, just for fun.

Now, I twist his bracelet around and around. There are still bits and pieces of Mike strewn about my room: his sweater, out of sight but neatly folded beneath my bed. A picture of the two of us printed and framed on my dresser. That same picture is the background on my phone. Maybe I should've removed all traces of Mike before I headed for Principal Scott's office on Monday. That's what women do in movies and books, isn't it? I shouldn't want to be reminded of him after everything that happened.

But I framed that picture of the two of us *after* he hit me the first time.

I cross the room and look at my reflection in the mirror above my desk. I can't decide what to do about my makeup. It would be easy enough to cover up my bruise—it's fading now, turning more yellow than pink, but still visible, a shadow beneath my skin. Covered up or not, everyone knows it's there—my class-mates saw it all week long. If I do conceal it, will they think that means I'm ashamed of it? Or will they think maybe it's already healed and I made too big a deal out of too small a hurt?

I put on bronzer, tap blush onto the apples of my cheeks, run a comb through my eyebrows. I brush mascara onto my lashes and lip gloss over my lips.

I wear concealer almost every day because I've always had circles under my eyes. Mom even complained about them to my pediatrician, and he said they were hereditary—from my dad's side, Mom insists—and the only thing that might improve them was to take a decongestant every day. And Mom may have wanted her little girl to look nice, but she didn't want me to be overmedicated, so the dark circles stayed put. But as soon as I was old enough for makeup—and my mom wasn't the kind of mom who made me wait until I was a certain age or anything like that, it was more that makeup didn't occur to me until I was fourteen—I started covering the circles with concealer.

Which means I was self-conscious about my looks *before* Mike ever asked me out. So maybe I would've started throwing up anyway.

Then again, I always enjoyed wearing makeup and trying on clothes. I don't *enjoy* sticking my fingers down my throat. Sometimes I have to silently beg my mouth to open wide enough for my fingers to slide inside.

"You look beautiful," Mom says. I always thought that was something mothers *had* to say, no matter how their children actually looked. I look fine, but surely I don't look beautiful, not with this bruise messing up the symmetry of my face.

Or maybe she thinks I'm beautiful despite the bruise. Maybe she loves me so much that I'm beautiful to her no matter what, under-eye circles and all.

Or maybe she thinks I'm beautiful because of the bruise. Because Mike hit me and I stood up for myself and said *enough*.

Eventually.

What would Mom say if she knew about the part of me that's excited to see him? The part of me that hid his sweater under my bed instead of throwing it away. The part of me that doesn't want to take his bracelet from around my wrist.

I rub concealer on my under-eye circles, but leave the bruise bare.

six

JUNIE

I shouldn't be thinking about the fact that Tess will be at the party. Shouldn't be thinking about the fact that just a week ago, I thought I'd walk into Big Night at Tess's side, maybe even holding hands, and everyone would cheer. (Not for me, of course, but for her, because she's the best runner on the girls' team.) I shouldn't be thinking about the fact that for once I didn't think I'd mind everyone looking in my direction, because mostly they'd be looking at Tess, and if they *were* looking at *me*, they'd be thinking how lucky I was to be with her. Which gets me thinking about the way our classmates used to look at Maya. Which gets me back to what I *should* be thinking about, which is Maya and whether she's going to be okay tonight.

Actually, that's not even what I should be thinking about. I mean, that's important and deserves my attention, but at the moment I should really be concentrating on one thing more than anything else—how I'm going to get out of the house without my parents knowing.

I am not a sneaking-out kind of daughter. Okay, sure—I snuck around cutting for months, but that's literally my only sneaking experience. And that's not the kind of experience that's going to help me get out the door tonight.

I'm not planning to shimmy down the drainpipe or tie my sheets together into a makeshift rope to rappel down from my bedroom window. Maybe it's not the most creative plan, but I've decided to simply wait until my parents go up to their room—they almost always watch a movie in bed on Saturday nights, and they inevitably fall asleep with the TV on. When I was younger, all three of us would watch together, usually some movie I probably wasn't old enough for, but I never minded. I almost always fell asleep before they did, but the next morning, I'd wake up in my own bed. (My dad carried me to my room after I fell asleep.) As I got older, I started spending my Saturdays with Maya, and then with Tess, or maybe I was in my room studying, or in the bathroom cutting. Whatever the reason, I stopped spending my Saturday nights with my parents.

But anyway, my plan tonight is to wait till they go to their room and then tiptoe down the stairs and sneak out the back door. Am I a Goody Two-shoes because—despite the fact that I'm sneaking out—I also plan to leave a note on my unmade bed letting them know that I'm okay, I'm with Maya, I won't be too late—just in case they happen to check up on me before I get back?

I mean, I won't be gone that long. Maya and I are going to

make an appearance to prove she's not scared to show up where Mike might be (and I'm not scared to show up where Tess might be), and then we'll leave after we've made our point. I can be there and back before my parents even know I'm gone.

Right?

I have literally no idea. Because like I said, I've never actually snuck out before. The only rule I ever broke (other than the kind of rules my dad encouraged me to break, ones that he thought were socially unjust) was cutting, and to be fair, it's not like my parents had ever explicitly forbidden cutting. At least, not before we made our three-month deal.

Which brings me to another thing I shouldn't be thinking about. My hands are shaking while I pick up a T-shirt and jeans from the pile of (clean) clothes on my bedroom floor. (Mom's rule is she'll wash my clothes, but she's not going to clean my room for me, so if I can't be bothered to put my clean clothes away, that's my problem, not hers, as long as I confine my mess to my room.) My hands are shaking while I brush my short hair. I tell myself it's normal to be nervous before going to a party your gorgeous ex-girlfriend will also be attending. And it's normal to be nervous before walking into Kyle's house, because he probably knows about the protest by now, and he probably knows that I planned it, and he definitely knows that I'm Maya's best friend. And it's normal to be nervous the night before a big event, even though Dad says he never gets nervous before a protest, that he's always too excited.

It's impossible to sit on my hands or stuff them in my pockets while I'm getting dressed. I'd been planning on wearing mascara tonight—I almost never wear makeup, once in a while just mascara and lip gloss—but my hands are shaking too hard to hold the mascara wand steady. I put the unused tube back in the medicine cabinet.

There's a pair of teeny tiny scissors in there, the kind that come in manicure kits. Somehow they survived my mother's sharp-objects purge. Maybe she thought they were too small to do any damage.

The blades curl into a point, almost as sharp and thin as a needle. I guess they're meant to curve around your fingernails. The tips of the blades are so narrow, I could make a tiny little cut, just enough to relieve the pressure. I wouldn't bleed much. I wouldn't even bleed for very long.

Before this week, I never wanted to use anything but my special razor blades, the ones I kept clean with cotton balls soaked in alcohol. But on Monday, I considered using the mirror in my glove compartment. And now, I can't stop staring at these scissors.

I mean, this is a special night, unusual circumstances. Maybe I *should* cut, if cutting would make me calm. After all, I'm already in trouble, so what's one more infraction?

No. It's one thing to be in trouble for missing class and sneaking out. (If I get caught.) Quite another to break our three-month deal. I force my shaking hands to grip the sides of the sink. If I'm holding the sink, then I can't reach for the scissors. But I'm shaking so hard that my hands slide right off the porcelain. I leave the bathroom without closing the medicine cabinet because I'm scared I'll slam it so hard, it would break. (More sharp objects.)

What if everything goes wrong? What if the protest tomorrow is a disaster and when I apply to college next year, the scope of my failure shows up on my records somehow? What if Kyle won't even let us in the door tonight? What if Maya looks to me for help and I don't know what to say? What if Tess is there with some other girl on her arm, someone who hasn't been diagnosed with anxiety and OCD, some girl who won't sabotage her relationship and who can get undressed with the lights on?

I shake my head. Yesterday, I kissed Tess. (Crap, what was I thinking?) But what I mean is that yesterday, I felt *good enough* to kiss Tess. Yesterday, I was ready to sit at our lunch table before the boys could stake their claim. I need to feel tonight the way I felt then.

Only tonight. And tomorrow. That's all. That was my plan, right? That's what I have them for. They're better for me than cutting would be. (Aren't they?) At least, they're not explicitly against the rules. (Except, of course, they are. Just not the *particular* rules of the three-month deal.)

I dig around in my backpack until I find the bag Hiram gave me. I shake out a red pill—red for daytime, even though it's dark outside—and put it under my tongue. I don't want to go back into the bathroom to get a drink of water, so I suck on the pill like it's candy, waiting for it to soften and shrink before I swallow. It tastes so bad that I gag, but I manage to force it down eventually.

I watch the clock, and when the time is right, I tiptoe down the stairs. I'm not driving, because my parents would definitely hear the sound of the garage door opening. Maya said she'd borrow her mom's car. She said she'd turn off her headlights and wait down the block so my parents wouldn't see her.

I open the back door, the one next to the kitchen sink, careful not to let it slam shut behind me. I run down the block on my tiptoes. Maya's right where she said she'd be. I open the passenger side door.

"Good idea," I say, "waiting down the block like this."

She shrugs. "Mike used to do it," she says. "Bringing me home after a date. Whenever I didn't want my mom to see us together."

Crap. I shouldn't have called it a good idea. I didn't mean to compliment Mike. What was I thinking? Why couldn't I keep my mouth shut? Why couldn't I have simply said *hi* the way any other person would? Commented on her cool outfit? Asked how she was feeling? Something, anything normal.

I take a deep breath and slide my hands beneath my thighs. It's just a matter of time, I tell myself, before the false sense of well-being kicks in.

I only have to feel like *this* for a little while longer.

seven

MAYA

Kyle's house is the sort of house that—before we went to Hiram's place last night—I would have described as the nicest home I'd ever been to. It's tucked into the hills with a view of the bay, though not nearly as nice a view as Hiram's. The house has a long driveway, and I park my mom's car—she was only too happy to lend it to me for the night—down the street because there are already a bunch of cars parked on either side of the driveway, which has a gate across it, though it doesn't have a keypad like Hiram's. The walk up the driveway is steep and long, and if I weren't so nervous, I think Junie and I would be laughing about how out of shape we are, huffing and puffing our way up the hill.

Mike likes to jog up and down this driveway. I used to sit on the grass by the side of it—because Kyle's parents are the sort of people who have green manicured grass even during a California drought—and cheer for him. I liked to think that my encouragement helped him, but the truth is, Mike would've been running up and down this driveway whether I was there or not. If it hadn't been me, maybe there'd have been some other girl cheering him on, maybe Eva Mercado, the sophomore who's always had a crush on him. I was never jealous of Eva, though. Mike always said he only had eyes for me, a line from a cheesy old love song.

The party is so crowded that no one seems to notice when Junie and I walk in, hand in hand. What was I expecting? That we'd walk in and the place would fall silent, someone would cut the music off, and everyone would turn to stare at us?

Yes, actually. That was exactly what I was expecting.

Instead, the music is so loud that I can't even hear the lyrics, I just sort of feel the rhythm of the bass. The wall of sliding doors that lead to Kyle's backyard are open, but I'm sweating despite the breeze coming in from outside. It's only a matter of time before my makeup runs and my hair falls flat, and all the effort I put into getting ready tonight will be for nothing. Junie leads the way through the crowd—there are so many people in here that we have to walk single file, but she doesn't let go of my hand. My palm is clammy, but Junie's is cool and dry. How can she be so calm? I feel like I need to throw up—not like when I make myself throw up, but like I'm sick and I actually *need* to throw up. I'm tempted to turn around and run down the steep driveway back to my mother's car. Junie gives my hand a squeeze.

"Maya!" someone shouts. I turn and see Maggie Haobsh, a girl I've known since first grade. "What are you doing here?"

"It's Big Night," I answer lamely, as if I'm not fully aware that most of my classmates probably didn't think I'd show up.

"Why wouldn't she be here?" Junie asks, leveling her gaze with Maggie's.

"No, it's *awesome* that you're here, it's just—I didn't know you were up for a party after everything that happened."

I think about all the parties and track meets I've attended in the last six months, while I was with Mike, sometimes with bruises beneath my clothes.

"Don't worry," Maggie says. She reaches out and rubs my forearm. "Hiram's not coming tonight."

"Hiram?" I echo.

"He may be a loser, but he's not an idiot," Maggie says. "And Kyle told him he's not welcome. But I'm around if you need to talk." Her voice is syrupy-sweet. I guess in a way, I confided in the whole student body when I went public with what was going on, so maybe they think we're all really close now. Then again, everyone always treated me like that—I may not have known them well, but they knew me well. That's part of being popular.

Junie would say I went public with *Mike's abuse*, not with *what was going on* between us.

I turn to Junie. "Do you know what Maggie's talking about?"

"No clue." Junie shrugs. "Maggie's always been a flake, right?"

"Right." I nod and continue following Junie across the room. Someone's hand falls on my shoulder. "Whoa!" It's Kyle. "Didn't think you'd show up. You here to apologize?"

Junie and I echo the word *apologize* at the exact same time, but we don't say it the same way. I ask it like a question. Junie says it like it's a dirty word.

"Yeah," Kyle adds. He leans in, so close I can smell his breath. Kyle's on the track team, and he shouldn't be drinking with the meet tomorrow, let alone hosting Big Night. Then again, Kyle's a pretty weak runner. Coach probably won't let him compete tomorrow anyway. I always thought Mike convinced the coach to let Kyle on the team, but I never asked, because it was the kind of question he wouldn't like.

"You know, about your little mix-up." Kyle winks. "Or not so little, I guess, but don't worry. Mike set us all straight."

"What are you talking about?" Junie asks.

"I'm talking about that shiner." Kyle gestures at my face. "I told Mike he should kick that loser's ass, but he said he didn't want to stoop to Hiram's level. Or maybe he didn't want to defend the honor of a cheat like you."

"To *Hiram's* level?" Junie spits. She sounds confused, but I'm not. In fact, it all makes perfect sense.

Mike rarely comes up with a plan at the spur of the moment—he likes to strategize—but I think he might have made an exception yesterday. Because the instant Hiram tried to defend me, he provided Mike with a cover story.

When Hiram got out of his car to confront Mike, Mike guessed that something was going on between Hiram and me. (Even if it was just that we were friends.)

And then Hiram hit Mike, and Mike fell backward, showing

everyone that Hiram was the violent one, and Mike was the pacifist.

So Mike said it was Hiram who hit me, the same way he hit Mike. He called me a cheat and a liar.

And now everyone at this party believes that because it's easier to hate the loser with whom we all reluctantly interact than the golden boy we all love.

Kyle walks away, and I explain it to Junie.

"But that's ridiculous," she says. "You said it was *Mike*. You never even mentioned Hiram. Did you?"

I didn't, not to Principal Scott. In fact, I didn't actually *mention* Hiram to Junie, not even when he was driving us away from school, to the beach, to his house, and home again after. I've never mentioned Hiram, not once. I kept him a secret.

No. I kept Mike a secret.

No. I kept *Mike's* secret.

Or was his hitting me *my* secret?

I shake my head. Junie hands me a drink. I take a sip. And then another, and then another, until the plastic cup is empty.

"Maya!" It's Erica Black. She's in my history class. "I'm so glad you're here." Erica is the third person who sounds surprised to see me. A few days ago, they'd have been surprised if I didn't show up.

"You are?"

"Of course. I've got my pink shirt all ready to march tomorrow." Junie shushes her harshly, but Erica shakes her head. "Oh, you can't keep something like this quiet, Juniper. Isn't the point to spread the word?"

"Of course, but—"

"So?" Erica says. "Word has been *spread*. Believe me, everyone here is ready to march."

"Everyone?" I echo, glancing at the crowd about us. Mike never really liked parties—he said he preferred to hang out just the two of us—but we always went. *We have to at least show our faces*, he'd say.

Thinking about the state of my face tonight, Mike's choice of words is almost funny.

"Almost everyone." Erica practically giggles. "It's a miracle that loser wasn't expelled a long time ago."

Erica is also the third person I've heard call Hiram a *loser*. I try to remember if I ever called him that, before I started hanging out in his car. Maybe since then too.

"Hey," Junie says softly, leaning in close so I can hear her above the music. "I'm going to try to figure out what's going on. Will you be okay for a few minutes?"

"I told you what's going on," I begin, but Junie's already dropped my hand and disappeared into the crowd. And Erica's still talking. She's practically shouting, because otherwise I wouldn't be able to hear her.

"Just so you know, no one blames you."

"Huh?" I ask dumbly.

"No one blames you, you know, for getting confused. You're the victim here, and none of us would ever blame the victim."

"Of course not," I agree. I know it's what she wants me to say. I've always been good at knowing what people want to hear.

246

"Trauma can confuse a person. PTSD and all that. I read it can even give people hallucinations, you know?"

I nod, though I don't know.

"It's not like anyone doesn't believe someone hurt you." Erica takes my arm like it's urgent. "You have to know that, right? That everyone believes you."

I nod again, but they don't believe me. They believe *Mike*.

Can I blame them? Mike spoke up as soon as he got hit. I didn't.

"At least Hiram showed us all who he really is. My god, did he *force* you?" The urgency is back in Erica's voice again. "No one would blame you for that either."

She adds, "If it were me, I would've gone to the police the first time he hit me."

I blink. Erica believes that it was going on for months, but she doesn't believe that I know who was doing it.

"Why did you wait?" Erica asks. "Did he say he'd hurt you worse if you told?"

Here she is, on my side, ready to march tomorrow—and yet, she still thinks I did something wrong. She believes that if it happened to her, she'd have stood up for herself right away.

Maybe she would have. Maybe Erica is strong like that.

Mike never threatened me. Threatening me would've been acknowledging what he'd done, and he never did that either. Unless you count the way he kissed my bruises.

But then, why *did* I wait? Why didn't I come forward sooner? What kind of girl stays after her boyfriend hits her?

What kind of girl gets hit in the first place?

Did Mike see something in me, some sign that I'd keep quiet, at least for a while? He'd have been as thoughtful about choosing me as he is about everything else. Why else would he have picked me when he could have had anyone?

He could have chosen Erica, but maybe he could tell she'd stand up for herself right away. Unlike me.

Erica interprets my silence as discomfort and says, "Don't worry. You don't have to talk about it if you're not ready." Then she says, "Mike didn't even try to fight back, poor guy, even after everything that happened."

Poor guy. Why is it easier for her to believe I cheated on Mike than to believe Mike hit me?

But then I remember: I *did* cheat on Mike. Maybe they can all tell it's true, like my bruise is Hester Prynne's scarlet *A*.

But *Mike* gave me this bruise.

"You look like you could use another drink," Erica says.

I nod again. Nodding seems to be more than enough to keep this conversation going.

eight

JUNIE

I'm looking for Tess.

And not only because I'm feeling good (false sense of well-being) and I want Tess to see me feeling good. And not only because the last time I was feeling this good and I saw Tess, I kissed her. And not only because I want to see Tess, period.

I'm looking for Tess because I think Tess will know what the heck Erica was talking about, how everything got so twisted and turned around.

I can't remember why I was embarrassed about kissing Tess yesterday. She's my ex-girlfriend, and we had a moment. Things like that happen between exes all the time. Plus, I want her back. (Don't I?) How else was she going to know I'm interested?

It's easy to find Tess, since she's taller than every girl in our class (and taller than at least half the boys too). Her hair makes her taller still. Her dark eyes are rimmed with black eyeliner that swooshes into wings at the edges (she told me she calls it her Cleopatra look), and slick-looking clear gloss makes her lips shine. Unlike me, Tess knows how to wear makeup. She tried to do mine once, but I thought I looked like a clown. She's wearing tight black jeans that stop above her ankles, black ballet flats, and a high-necked black tank top. I can tell she's not wearing a bra.

"Hey!" I stand on my tiptoes to hug her hello. Her skin is warm. "I just ran into Erica Black," I begin. "She said that news about the protest has spread."

Tess's plush lips widen into a smile. Her teeth are so white, they practically glow in the dim light. "Isn't it great?" she says. "Kids from East Prep are planning on marching with us. Even if it means postponing the meet."

"But they don't even know Mike and Maya." I don't stop and think before I speak, don't go over the words in my head and wonder, after they've been said, if they're okay.

"Sure they know Mike." Tess shrugs. "They've been racing against him since freshman year. And they don't need to know Maya to want to march against domestic violence."

"But this isn't supposed to be about domestic violence. It's about getting Mike expelled. We wanted the board going into their meeting on Monday seeing that the student body had a united front." It's all so clear. Why can't she see it? Why can't everyone see it?

Tess's smile falters. "Well, I think that as more information got out—"

"Information?" I echo. "You mean these ridiculous rumors

about Maya and Hiram?" I shout to be heard over the music. Or maybe I'm just shouting.

I roll my eyes. "God, you're as bad as they are." I don't worry that my words might hurt Tess's feelings. I don't worry that I'm doing the same thing she did to me on Monday, assuming she's wrong without giving her a chance to explain. I don't worry at all. Instead, I gesture at the crowd like they're lemmings following wherever Mike tells them to go, believing what he tells them to believe. I turn on my heel, but Tess grabs my arm.

"I heard he's planning on marching tomorrow," she says. "He wouldn't be doing that if he hit her, would he?" She doesn't sound like she's certain, more like she actually wants my opinion.

"Of course he would," I answer confidently. "What better way to look like a hero instead of a villain?"

Tess's face falls, but I shake off her grip and storm back through the party, looking for Maya. Was it always this hot in here? I fan my face with my hands. Even though the room is pretty dark, I can see that my palms are pink.

I grab Maya's hand just in time to hear the word *Slut!* being hurled across the room. I turn around.

"Who said that?" I shout. (No hesitation. False sense of well-being. Inner monologue silenced. Well, except for the part of me that's acknowledging the silence.)

No one answers.

"Wow, whoever you are, you're really brave, aren't you?" I laugh. "And seriously, *slut*? Can you think of a more anti-woman, anti-feminist, anti-victim thing to say? Let's say, for the sake of argument, that Maya did cheat on Mike—does that mean it was okay for him to hit her? And she didn't, you know—Maya was the perfect girlfriend, and Mike still hit her. What is *wrong* with you people?" I spin around to face Maya.

"What is wrong with these people?" I repeat.

Maya's eyes are very bright.

"Are you okay?" I ask. "Don't listen to any of it. They don't know what they're talking about."

Maya shakes her head. She says something so softly, I can't hear it. I lean in, my ear close to her mouth. Her breath is warm on my skin. God, I'm so hot.

"They *do* know what they're talking about, Junie." Maya's voice is shaking.

"What do you mean?"

"I was hooking up with Hiram."

Maya blinks away her tears. I take a step back. "What do you mean?" I ask again.

"It wasn't all the time," Maya says. "Only—once in a while. And just kisses, mostly."

I shake my head and take another step backward. After everything that happened yesterday, everything I told her, how could she keep this from me?

Crap, I'm so stupid. The way Hiram burst out of his car to hit Mike, the way he held open the passenger-side door for Maya afterward, how he knew where she lived—of *course* there was something going on between them!

All day yesterday, at the beach, at Hiram's house, I thought

252

we were bonding, getting back to where we used to be. And that whole time, she and Hiram were probably wishing I'd never gotten into the back seat of his car, wishing I'd make myself scarce, cursing me for being such a heavy third wheel. No wonder he took me home first last night—obviously, he wanted time alone with her. And that must have been why he gave me the pills in the first place. He was only being nice to me to get on Maya's good side.

"You lied to me?"

Maya shakes her head. "I didn't lie—"

"No, you just didn't tell me the truth." Like she didn't tell me about Mike. Like she didn't tell me about throwing up.

"I'm sorry," she says, but the words sound empty.

"What else did you lie about?"

"Nothing, I promise. It's just—like we said yesterday, we weren't as close over the last six months—"

"And whose fault is that? You're the one who disappeared, not me."

"I told you, Mike wanted us to be together."

The question that's been dancing around my brain since Monday bubbles up in my throat. Later, I'll think that there are so many versions of this question, versions that have been asked thousands of times by thousands of people thousands of different ways: Why didn't some girl scream even when there was a knife to her throat? Why didn't another girl bite and kick and scratch even when the man forcing himself on her was a foot taller and twice her weight? Some version of this question has been asked by judges and defense attorneys and journalists and random observers because they think they know something about survival; because they believe they know how they'd behave under circumstances they've probably never experienced.

But right now, I'm not thinking about any of that (no inner monologue), so I ask: "You said he hit you for the first time in January. Three months ago! How could you stay for three months?"

I turn away before Maya has a chance to respond. Suddenly, I'm grateful this party's so crowded. It makes it easier to put a bunch of people between Maya's body and my own.

A cool hand lands on my arm. I spin around. *Tess*.

"Hey," she says. "Look, I'm sorry about before. You're right. Of course I believe Maya."

I shake my head. "Maya lied." Not about Mike. About Hiram. But a lie's a lie's a lie. That's what my father taught me. Black and white. Good and bad. Lies and truth.

Tess's lips curl into an almost-smile. "Are these things always so confusing?" she asks. "I mean, when I read about it happening at other schools, I always know exactly who to believe."

I reach up and slide my hand to the back of Tess's neck. She gasps. "Your hands are so hot."

I pull her head down toward mine. "Let's get out of here," I whisper.

nine

MAYA

I can't see who says it, but the word rings out so clear and loud that you'd think there was no music playing, no friends chattering.

Slut.

Junie starts shouting at the crowd, as if everyone said it, not just a single girl. (I think it was a girl's voice.) But maybe Junie knows what I suspect—even if all of them didn't *say* it, they're all *thinking* it.

Slut.

"What is wrong with these people?" Junie asks, turning back to me. I don't think she expects an answer.

"Don't listen to any of it," she adds. "They don't know what they're talking about."

I shake my head. Or anyway, I try to shake my head, but my muscles aren't cooperating. They *do* know what they're talking about. I cheated on Mike.

Is that why he hit me?

But I didn't start cheating until after he hit me.

Maybe that's why he hit me *again*.

But he didn't know about Hiram and me until yesterday.

Maybe I deserved it anyway. Maybe Mike knew, somehow, that I was going to hook up with someone else. Maybe he knew I was a bad girlfriend. A bad girl.

A *slut*.

I lean in, so I won't have to shout for Junie to hear me. I tell her that *these people* know exactly what they're talking about.

"I was hooking up with Hiram." My voice shakes.

"What do you mean?"

"It wasn't all the time," I add quickly as though the frequency—or lack of frequency—makes it better, less of a crime. "Only—once in a while. And just kisses. Mostly."

Mostly kisses. Mostly Hiram's gentle mouth over mine. But sometimes, his gentle hands traced my skin. Sometimes they slipped up under my shirt, down beneath my waistband. Always slowly, always hesitantly. Always like he was asking permission, giving me a chance to say no.

Sometimes Hiram really did ask permission. He didn't whisper it, but said it clearly. *Is this okay?* He never seemed the least bit scared that the question would spoil the mood. He never seemed worried that it might give me a chance to rethink my actions and change my mind. I think he actually wanted me to have time to consider my actions, that he would have simply shifted back to his side of the car if I changed my mind.

But I never did.

Slut.

Even Junie thinks so. I can tell from the look on her face, the way she's backing away from me. She thinks I'm disgusting.

A liar.

A cheater.

A girl who got what she deserved.

"How could you stay for three months?" Junie asks before she disappears into the crowd. I don't have an answer.

Junie wouldn't have stayed. Erica Black wouldn't have stayed.

Maybe the kind of girl who gets hit in the first place is the kind of girl who stays. The kind of girl who cheats rather than leaving.

If it were some other girl, some story I'd heard in which I didn't actually know any of the people involved, I'd say there was no excuse for her boyfriend's hitting her, even if she did cheat on him, even if she did stay.

Wouldn't I?

Isn't that what I believe?

"You really screwed up, you know."

I spin around. Eva Mercado is standing behind me. Or, rather, standing in front of me.

"What?" I ask dumbly.

"You really screwed up. Thanks to your little mix-up, Mike could get into real trouble."

"My little mix-up?" I turn back, then remember Junie isn't there anymore.

"Or did you lie on purpose? Because if it were me, I'd sure as hell be able to tell the difference between Mike Parker and *Hiram Bingham*." She spits Hiram's name like it tastes bad. Eva barely knows me, but I can tell from the look on her face that she *hates* me. Before, she hated me because I had Mike and she didn't. And now, she hates me because I gave him up.

Did I give him up? We still haven't broken up, not officially, not technically.

She continues, "Did you think your little cover story was the only way to save yourself from getting dumped? You know, Mike deserves someone who would appreciate him. Someone who would never hurt him. Never cheat on him."

"Someone like you?" I ask before I can stop myself.

I wasn't thinking about a hypothetical next girl when I came forward. I wasn't thinking that Mike might end up with someone else and hurt her too. I wasn't even thinking about whether Mike might be expelled, what kind of consequences he might face. I was thinking about myself.

I just wanted it to stop.

Eva thinks I came forward to save myself. Not from being hit, but from being dumped. She thinks I accused Mike to get ahead of the story, save face. But who would come forward and say her boyfriend was beating her to *save face*?

It only saves face if you're also something else that's worse than a girl who stayed.

If you're also a cheating, lying *slut*.

Which is exactly what Eva thinks I am.

"Maybe me." Eva shrugs, answering a question I forgot I asked. "I'd be better to him than you were."

Maybe she'd be a good enough girlfriend that Mike wouldn't hurt her. Maybe she wouldn't cheat on him even if he did.

An achingly familiar voice enters the conversation. "All right, Eva, I think that's enough."

I wish it were Junie. Or Hiram, coming to my rescue again. Actually, I wish I weren't the sort of girl who needed someone to come to her rescue.

The kind of girl who gets hit.

The kind of girl who stays.

What would I have done in the parking lot yesterday if Junie and Hiram hadn't been there? Maybe I'd have let Mike take my arm and pull me away to some quiet corner. Maybe I'd have nodded when he said, *This is all a misunderstanding.*

And,

Don't you remember it was an accident?

Then,

I just want to talk to you.

Until,

We can work this out.

◇◇◇◇

I let Mike lead me down the stairs to Kyle's room. He keeps his hand on my upper arm, right below my sleeve, almost exactly where he held me in the parking lot yesterday. I can feel each one of his long fingers on my skin. He closes the door behind us without letting me go. We've been alone in this room before. We made out on Kyle's bed less than two weeks ago. This house is so well insulated that I can barely hear a sound from the party above us.

Mike is standing in front of the door. Did he stand there on purpose, to block my escape, or was it just because he closed the door behind him?

Everything Mike does is on purpose.

I'm surprised to discover that my heart is pounding. I read somewhere that the most dangerous time in an abusive relationship—if that's what our relationship is—is right after the woman tries to end it.

But Mike wouldn't do anything to me now, here. Would he? Not in Kyle's house. Not with everyone upstairs. Not with the rumors swirling. He's too careful for that.

He's standing close enough to me that I can smell him: Ivory soap and Tide. (Not that Mike would know the difference between Tide and any other detergent. I don't think he's ever done his own laundry.) And there's some other scent, the one that always clung to Mike like it was coming from inside of him, a combination of sweat and breath and *boy* that I memorized months ago.

Two weeks ago, being alone with him in this room was exciting. I didn't know how far Mike would take things. Kyle might have come in at any moment; he wouldn't have bothered knocking on the door to his own room. My pulse quickened, my palms were moist. Mike didn't ask permission the way Hiram did. Not that he

260

was aggressive about it, but he never asked either. He moved from one step to the next, as methodical as he was about everything else.

Two weeks ago, in between kisses, my eyes kept darting to the door, to the windows, to the closet. Escape routes. Hiding places.

For the first time, it occurs to me that maybe I wasn't excited. Maybe I was *scared*.

"Man, talk about a rough week," Mike says. He lets go of me and collapses dramatically onto Kyle's bed. His legs are so long that I can see his ankles between his jeans and his sneakers.

I don't say anything, and I don't leave the room even though he's cleared the way to the door. The kind of girl who stayed doesn't make a run for it, right? I stand in the middle of the room. My legs feel rock solid. I don't think I could leave if I wanted to. Mike stands and crosses the room, not quite touching me, but close enough that I have to tilt my head up to see his face.

"I'm not mad at you, My, if that's what you're worried about."

Mad at me? For cheating on him, or for reporting him to Principal Scott?

"I could never be mad at you. I love you."

Did I always feel this frozen in his presence? Did I always worry that I might say the wrong thing? Was my throat always this dry? I manage to nod.

"*Still*," Mike adds emphatically. "In case you thought that had changed."

I nod again. He leans down, his face closer to mine.

"I won't always be under so much pressure—track and grades

261

and my baby brother. You know how it all gets to me." He runs his hands though his tawny hair.

Does he mean he won't always hit me?

"It takes two, you know," he adds, so close that I can feel his breath. I nod again. I'm half of this relationship, just like he says. A person can't hit another person if that other person isn't *there*.

His brow furrows, then relaxes. "All you need to do is take it back. Just tell them you were confused, and everything can be the way it was before." His voice is soft.

I nod. Again. I don't move away when he leans down, his lips lingering over mine. "We have so many plans, My. We're going to college together. We're going to be together forever."

He kisses me. I never noticed before that his nickname for me sounds like I belong to him.

I kiss him back. Is it a reflex, muscle memory? Am I scared that if I don't kiss him back, he'll get angry?

Or is it that the future he laid out—the one in which we spend our lives together—sounds so much better, so much easier than whatever *this* is.

Is it that I love him *still*, too?

I feel my body unfreeze and lean into him, pressing my chest against his. I always loved feeling his heartbeat speed up even as he kept his voice calm and even. But tonight, his pulse feels steady and slow.

As always, Mike ends our kiss, not me. "Just say it was Hiram. Whatever went on between you two, it's over now. I'll forgive you. I'll make sure everyone knows it."

Mike doesn't ask *what* went on between us. Does he care? Even if I never kissed Hiram, my friendship with him was still cheating because I kept it to myself, did it behind Mike's back.

But he'll forgive me. If I say Hiram was the one who hurt me.

"Everyone already knows the guy's a creep." Mike gestures to his face. There's a shadow of a bruise there, but it's not nearly as pink and angry as my eye looked the day after Mike hit me. "I mean, he gave *me* a black eye too."

Too? But Hiram didn't give me a black eye. *Mike* gave me a black eye. Yesterday, in the school parking lot, he said it was an accident.

As if Mike can hear my thoughts, he says, "It's better than saying it was an accident, My. People will still suspect me if you say it was an accident. But if you say it was Hiram, there won't be any more questions. He's getting expelled anyway," Mike adds, like the board has already decided. "And it's not like *he* has a scholarship riding on this."

As always, Mike's given thought to his plan. It's true: Hiram doesn't need a scholarship. But couldn't Columbia rescind his admission if they found out he got expelled?

"You're the best, My." Mike kisses me again, a stiff, quick kiss this time. "I better go, though," he adds. "Gotta get up early for the meet tomorrow."

I nod. I know Mike's routine before every race: in bed by eleven, up by seven, an hour of stretches before heading to campus. We scheduled our dates around it.

Mike adds, "Hope the rally won't delay the races too much tomorrow."

The rally. Mike's going to march tomorrow, protesting domestic violence.

Does *domestic violence* even apply to us, to Mike and me, a couple of teenagers? We're not married. We don't live together. Like my mom said, there's no house to sell, no child custody to negotiate. We have our whole lives ahead of us. In one of the articles I read last week, I saw words like *dating abuse* and *relationship violence*. Do those words apply to us?

"Love you," Mike says before he closes the door behind him and leaves me alone. His scent lingers even though he's gone. My legs aren't frozen in place anymore. Instead, they're shaking. I sink onto Kyle's bed.

Maybe Mike doesn't deserve to be expelled, doesn't deserve for his whole life to change. He's under so much pressure now, like he said. It won't always be like that.

Mike never put me in the hospital, never broke a bone. Other women—the ones I read about, the ones who are in danger after they end it, report it—have it so much worse than I did.

I spin his bracelet around my wrist. The silver is cold against my skin.

Everything can be the way it was before.

Mike doesn't think I'm a slut.

Mike still loves me.

If we get back together, no one would dare call me *slut* again.

He wants to be with me forever.

That's what every girl wants to hear.

Isn't it?

ten

JUNIE

Tess is running tomorrow—assuming the meet goes on after the protest—which means she needs to leave the party early. I don't have my car, so we take hers. I roll the windows down and feel the sweat at the nape of my neck, under my arms, between my fingers, cool in the breeze. Still, I'm hot. This warmth is coming from somewhere *inside* of me.

I lean over and rest my cheek on Tess's cool, bare shoulder. With my nose, I nudge the strap of her tank top aside and I kiss the skin on her upper arm, then her neck. She leans into my touch. When Tess turns onto my street, I pull away abruptly.

"Stop the car!" I shout.

"Why?" Tess pulls over several houses down from my own.

I giggle. "Frida and Aaron don't exactly know I'm out tonight."

"You snuck out?"

"Well, I *was* grounded."

"You were? For what?"

"For cutting class yesterday." I laugh again. Who decided to call it *cutting* class?

"You weren't cutting class," Tess insists. "You were supporting a friend who needed you."

I shake my head. I don't want to think about Maya. And just like that, the thought of her is gone. I almost start laughing again. Who knew a person could simply *decide* not to think about something? I've spent so many nights wishing I could turn my thoughts off, unable to sleep because I can't stop going over the day's conversations in my head, promising myself that I'd keep my mouth shut the next day, that I'd like to bite my tongue to avoid another sleepless night.

It never worked.

The only thing that made it feel better was cutting, but I'm not allowed to do that anymore.

Correction: The only thing that made it feel better *used* to be cutting. Now it's Hiram's red pills.

I unclick my seat belt. Tess looks at me like she's waiting for something. I'm not sure which of us starts kissing the other first, but for once, I don't care if it was me. She's kissing me back, isn't she? She's putting her hands in my hair, sliding her fingers down my arms. She wants me as much as I want her.

When we get back together, I won't wait for her to take my hand when we're walking down the hall at school. I won't wait for her to lean in to kiss me goodbye after class. I'll say *I love you* first, and I won't wait for her to text me to make plans.

We kiss and we kiss and we kiss. I don't check the clock on Tess's dashboard. I have no idea how much time goes by.

We could double-date with Hiram and Maya. No—I'm mad at Maya. She lied to me about Hiram. Well, technically I guess she didn't lie to me—she just didn't tell me the truth. When my parents found out about my cutting, my dad said that *withholding information* was a kind of lying. He said I had to prove they could trust me again. Hence the three-month deal, the honor code, et cetera.

I told Maya about the cutting, but I didn't tell her about the pills. I withheld information too.

And Hiram can't have given me the pills just to get on Maya's good side because he didn't tell Maya he gave them to me. When she asked what we were talking about yesterday, he covered for me.

Wait—why am I thinking about Hiram, about my dad, about Maya, when Tess is kissing me? I should be thinking about her, only her, and nothing else. Why can't I make these thoughts disappear anymore? Why can't I stop thinking about the words I said to Maya before I left Kyle's house tonight?

You lied to me.

What else did you lie about?

You're the one who disappeared, not me.

How could you stay for three months?

Oh, god, I'm as bad as they are. Insisting that a victim has to be perfect to be believed. I'm like one of those prosecutors interrogating a sexual assault victim about what she was wearing, how much she had to drink, as though that makes what happened her fault.

The truth is, I don't know how Maya stayed for three months. I might want to believe that I'd have left or asked for help right away if it happened to me—but how can I possibly know that's true? I've never been where she was. Like I said yesterday, I hurt myself for months without asking for help. I'm in no position to judge.

Oh, god, I'm sorry.

I pull away from Tess.

"What's the matter?"

"I have to go back to the party."

Tess blinks. "Go back?"

"I have to make sure Maya's okay."

"Oh, baby," Tess says, running a hand up and down my arm, making me shiver. (Since when am I *cold*?) "You're such a good friend."

"I'm not." I shake my head. "I'm really not."

"Of course you are," Tess counters. "Didn't you just say you got grounded for looking out for her?" I shrug. "And here you are, planning this protest for her."

The protest. The protest that's taken on a life of its own. The protest that's supposed to be about Maya but isn't anymore.

"They all think it was Hiram."

Tess shakes her head. "Not all. And no matter what, everyone agrees that someone hurt Maya, and she needs our support."

"But do you think it might have been Hiram?"

Tess considers. "It would be crazy for Maya to accuse Mike if it was really Hiram. Maya may be traumatized like everyone says, but I think she knows exactly what happened."

Maybe Tess would call me *crazy*, if she knew I feel better after cutting myself than when I'm not bleeding.

"Hey," Tess says. "It's going to be okay. I love you."

I should be so happy to hear her say it, but instead, I'm thinking that Tess doesn't know about the anxiety, about Dr. Kreiter and my diagnosis. (Diagnoses?) When Tess broke up with me, she said she didn't know me anymore. But maybe she never knew me at all.

I'm so cold that I'm shaking.

No. My *hands* are shaking.

"I've got to go."

"You're leaving?" Tess sounds incredulous.

I nod.

"Didn't you hear what I said?"

I nod again.

"And you're still leaving?"

I open the car door and stumble onto the sidewalk. I don't turn around to watch Tess drive away, but I shudder when I hear her engine roaring to life, her car speeding past me. She thinks I rejected her. A few days ago, I'd have preferred it that way. Now, I'm not sure what's better: Do I want her to think I left because I'm cool and aloof, or because I'm freaking out?

I walk up my driveway and open the back door slowly, quietly. I take off my shoes. The house is quiet and dark.

I tiptoe up the stairs, close my bedroom door behind me with a soft *click*. I turn on my desk lamp and dig into my backpack for the bag of pills. I google the name printed on the capsule.

Turns out, a false sense of well-being isn't the only side effect. These pills make patients feel hot, light-headed, impulsive. Their effects come on strong and wear off quickly. (I learned that much yesterday.) They were taken off the market—like Hiram said—because of concerns they could be habit-forming. No kidding. Yesterday, after only one dose, I was already thinking about asking Hiram for more.

I get out my phone and send a text. **Why did you give me those pills when you knew they were addictive?**

The phone buzzes almost immediately with an answer. **You said you needed them.**

Did I? I scroll up the screen, looking at the short history of texts between Hiram and me. Hiram's right: I begged for the pills, promised not to tell anyone, promised never to ask again.

Don't worry, Hiram continues now. **I don't have any more. And they don't make them anymore. So you couldn't have more even if you wanted to.**

That does make me feel a little bit better. But then—what if I need them again?

There are still a few in the Ziploc bag that's currently sitting on my desk.

I count. Three. Three more chances for a false sense of well-being. Three more chances to kiss Tess without worrying whether or not it's the right thing to do.

Until the pill's effects wear off.

How can I even know if I really wanted to kiss Tess tonight, if I really wanted to stop kissing her—was it me or the pills calling the shots? I pick up the Ziploc and twist it in my shaking hands, so the pills slide around inside. I could take a blue one now and go to sleep without going over the night's events in my head, all the things I said wrong.

I shake my head and toss the bag into the garbage can beneath my desk, then glance at my closed bedroom door. The bathroom is just down the hall. I could break open my Gillette ladies' razor. Mom confiscated it after Valentine's Day, and I told myself I didn't mind, that not shaving was a stance against the patriarchy. But I hated having hairy legs, so, after a month, Mom let me start shaving again.

It would be so easy.

But it hasn't been three months yet.

Did my parents and I ever discuss exactly what would happen at the end of three months? I assumed it would mean that Dr. Kreiter was wrong: that I don't need medication, or group therapy, or even to see the doctor anymore. If I could go without cutting for three months, I'd have proved that I could handle this by myself, that I can stop myself from slicing my skin.

But now I wonder…have I just been running out the clock? Did part of me think that if I made it three months, I could go back to cutting? Like someone on a diet who reaches their goal weight and goes back to eating the way they did before. Their diet was a means to an end, not a lifestyle change. Maybe that's why Dr. Kreiter disapproved of the deal I made with my parents. I sit on my hands.

I will not cut. I will not cut. I will not cut.

My phone vibrates with another text from Hiram. **You okay, Juniper?**

My hands are shaking so much that it's hard to write back. **I'm fine**, I type, even though it's not entirely true.

I shouldn't have given you the pills, Hiram responds. **I'm here if you need to talk.**

Why is Hiram being so nice to me? Then I remember: It's probably because he thinks being nice to me will make Maya like him more. He doesn't know what happened at Big Night. He doesn't know that Maya must hate me now.

But he covered for me with Maya about the pills yesterday. I picture him alone in that big house—his dad at work, his mom out of town, all of his classmates at Big Night. Like me on New Year's Eve, on Valentine's Day.

Hiram says he's here if I need to talk, but if I told him what happened tonight, he'd hate me for hurting Maya. Like Tess would hate me, if she knew what I'm really like. She'd never say *I love you* again.

Good night, I type quickly. I put my phone down and change into my pajamas. I kick the clothes I wore out tonight under my bed because I know I won't want to see them in the morning, a reminder of everything that happened.

It's all running through my head: the words I said, the words I heard, the things I did. Not cutting means I have to lie here feeling hurt because Maya didn't tell me about Hiram. Feeling bad because I said terrible things to her. Feeling guilty because I kept something from her too. Feeling humiliated because of the way I stumbled out of Tess's car. Feeling certain Tess will never give me another chance. Feeling uncertain of whether or not I want one.

When I was a little kid and I had to get a shot at the pediatrician's office, Mom would squeeze my hand so tight it hurt. She said it was to distract me from the pain of the needle.

Maybe that's all cutting ever was. A distraction from all the other pain.

Sunday, April 16

eleven

MAYA

It's after midnight when I get home. Not because I stayed at the party, but because I got into Mom's car and drove up into the hills. I slowed down when I neared Hiram's house, as though I thought there was a possibility I might run into him. But if he was home, he was secure behind the front gate. Eventually I stepped on the gas and drove past.

Now, I go into the bathroom and crouch over the toilet. In the months we were together, Mike never actually said I was fat. But there was something about the way he gripped the skin on my upper arm, around my rib cage. Like there was too much flesh for him to hang on to, too much there for him to dig his fingers into.

I throw up. I haven't eaten in hours, so nothing much comes up. A little bit of whatever I drank at the party. Some water. Some toothpaste, maybe, because I brushed my teeth before I left the house tonight. Maybe some lipstick, because I chewed my lips on the way to pick up Junie.

I stand and flush the toilet. Wash my hands. Brush my teeth. (Again). I change into my pajamas and get into bed. When we first started dating, I'd hug the pillow and imagine it was Mike. I missed him so much when we were apart, and I hated that we couldn't spend the night together. The lyrics to one of my dad's favorite old songs, "Wouldn't it be nice?" would get stuck in my head. The song is about being in love with someone but being too young to spend the nights as well as the days together. Too young to wake up together each morning. Too young to hold each other close all night long. I wondered how the Beach Boys—years and years before I was born, before I met Mike, before we fell in love—understood exactly how I felt.

I can't help it; the song is stuck in my head now. Again. Tonight. Even after everything that's happened.

I kick off the covers.

Why did I want to spend the night with him after he'd hurt me?

Because I'm *the kind of girl who stays.*

Why did I let him kiss me tonight? Why did I kiss him back? Why do I still have his sweater folded neatly under the bed, his bracelet wrapped around my wrist?

Because I'm *the kind of girl who goes back.*

But if I loved him, why did I cheat on him with Hiram?

Because I'm a *slut.*

But if I didn't love him, why did I miss him all those nights?

Because I'm *the kind of girl who stays.*

Why *do* I miss him now?

Because I'm *the kind of girl who goes back.*

I sit up. I miss Hiram too. Not in the aching way I missed Mike. It's an easier feeling. I'm certain that if I asked, Hiram would come right over, even in the middle of the night. He'd climb the tree outside my window and sneak inside through the window. He'd spend the whole night by my side if I asked him to. He wouldn't kiss me if I didn't want him to. He'd wait for me to kiss him, not the other way around.

I rub my eyes with the heels of my hands. I can still smell vomit on my fingertips.

For months, Mike told me that he wanted to be together forever. He held my hand in public every day, and he kissed me goodbye before we headed into different classrooms. And yet, I always felt so desperate over him, like I was always at risk of losing him.

Maybe because I knew—I *know*—he wouldn't come if I asked him to. He'd say he needs to rest before the meet tomorrow. In fact, he'd be angry at me for calling in the first place, for waking him up. I'd apologize, of course, but it would be too late.

My heart beats fast, the way it did when Mike and I were alone together in Kyle's room. Out loud, I say, "It's okay. You didn't actually call him. He's not actually mad at you."

If I told Eva Mercado about this feeling, maybe she'd insist Mike would have every right to be angry at me—I should know better than to disturb him the night before a race. She'd say being angry at me isn't the same thing as hitting me. Maybe she'd say that she would know better, if *she* were Mike's girlfriend.

I lie back down, twisting Mike's bracelet around my wrist. Sometimes I wake up having slept on my arm, and my wrist hurts from where the silver dug into the skin all night. But I haven't taken it off since the night he gave it to me. Valentine's Day. I was so certain Mike would be my Valentine for the rest of my life. I'd never have to worry about having a date on February fourteenth again.

I hug my pillow the way I used to. Tonight, Mike didn't yell, and he didn't squeeze, and he certainly didn't hit.

He says he still loves me.

He says none of this has changed his plans.

Our plans.

But even though he was gentle—even though I kissed him back—I was *scared* being alone in Kyle's room with him. Some part of me knew that one wrong move, one wrong word, and he'd be angry all over again.

Was it worth it, that little bit of fear, to get to be with him?

Maybe he was always angry. Maybe every time he was careful and loving, he was really hiding his fury underneath. Maybe he's so methodical because it's the only way he can keep his rage under control when everyone else is watching. Or even sometimes when it's just us. Maybe even sometimes when it's just him. That must be exhausting.

I shake my head. I shouldn't be feeling sorry for him! What kind of woman am I, worrying about what *he's* going through?

What kind of girlfriend would I be if I didn't?

I never saw the slightest hint of anger in Hiram—not when I pulled away after we made out, not when I didn't want to kiss him at all, not when I pretended I didn't know him when we passed in the halls at school.

I twist the bracelet again. I press it so hard that I actually bend the thin metal, making it even tighter.

I shouldn't be so confused.

I shouldn't have kissed Hiram.

I shouldn't be worrying about Mike.

I shouldn't be making myself throw up.

I should have said something the first time Mike hit me.

I shouldn't have stayed.

I should have kept my mouth shut.

I shouldn't go to the protest.

I should go.

I shouldn't be missing him.

I should be sleeping.

I shouldn't—

I should—

I shouldn't—

I should.

twelve

JUNIE

I wake to the sound of my parents' raised voices. At first, still fuzzy with sleep (I don't actually remember falling asleep last night), I think they're yelling at me. They must have found out that I snuck out. I'm grounded—no, I'm already grounded. What new punishment will they come up with? What new deal will my dad propose? Six months without sneaking out to regain his trust?

But then, as I open my eyes, it becomes clear that my parents' voices aren't directed at me. That they're not yelling here, in my room, but at each other in their bedroom on the other side of the wall. I force myself to wake all the way up so I can concentrate on exactly what they're saying.

"We have to let her go, Fee."

"She's grounded," Mom counters. "What's the point of punishment if we're not going to enforce it?"

"She's still grounded," Dad insists. "But this is a school event. Being grounded doesn't mean staying home from school."

Mom says something I can't quite make out. Dad answers, "This is what we want for her, Fee. We'd be hypocrites to keep her home."

I know they'll let me go today. Because of all the reasons Dad says—they raised me to fight for what I believe in, and this is a school event that I helped organize.

I could march into their room and tell them the protest has grown beyond my control, that it's not about Maya anymore. I could even say I snuck out last night, I deserve *more* punishment, not less.

If they heard all that, they might make me stay home. And then I wouldn't have to watch Mike march in a demonstration that was supposed to be against him, and I wouldn't have to see Tess looking pleased that the event grew beyond our initial expectations, and I wouldn't have to explain to her that this isn't what I wanted.

And I wouldn't have to see Maya, wouldn't have to see the look on her face because I called her a liar and blamed her for staying with Mike. I wouldn't have to hear what she'd say now that she knows her best friend is just as bad as the rest of them.

I listen as Dad wins the fight (Mom never had a chance), then I get out of bed and into the shower. I rub my short hair dry with a towel. I have to dig a little to find a pink shirt because most of my tops are shades of white and black and navy and gray. I slather sunscreen on my face because Dad always said to wear sunscreen to a protest, because you never know how long you might be standing outside demanding that justice be served. In the picture of us at my first protest that's displayed in the living room, my face is smeared with white streaks of lotion that Dad didn't rub in properly.

"Morning," I say as I trot down into the kitchen. The races are scheduled to start at ten o'clock. On Wednesday, we agreed to gather on the track by nine. I don't know if the plan's changed.

I grab a banana from the bowl by the sink. Dad's sitting at the table spooning cereal into his mouth while he reads the paper. Mom's rubbing phantom grease off the stove with a towel. For the first time, it occurs to me that maybe she has OCD too. The more well-known cleaning kind, not the disorganized kind. Dr. Kreiter said once that my problems could have hereditary roots as well as environmental ones. I thought she was just trying to let me off the hook. Or that she was trying to convince me I should take medication, that my problems were tied to a chemical imbalance and weren't entirely in my control. At the time, it made me feel helpless.

"Do you want us to come with you?" Mom offers.

Dad speaks before I can. "Don't be silly, Fee. It's *Junie's* event. She doesn't need her parents there, cramping her style. But we'll be there with you in spirit," Dad adds enthusiastically. "We're so proud of you for organizing all of this."

I shrug, grabbing my car keys from the bowl by the back door. There will be plenty of parents there. Mike's parents never miss a race. Neither do Tess's.

"Are you picking Maya up?" Mom asks. Before I can answer, she adds, "How's she doing—Mrs. Alpert said she went to a party last night?"

"I haven't talked to her since then." It's not a lie. "So I don't know how the party went." That's half a lie. I know how her night began. I don't know how it ended.

"Well, be sure to send Maya our love and support."

I nod. I'm scared if I say anything, I'll start to cry. Then Mom wouldn't let me go to the protest. And Dad would know I'm not as strong as I'm supposed to be.

"Call if you need anything," Mom says. She kisses my forehead before I leave. We're almost exactly the same height now.

I need you to come with me.

I need you to say you're too worried about me to let me go.

I need you to say that you'll love me whether I change the world or not.

I almost gasp at that last thought. It's not one I've ever thought before. Or maybe I've always thought it. Maybe it's been there, humming in the background, for a very long time.

◇◇◇◇

Of course I'm late. It's nine twenty-one when I park my car in its usual terrible spot and the track behind the school is a sea of pink. I mean, our entire student body is only a few hundred people, and it looks like they're all here. Plus some East Prep students are marching. Everyone is holding signs that say END

DOMESTIC VIOLENCE and ZERO TOLERANCE! and NO ABUSE IN OUR SCHOOL. Some of the signs are printed on hot pink paper. Some are big pieces of white poster board decorated with glitter and confetti. It's early enough that the fog hasn't entirely burned off yet, but people are mostly wearing T-shirts, no jackets. Once the sun breaks through, it's going to be a beautiful day.

I don't see a single sign that mentions Maya's name. Or any that call for Mike to be expelled. I wonder if they made those signs on Wednesday and then ripped them up and made new ones on Friday. Half the signs I see could apply to what happened in the parking lot between Mike and Hiram, not what happened behind closed doors between Maya and Mike.

I didn't stop by Maya's house. Maybe she'll drive herself or maybe someone else will bring her, some better friend. I know I must be the last person she wants to see right now.

Or maybe the second to last. Because there's Mike, in the thick of it. He's even dressed appropriately, in a North Bay shirt that's been washed so many times the red school logo has faded to pink. I shake my head and stuff my hands into my pockets. This is not the united front I had in mind.

I know I shouldn't, but I dig my fingernails into my thighs through the fabric. I can feel my Valentine's Day scar, and I wonder how hard I'd have to press to open it. I wonder if the people around me can tell what I'm doing but then I realize that—for once I have no trouble believing this—no one is looking at me.

They're chanting. Their voices are so loud it takes me a second to make out what they're saying.

End

violence

now.

End

violence

now.

End

violence

now.

Protests are always loud. Once, when I was thirteen, at a demonstration in the city (I honestly can't remember what for), someone placed a couple of speakers right next to my parents and me and started playing music so loud and deep that it made the ground shake beneath our feet. Then he pulled out a bullhorn and joined the chant. My parents didn't notice when I stopped chanting. Unable to hear anything but the music, anything but this man's voice, I was frightened. What if the police came and I couldn't hear the sirens? What if this man wasn't really on our side, what if he was infiltrating the protest with the intention of setting off a bomb, opening fire, throwing punches? What if he was playing his music that loud to drown out the sound of people screaming when his counterprotest began?

I feel now the way I did then, even though there's no one here blasting loud music, no one voice rising above the rest. Somehow, even though they're chanting against violence, these voices *sound* violent. It feels as if someone in the crowd might turn against us. After all, Mike is in the crowd.

But Mike would never blow his cover. Maya was right—he showed up today because he knows it looks better that way. It would have been strange if he stayed home now that he's told everyone it was Hiram who hurt Maya. He's playing the victim and the hero—even though she cheated on him, even though she accused him, he still doesn't think she deserved to be hurt.

So why am I scared? Why are my hands shaking so hard that even digging my jagged nails into my skin can't steady them? Why is my heart pounding? Why can't I open my mouth to add my voice to the chorus? Why does my short, tiny ponytail feel like it weighs a thousand pounds? Why do I feel like crying, like running, like hiding? Oh, god, what's happening to me?

Why can't I breathe?

thirteen

MAYA

I didn't know we were supposed to wear pink. I suppose I should be focused on something else, something more important, but all I can think about is the fact that I didn't wear the right thing. I *always* wear the right thing. I even set my alarm this morning to make sure I'd have extra time to decide on an outfit, but now, here I am, wearing the wrong thing. At Kyle's house last night, Erica said she had her pink shirt all ready to march—I should have realized what she meant. But I didn't, so now instead of pink I'm wearing red and white. North Bay colors just in case the meet still goes on after the protest. I wanted to show that no matter what happened, I still support my school. I'm still rooting for us to win.

I walk from the parking lot toward the track. When I asked to borrow the car this morning, Mom offered to come with me, but I said no, I wanted to do this myself. That wasn't entirely true—it's not that I wanted to be alone, but I didn't want to spend the whole day assuring Mom I was okay, offering her tissues to dry her tears.

The protesters are a sea of pink walking around the oval track, holding up signs, chanting words I can't quite make out.

I see Mike before he sees me. He's right in the middle of the crowd, but he's not chanting. I watch his Adam's apple bob up and down as he swallows. His hands ball into fists and then release. He's saving his energy for the race. He's waiting to run.

His eyes dart from one side of the crowd to another like he's looking for something. Then his gaze lands on me and keeps still, even as he continues to march. The group is moving slowly around the track, so slowly it must be very frustrating for him. He nods at me, and I realize it's not the race he's been waiting for.

He's been waiting for me.

My heart starts to pound like it did when we were alone together last night. I break Mike's gaze and turn back to face the parking lot. There, in the back, is Hiram's brown car. Hiram stands leaning against it, showing his support despite what everyone marching on that track—or at least, some of them— thinks about him. I can't make out the features of his face from here, but I imagine he sees me too. Maybe he's nodding too, but not like Mike. His nod would be one of support, not expectation. Of course, Hiram doesn't know what Mike asked me to say, but I think he would've come even if he did.

My pulse slows, dropping back to normal.

Hiram never hurt me.

Hiram, my secret friend. But everyone knows about him now. *Mike* knows about him now.

Mike doesn't care about what went on between Hiram and me. He says he'll forgive me. Mike doesn't know that *I* kissed Hiram first, not the other way around. I wanted to know what it would feel like, to kiss someone like Hiram, who let me come to his car day after day and never asked for anything in return.

I thought Mike wasn't aggressive about that, but maybe he was. Because he never did ask—not the first time he put his hands up my shirt or down my pants, not the first time he unhooked my bra or moved his mouth from one spot to the next. It was as though I'd given him all the permission he needed as soon as I said *yes* the day he asked me out. I don't know if I would've stopped him, had he asked along the way—I wanted to be with him too. But maybe he should've asked. At least once.

Standing on the grass between the cars and the track, it occurs to me that my friendship with Hiram is the only one that Mike never interfered with. Spending time with Mike couldn't keep me from spending time with Hiram because Mike never knew I was spending time with Hiram in the first place.

I told Junie that Mike wanted us to be together all the time, as much as we could. I press my fingers to my temples. Maybe he really was keeping me from Junie so I couldn't confide in her.

I close my eyes, remembering all the nights I sat next to Mike, rooting for his favorite basketball team. Did I forget that I don't even *like* basketball?

I nodded along when he talked about going to college

together—Berkeley, UCLA—and I never told him that I'd always wanted to go to college on the East Coast because that would've interfered with our plans.

His plans?

He said we'd move in together after college, and I thought that meant he loved me. But maybe if he'd loved me, he'd have asked where *I* wanted to go to college, where *I* wanted to live after graduation. *If* I wanted to live together.

I shake my head. They were always *his* plans.

I open my eyes and face the track. There's Eva Mercado, a few steps behind Mike.

Will he ask her out, the same way he asked me? Will he laugh at her, the way he laughed at me? Will he laugh at her mother, the way he laughed at mine?

For the first time, I wonder whether Mike isn't as *good* as I thought he was. Like, maybe he isn't always a good big brother—maybe he insisted on having the good bedroom upstairs instead of letting Ryan have it. And maybe Ryan has activities after school every day because Mike never offered to babysit.

Maybe it doesn't matter if Eva—or anyone else—might be a better girlfriend than I was. Maybe Mike didn't hit me because I wasn't a good enough girlfriend. Maybe Mike hit me because he was—is—a guy who hits.

And maybe he's not a good boyfriend either.

And how can he love me like he says he does when I stayed so quiet? Not just in Kyle's room last night, but all this time. Mike can't *know* someone who never spoke up: who never told him where she really wanted to go to college, what she really wanted to watch on TV, when she wanted him to stop.

Hiram listens to me. Junie listens.

They do more than listen—they *ask*.

And maybe sometimes I'm frightened to answer, scared that my answers might make them like me less. But I'm never scared that my answers will make them hit me.

Mike hasn't texted, hasn't called, hasn't even emailed, since Monday. What if I hadn't been at Kyle's last night? What if he never had a chance to pull me aside and tell me to blame Hiram?

What was his backup plan? (Mike always has a backup plan.)

Was he going to stand up, in front of everyone, point to his lightly bruised eye, and accuse Hiram? Maybe he'd have called himself a victim of violence too. Would he lie so well that everyone would believe it? Maybe *he'd* even believe it.

I take a deep breath. Maybe Mike did learn to hit from his father. Or maybe he really is missing a magic gene that everyone else has.

But maybe it doesn't matter why.

Okay, yes, I know it matters. If he's going to get help, if he's going to stop himself from doing this to the next girl and the next girl, of *course* it matters. He needs to hash it out in therapy and confront his demons in order to overcome them. And I hope he does. I hope he admits what he's done and asks for help someday. Someday soon.

But maybe—just for now, just this once, just for today—the *why* of it all also doesn't matter.

Because no matter *why* he hit me, it wasn't justified. No matter *why*, it was wrong.

And no matter *why*, he deserves to face the consequences.

If Mike gets expelled, he'll never win a scholarship. He might never run competitively again. It could change the course of the rest of his life.

But maybe what happened *should* change his life. He'll surely still go to college somewhere, and he'll probably still get to run one way or another—he has his whole life ahead of him, just like I do. But maybe the things that happened between us should at least *shift* his future.

Because what happened between us changed *my* life.

I didn't always think so. While we were together, even after Mike hit me, I got the same good grades, still wore the right clothes (except for today) and still said the right things so no one—not my parents, not my best friend, sometimes maybe not even me—knew what was happening. I thought that as long as they couldn't tell, it was proof that it wasn't really that bad.

But maybe the things I said and did—or didn't say and didn't do—weren't the right things. Maybe those were the *wrong* things.

I thought it was okay because Mike never hurt me so badly that I needed a doctor's care. But the first slap didn't leave a bruise and the last one did. It was getting *worse*, not better. With our whole lives ahead of us, we had a lifetime for things to get worse,

and worse,

and worse still.

Maybe I'm not so different from the women I read about, the ones who were in danger when they broke up with their husbands and boyfriends. I close my eyes, remembering an article I read about a girl whose abusive boyfriend killed her in their college dormitory. She wasn't that much older than I am; her boyfriend wasn't that much older than Mike.

Did that boy tell his girlfriend he loved her, that he wanted to spend the rest of his life with her? Did she root for his favorite teams? Did she attend that college because it was *his* first choice? Did that girl keep quiet about what she really wanted, scared that if she spoke up, he'd hit her again?

I grab my left wrist with my right and twist Mike's bracelet. I can't get the clasp to open, so I slide it over my hand, even though it's so tight that it hurts. I wish I were wearing Mike's sweater so I could take it off and stomp on it, but it's still folded neatly under my bed.

The march has slowed because everyone is looking at me. They always looked at me—the popular girl in the right clothes, the lucky girlfriend.

It takes me a second to find Mike's face again. But then, there he is—his height and his tawny hair and his tightly held fists.

He's looking at me too.

He's waiting for me to take it back.

He's waiting for me to say I was confused.

He's waiting for me to let everything go back to the way it was before.

And he's not the only one. Surely some of those other

295

marchers are hoping I'll say something to set their minds at ease. Then they'll get to keep their golden boy, they'll get to go back to admiring my good luck in being with him, and they'll never have to wonder why I retreated to Hiram's car for a few minutes of relief.

I guess I can't blame Mike for thinking I'd go along with his plan today. I went along with everything he wanted for months.

My skin feels hot and my throat feels tight.

I drop Mike's bracelet to the ground and begin walking toward the crowd.

fourteen

JUNIE

I'm in the middle of the track, surrounded by other protesters. I look down. Am I hiding? Or just watching their feet so I know when to step, where to step, *how* to step?

What was it Dr. Kreiter said to do? Count backward.

One hundred.

Ninety-nine.

Ninety-eight.

Ninety-six.

No. *Ninety-seven.*

Ninety-eight.

Ninety-nine.

One hundred.

Crap. Wrong way. I picture a blinking red light and sirens and a loud voice telling me to go back. I look desperately at the feet around my own, relieved to discover that at least I'm still facing the same way everyone else is.

It's going to be okay. I just have to breathe. I know how to breathe. I mean, I've been doing it my whole life, haven't I?

In.

Out.

In.

Out.

In.

In.

In.

I'm holding my breath. Why am I holding my breath? I'm going to hyperventilate. I'm going to pass out. Maybe no one will notice. Maybe no one will see. Maybe there's enough of a crowd around me that I'll still be able to blend in and they'll drag my unconscious body along with them.

No. They'd notice. It would disrupt the protest. Everyone would see. My parents would find out. Dr. Kreiter would find out.

I have to breathe.

I have to breathe.

I have to breathe.

I *can't* breathe.

fifteen

MAYA

Principal Scott stands in the center of the track with a bullhorn.

"It warms my heart to see the student body come together to protest violence," she says. She doesn't say violence against women. She doesn't say violence against *me*.

"I commend you for your activism," she continues. "At North Bay, we condemn violence." The crowd cheers. Is she talking about Hiram because he hit Mike out in the open where everyone could see? Is *that* what my classmates are applauding?

I don't know exactly how I get to the center of the track, how I end up standing next to Principal Scott. I look behind me—I can't remember where I was standing when I dropped Mike's bracelet. The principal puts her arm around me, a very public display of support.

Could I lose my scholarship if I make a scene? All this time worrying about Mike's potential scholarship, I almost forgot about the one I already have. (Junie would say that they *can't* take my scholarship away. It's supposed to be for academic excellence, and my grades haven't faltered.)

Maybe somewhere inside, deep down, Principal Scott is conflicted and confused. Maybe, as an administrator, she wants to keep the peace, wants the races to go on as planned, wants her school to win. But maybe there's another part of her—the part that's a mother (I know she has two sons)—that's wondering how she'd react if her child were accused. Or if her child was the accuser. Maybe there's a part of her that remembers the girl she was when she was my age. Maybe her first boyfriend tried to control her, or maybe she was riddled with self-doubt, or maybe she fell for the wrong guy.

For the first time in a long time, *I* don't feel conflicted and confused.

The principal continues, "As you know, the board of trustees is meeting tomorrow night. There are decisions to be made, but no matter what happens, I'm so proud of the unity you've shown here today."

She pauses like she wants to leave time for her words to sink in. I go over what she said in my head. She condemned violence, but she didn't mention Mike, or even Hiram. She didn't say *what* decisions had to be made, or what *she* believed should happen. She said a lot of words, but managed not to actually *say* anything at all. Finally, she adds, "Now, let's celebrate your successful event by competing against East Prep—and winning!" The crowd cheers again, though not as loudly as they did before.

Half the crowd probably thought the meet would be canceled. Maybe some of them don't want to see Mike—our best chance at beating our rival school—run.

At least, I hope some of them feel that way.

I feel that way.

For the first time ever, I don't want to see Mike crouch before the race. I don't want to see him putting his hands just behind the line, raising his hips as he prepares to spring. I don't want to see him shoot off into a sprint. I don't want to see him raising his arms overhead in victory. I don't want to see his jaw working as he mentally goes over whether he beat his own best time—whether or not he beat someone else comes second to beating himself—and I don't want to see the smile that spreads over his face when he realizes he did, or the scowl when he discovers he didn't.

I can't believe how much I cared about all of that, and for how long. Even before we were together, I showed up to every race, I cheered him on, I rooted for him. Now, all of that seems unbelievably *dull*.

I turn to look at our principal. She's smiling. Is she glad this is over? Glad the protest went off without any drama? Glad no one pointed out how empty her platitudes were, how toothlessly she condemned violence? Is she hoping this will all blow over?

When I told her what Mike did, she said it was a *serious accusation*. I actually felt bad for putting her in an uncomfortable position, forcing her to consider that one of her favorite students might have done what he did.

She offered me an ice pack. She offered to call my parents. She offered to send me home early.

But she didn't offer to send *Mike* home. She certainly didn't offer to expel him. Maybe in a few weeks, when the tumult has died down, she'll be praised for how she handled this week's events—elevating the issue of violence among students, allowing them the freedom to protest—without actually making any difference at all, without so much as disrupting a track meet beyond a fifteen-minute delay.

There was something else in that article about the college student whose boyfriend murdered her: In the weeks before she was killed, she reported the abuse to campus security, but the administration didn't take any action. Maybe they thought the tumult would die down too.

No.

It's not enough that I told Principal Scott, tucked behind the closed door of her office. I need to tell them *all* the truth about what happened between Mike and me. I know that some of them won't believe me. So I'll tell them again, even if that means some of them will never look at me the same way. And again after that, even if it means some of them will hate me for it.

This is a part of myself I've never felt before. This part of me wants to stand up and fight. It feels bigger than the part that wants everyone to like her, bigger than the part that hates her body, bigger than the part that wants to check out, bigger than the part that loved her boyfriend.

Or maybe not bigger. Maybe just newer. And right now, *louder*.

Angrier.

I'm angry that I kept quiet, and I'm angry that my world got smaller. I'm angry that they called me a slut, and I'm angry that I kept so many secrets. I'm angry that I tried so hard to remember what led to that first slap, and I'm angry that I ever believed anything I said or did would make a difference. I'm angry that Mike thought I would lie for him, and angry that I ever considered going through with it.

But I'm not angry at *me*.

I'm angry at *Mike*.

I twist myself from Principal Scott's embrace, then reach out and slide the bullhorn from her grasp.

"I'm Maya Alpert," I begin. The crowd cheers. Principal Scott's mouth widens into an *O*.

"Thank you so much for gathering today to protest violence."

Another cheer.

"But please remember what started all this—I came to school last week with a black eye."

I gesture to my face, to the bruise that's fading steadily.

"I came to school with a black eye because my boyfriend, *Mike Parker*, hit me." I emphasize Mike's name, like if I say it loud enough, I can erase any trace of the story Mike told, blaming Hiram.

No one cheers.

I take a deep breath. "Mike Parker should be expelled."

I see Mike, standing head and shoulders above most of the other kids. *Ex-boyfriend*, I think suddenly. I'm not going to wait for him to make it official. I've already decided.

303

There's a look on his face that I don't think I've ever seen before: surprise. One of his carefully thought-out plans finally fell through.

The expression on his face—his mouth hanging open, his eyes wide, his brow furrowed—doesn't make him look handsome. It doesn't make him look ugly, not exactly. But he looks younger, somehow. Like a kid who's used to getting his way. He blinks once, twice, like he can't believe it's me he's looking at, like he still expects me to run into the crowd and throw my arms around him, tell him all is forgiven, it was all a misunderstanding. To *apologize*. Slowly, carefully, I shake my head. I think it may be the first time I've ever told him *no*.

Maybe Mike hid parts of himself from me every bit as much as I hid from him. Maybe somewhere there's a part of him that's frightened and hurt. Maybe I'm getting a glimpse of that part of Mike now, in his surprised face, his open mouth, his wide eyes. I shake my head again, then blink, breaking his gaze.

The crowd doesn't seem to know how to react to my announcement. They're staring at me, and they're staring at Mike. The arms holding up the signs droop. The chants don't resume.

Maybe every single person in this crowd is a puzzle. Maybe part of each of them wants Mike expelled and part of each of them can't believe he'd ever hurt me. I can't really blame them for being confused. I was confused for a long time, and I was the one it was happening to.

I hand the bullhorn back to our principal. She looks at it like she's not sure what to do with it. Should the races begin? Should she postpone the meet? This time, I don't feel bad that I put her in an uncomfortable position.

Maybe Mike won't get expelled, won't lose his scholarship, maybe (some of) our classmates won't ostracize him. But it still matters that I said what I did. It will still make a difference.

It already has. Right now. For me. I *feel* different. I'm not sorry for causing trouble.

I'm angry that I ever felt sorry.

I scan the crowd again. Despite everything that happened last night, I know Junie will be proud of me for speaking out.

But when I see her, she's not looking at me. She's not looking at anyone. She's crouched on the ground, her arms crossed over her chest. She's shaking so hard, it looks like she's freezing, but her short hair is matted around her face with sweat. I rush toward my best friend.

sixteen

JUNIE

The crowd stops walking. Everyone's standing so close together that I'm not sure whether the people on either side of me notice how I'm sort of leaning against them, counting on them to hold me up. Someone says something so loud it hurts my ears. The crowd cheers.

Someone says something else. The crowd cheers again.

A pause and then another voice speaks just as loudly. Whoever it is must have a microphone, a bullhorn, something.

Another cheer.

And again.

And—wait. This time, when whoever it is speaks, no one cheers.

The voice speaks again.

I know that voice. That's *Maya's* voice. What's she saying? Why can't I make out the words? What is this other booming sound that's so much louder?

I try to concentrate, but all I can hear is the booming noise. I glance at the people I'm leaning on, but they don't seem to hear it. Everyone else is looking straight ahead, at Maya in the center of the track. I want to look too, but I can't see. Not just because I'm so short, but because my eyes are blurry with tears.

And still, all I hear is *boom, boom, boom.*

It's okay. Maya doesn't care whether I'm listening to her anyway. Not after the things I said last night.

Boom, boom, boom.

Oh, god, what is that?

Boom, boom, boom.

Oh, god, it's my heartbeat.

Boom, boom, boom.

Can a sixteen-year-old have a heart attack?

Boom, boom, boom.

The crowd's dispersing. I want to shout *Wait! Please!* but I can't make my mouth cooperate. The only sounds I make are heaving breaths. Without anyone left to lean on, I'm going to fall. Crap, I'm going to faint. I can't stop shaking. I'm going to lose it. I've already lost it. If I ever had it to begin with, which, I mean, I probably never did.

Boom, boom, boom.

My shaking hands are still tucked into the pockets of my jeans. How is *this* feeling better for me than cutting was? I press my nails through the fabric into my skin. I want to go home, close the bathroom door, take out my razor, and cut.

Then I remember my razor isn't there anymore. I threw it

away. And I couldn't get home now, anyway. I can barely stand upright, let alone drive.

I rip a hole in my pocket and press my fingernails—bitten almost to the quick but still sharp—against the scar on my left leg. I close my eyes and imagine slicing it open, imagine the skin and the scar tissue and the blood. Could I go deeper than I went before, deep enough that I could see the fat and the muscle and maybe even the bone? Can a person survive cutting herself that deeply? Would I pass out before I made it that far?

When I overdid it on Valentine's Day, I drove myself to the hospital.

I wasn't scared then, but I am scared now—of what I might have done to myself, what I might still do, what I *want* to do. Back then, I was so sure I was in control—I was certain I'd never end up like one of those accidents I'd read about, the ones that made suicide rates among cutters so hard to determine—because I drove myself to the hospital.

But I needed to drive to the hospital because I'd had an accident in the first place.

And now I realize I was lucky I was *able* to drive myself to the hospital.

What's more, what happened that night wasn't *entirely* an accident. I mean, I hadn't meant to hurt myself so badly I'd need stitches, but I *had* meant to hurt myself more than I ever did before. That night, I knew that Tess was out with some other girl, that Maya was out with Mike, that my parents were out together—and all the while, I was home alone. I didn't cut deeper just to see what would happen. I cut deeper because I *needed* to cut deeper. I needed the cutting to hurt more so the rest of me could hurt less.

And the rest of me hurts even more now.

If I had something sharp, I don't know how deep I would cut. Maybe all the way to the bone. Maybe right through to the marrow, like one of those people I read about, the people I thought were so much sicker than I'd ever be.

Maybe I'm just as sick as they are. Or anyway, maybe I could *become* that sick, given enough time. The fact that I cut as deep as I did on Valentine's Day proves that I was getting *worse*, not better, in the months since I made my very first cut.

Suddenly, there's a tentative hand on my elbow. Someone gently guiding me away from the crowd. Someone leading me to the grass beyond the track on the way to the parking lot. Someone lowering me to the ground, telling me to put my head between my knees. Someone reaching into my pockets, taking my hands in hers and holding them steady.

A voice saying, "Breathe, Junie. Just breathe."

Maya.

"You can do it."

Why is she helping me? I was so mean. But she lied to me.

A lie's a lie's a lie. That's what Dad says.

Maybe Dad's wrong. Maybe Dad has no idea what he's talking about.

"You can do it, Junie," Maya repeats.

I shake my head because I *can't* do it. Can't stop crying. Can't stop my heart from racing. Can't stop my lungs from refusing to take in any air.

"I'm sorry," I manage. Sorry for what? For what I said last night? For how the protest got so ridiculously out of control? For not being nearly as strong as she is—strong enough to hold it together, strong enough to speak up? Sorry that I'm such a mess.

"Just breathe, Junie," Maya says again. "In, out. In, out." She puts my hand on her chest so I can feel her breaths. I try to match my movements to hers.

"In, out. In, out."

I nod along time with her words. My heartbeat slows. I'm able to catch my breath. Maya wipes the tears from my cheeks.

"You okay?" she asks.

I nod, though my breaths are still ragged. At least I can breathe. "I've never felt like that before," I say.

"I think you were having a panic attack."

I nod again. I don't know much about panic attacks, but I can't think of two better words to describe how I felt.

"We could go to the hospital—" Maya offers, but I shake my head.

"It's getting better."

"If you're sure." Maya looks so concerned. Even after what happened last night, she still cares about me. She's still my friend. I take a deep breath.

"I shouldn't have left you at Kyle's last night. I'm so sorry."

"I'm sorry too. I should have told you about Hiram."

"I haven't told you everything either." I open my mouth to tell her about the pills, but before I can get the words out, another voice joins us.

"What are you guys doing over here?"

Tess. The boys always run first. She has time before she has to race.

"You were amazing up there, Maya," Tess adds.

Maya pulls me up to stand. I feel her shrug. "I just told the truth."

"They're starting the meet," Tess explains.

"Are they seriously going to let Mike run after all this?" I ask.

Tess shakes her head. "I'm not sure. If they do, we could try to stop it. I've got the girls' team on standby."

I meet my ex-girlfriend's gaze. Her hair is knotted into a tight bun as it always is on race day, the only time she tries to tame it. She's wearing a pink sweatshirt, but I can tell she has her uniform on underneath. When she got dressed this morning, she still planned to be ready to run. After all, she's a competitor. She can simultaneously want to march in a protest and want to win a race.

I watch Tess take in my face. I don't need a mirror to know I look terrible. My cheeks are streaked with tears, my skin is surely red and blotchy, my eyes bloodshot, my nose crusted with snot. I'm still breathing heavily, as though I was the one who'd been running.

"We were just leaving," I say finally.

Tess blinks. She knows something's wrong, but she's never seen me like this—*I've* never seen me like this—so she can't possibly understand *what's* wrong. "It's not like you to leave," she says finally.

I shake my head. "Actually, you don't know what I'm really like." It sounds harsher than I want it to (always the wrong thing), though it's almost exactly what Tess said when she dumped me last week, almost exactly what I thought as I stumbled out of her car last night.

Maybe Tess never loved me. Maybe she *couldn't*.

Tess opens her mouth to respond, but I speak before she can. "It's not your fault," I say. "It's mine."

seventeen

MAYA

I lead Junie to Mom's car. "Okay if I drive?" I ask. "You still seem kind of…" I pause. I don't want to say something that might hurt her feelings. "Shaky."

Junie surprises me by laughing. "That's the perfect word." She holds up her hands so I can see them trembling. "Definitely shaky."

Junie and I get into the car, but I don't start it. I read somewhere that you're not supposed to touch someone who's in the midst of a panic attack without their permission, but I didn't know what else to do but take her hands and beg her to breathe. Now, even though she's still shaking, my best friend seems better than she did a few minutes ago.

Junie nods in the direction of the track. "I couldn't hear what you said back there."

"I said I wanted Mike expelled." Even inside the car, with the doors and windows closed, I hear the crowd applaud when the runners take their marks. The sound makes me cringe. It hurts to think that some of the people sitting in the bleachers around the track still don't believe me. Or even worse—they *do* believe me, but it's not enough to stop them from cheering for their star.

"Mike's still out there," I say, "still running. They're still rooting for him." I swallow, but the lump in my throat doesn't go away.

"You don't know that for sure," Junie offers. "They might not let him run."

Our school's best chance at beating our archrival? Not likely.

"Or maybe he decided not to run after what you said," Junie adds hopefully, though she doesn't quite sound like she believes it. We both know Mike would never miss a chance to compete. A chance to win.

"Even if he does run," Junie decides finally, "there are a lot of people who won't cheer for him."

I shrug. "They still want North Bay to win."

"No one wants to win like this." Junie pauses. "Okay, I mean, maybe not *no one*, but plenty of people. I believe that. Really. It *matters* that you stood up there. It *matters* that you said what you did."

I nod, but I still feel like crying. I used to think that when Mike won, I won too. We were a team. I thought that when the crowd cheered him on, they were cheering for me too. Now, the opposite feels true.

My anger let me stand up there, in front of everyone, and say what I wanted. It helped me *know* what I wanted. But now—my heart isn't pounding anymore. Everything I felt when I took the bullhorn from Principal Scott—the fury, the adrenaline—has faded. It's like I had a limited amount of energy and I used it all up. Like a balloon that's been popped. I'm suddenly very, very tired.

"What's wrong with me?" I feel desperate as tears stream down my face. "Why am I crying?"

I don't want Mike. I don't want to watch him run. And yet—I still feel like I lost something.

"What's wrong with *me*?" Junie counters. "Why was *I* the one panicking back there? You kept it together while I was falling apart, even though *you* were the one who'd been hurt." Junie leans her head back and closes her eyes. "I wish I could be that strong."

"Strong?" I echo incredulously. "Are you kidding? Like you said, I kept quiet about Mike for months."

"No," Junie says firmly. "I shouldn't have said that. I mean, of course I wish you'd said something sooner, because I hate to think that he had more time to hurt you. But still—you came forward and told Principal Scott. You stood up for yourself the minute you went into her office on Monday."

I shake my head. "Only because it's too hard to hide a black eye."

"Give yourself more credit than that!"

"I can't," I explain. "I honestly don't know if I would've said anything if I could've hid it."

"But you *could* have hid it," Junie insists. "You could've faked the flu and stayed home, or slathered on concealer, or made up some kind of story about walking into a doorknob in the middle of the night."

I laugh, because I thought of the same ridiculous excuse just a few days ago. "Not all of us are small enough that doorknobs are eye level."

"Are you calling me short?" Junie feigns offense, then turns serious again. "You could've kept on protecting him if you wanted to, but you didn't. For whatever reason, that black eye was the last straw for you."

I circle my left wrist with the fingers of my right hand the way Mike's bracelet used to. "Why did it take me so long to reach the last straw?"

Junie considers my question. "I don't know. Maybe because—despite everything—you loved him?"

My tears finally overflow. Did I love him? *Could* I love someone who hurt me, someone who frightened me?

From our very first date, I wanted to be with him, and maybe that's part of the reason why it felt like everything that happened was my fault. I liked knowing that he chose me, when he could have had anyone. I liked the way it felt, when people looked at us, walking through the halls hand in hand. That felt like love to me.

"I should've hated him from the very first time. Why didn't I hate him?" It's hard to talk through my tears.

"I don't know," Junie answers. "I hid it for months when someone was hurting me. I mean, when *I* was hurting me. I was scared of what people would think. I was scared of disappointing them."

I nod, wiping my tears. The lump in my throat feels a little bit smaller. "I was scared too."

"Are you still?" Junie asks.

I rest my hands on the steering wheel in front of me, considering. "I know Mike could still hurt me," I begin slowly. If he doesn't get expelled—even if he never hits me again, even if we're never alone together again—he could probably turn half the student body against me. And that's not counting the kids who already hate me for what I said today.

Or he could bang down my door when I'm home alone some night. I used to think he'd never do something like that.

But I used to think he'd never hit me hard enough to give me a black eye.

"If he hurts me again, I'm not scared to speak up anymore."

"I'm still scared," Junie says. "Can you imagine what my dad would say if he knew how I lost it today?"

"He'd understand," I begin, but Junie shakes her head.

"He wouldn't."

"I don't even remember walking toward Principal Scott, taking the bullhorn."

"But you did it anyway," Junie says. "Doing something when you're scared is braver than doing something when you're not."

"Which means you were brave to come here today too." I reach across the car and take her hand. "There are lots of different ways to be brave. And if your dad can't understand that, then he doesn't understand you."

Junie's eyes are very bright. "Can I ask you something?" she says finally.

"Anything." I'm done keeping secrets.

"What made you decide that you wanted Mike expelled? On Friday, you said you weren't sure."

There are the obvious reasons: That it's simply fair for Mike to suffer the consequences of his actions, that the school rules should protect girls (and guys) like me. Or because I don't want to have to see him every day going from one class to the next.

And all of those are good reasons, but there's something more too. "I think it's because I finally understood that this *really* happened, that Mike *really* hurt me, that it was *really* wrong. I think—I don't know—I think for months, I was living in a kind of gray area, where I believed he could hit me and it was okay because he loved me so much."

"What do you think now?"

Before, I thought the only thing about our relationship that wasn't okay was when he hurt me.

Now, I know I was wrong.

With Mike, I was quieter, smaller. I *literally* tried to take up less space.

With Mike, being loved meant being hurt. Not just physically.

"I think it was bad love," I answer finally, remembering what Hiram said on Monday. "And bad love is no better than not being loved at all. In fact, I think it might be worse."

Maybe I did love him back. But maybe that was bad love too. I don't mean that loving him back was something I did wrong, something I should've been too smart to feel—but it *was* loving someone who hurt me. It was a love that made me confuse fear with excitement, control with devotion.

And that's not good love either.

Junie nods and squeezes my hand back. "Just so you know, *I* love you. I love you for standing up there today, but I would love you just as much even if you hadn't."

I smile. "I love you for coming here today even though you were scared. And I'd love you even if you'd had to stay home."

"You would?" Junie asks.

I nod. "Absolutely."

I know, without turning to look, that Hiram is still standing beside his car in the back of the parking lot. I know that he'll be my friend even if I never want to kiss him again, just like he was all those days when I showed up at his car during lunch and we sat side by side in silence, not touching.

Maybe he suspected what was going on with Mike and me back then, but he understood I wasn't ready to admit it. Maybe he thought the best way to support me was to sit beside me and wait, showing me he'd be there whenever I was ready.

I look at my best friend and say, "That's *good* love. The kind of love that's there even when you're a mess, even when you're so disappointed in yourself that you can't imagine you're worth loving."

eighteen

JUNIE

"Juniper Serra Mesa-Stern!"

Uh-oh. Mom using my full name is never a good sign.

No matter what Maya says about good love, I still believe it's harder to love someone you're disappointed in, or at least you can't love someone you're disappointed in as *much* as you can love someone who never lets you down. And however disappointed Mom and Dad are now (for whatever it is that made Mom use my full name the instant I walked in the door), they're not half as disappointed as they would be if they knew what happened at the track today. Not that I would ever tell them.

"Now, Fee, let's give her a chance to explain—" Dad begins, but Mom cuts him off.

"To explain?" Mom echoes incredulously. "There's no acceptable explanation for this." She slams a Ziploc bag onto the kitchen table. It takes me a second to see what's inside.

Hiram's pills. The red diet pills with the bonus side effect. The blue pills to put you to sleep.

My pills.

Why did I throw them in the trash? How stupid could I be? I mean, everyone knows you're supposed to flush drugs down the toilet if you don't want to get caught. But I read an article that said flushing pills was really bad for the environment, and I thought it would have been hypocritical of me to flush them for my own protection if it meant endangering the planet.

"What do you have to say for yourself?" Mom asks. I know I don't need to answer. She's going to keep talking.

It was like this at the hospital on Valentine's Day. Mom spoke, Dad defended, and I was mostly silent. Now, I sink into my chair at the kitchen table, the same chair where I eat dinner most nights, breakfast most mornings, right across from Mom. Though Mom never really sits, she usually sort of perches, because she's always bouncing up to get more food from the stove, to bring a dirty dish or glass or knife to the sink.

"I've already called Dr. Kreiter," Mom continues. "You have an emergency appointment scheduled for tomorrow afternoon." She doesn't ask what the pills are or why I'm taking them. Maybe it doesn't matter. Or maybe she's already guessed. For a second, she turns her anger toward Dad. "I should never have let you convince me to let her go today."

"Today was important," Dad insists.

"More important than this?" Mom asks, waving the Ziploc like a flag so the pills slide around inside. "This time, we're doing whatever the doctor recommends. If she says group therapy, you're going to group therapy. If she says family sessions, we're participating in family sessions."

"She wanted us to do family sessions?" I interject, but Mom keeps going.

"If she says medication—*proper* medication, supervised by a doctor—you're going to take it. No more deals, no more goals, no more work-arounds."

"Fee, let's not be unreasonable. This doctor isn't the be all and end all—"

"She said Junie wasn't progressing in their sessions together."

"And I said that was ridiculous—"

"Ridiculous?" Mom echoes. My gaze shifts from one parent to the other like I'm watching a tennis match.

Mom continues, "The doctor said that in nearly every single session, Junie sits on her hands or stuffs them in her pockets to hide the way they're shaking."

She did?

"And she said that when she so much as broached the subject of group therapy—bringing up that she'd worked with other patients who struggled like Junie—Junie completely refused to engage."

In our first session, Dr. Kreiter said she'd worked with kids like me before. Maybe she wasn't just reducing me to a type like I thought. For the first time, it occurs to me that maybe she was trying to make me feel a little bit less alone.

Dad says, "Fee, be reasonable. Junie wasn't supposed to cut herself again, and she hasn't."

"No, she's just started using drugs." Mom throws up her hands and storms out of the room. Dad looks at me and sighs, sinking into his usual chair next to mine.

"She'll calm down."

I nod.

"She's scared."

I nod.

"This is just a speed bump," he adds. "You've been doing so well, no matter what the doctor says."

Normally, I'd be relieved to hear Dad say that I've been *doing so well*. I'd be happy he thinks Mom just needs to calm down. He's the one who talked Mom out of making me go to group therapy. He said I made a good argument against it—my brilliant three-month plan—and I deserved a chance to prove myself.

But Mom just found pills in my trash can.

I *haven't* proved myself.

And Dad doesn't see it.

He doesn't see *me*.

"What did the doctor say?" I ask. "About my progress?"

Dad shrugs. "That you hadn't really opened up to her. But *of course* you've made progress. Look at what you did today." Dad pauses, then leans closer to me and says, "I know we weren't supposed to go to the demonstration, but I couldn't help myself."

Does he remember that I never said I didn't want them to come? *He* said that. *He* decided it.

He continues, "I watched from the parking lot. I saw Maya up in front of that crowd, and I was so proud of you. I drove away before you had a chance to see me there, though." He winks.

Proud of *me*, because Maya stood up and spoke out? Does he think I planned that, timed her speech perfectly for maximum impact? Could he ever guess that I was so out of it when Maya spoke I didn't hear a word she said?

I feel something twist in my stomach, but my hands don't start their familiar shake. Whatever this feeling is, it isn't anxiety.

Dad continues, "When I was your age, I could've only dreamed of organizing an event like that. Everyone marching in lockstep, chanting in unison. One goal, one voice."

I shake my head. The words they were chanting weren't my goal. They didn't reflect my voice, or (more importantly), Maya's voice.

"I saw you and Maya heading for her car before I left. It must have been a hard day for her. But don't worry, we can go back and pick up your car later."

I shake my head. *Maya* wasn't the one who was so upset she needed to leave. *I* was. Didn't he see that Maya was comforting me, not the other way around? Can't he see—I'm sitting right beside him—that my face is streaked with tears? Is he even *looking*?

"Imagine what you'll achieve at Stanford," Dad says. "You can write about today on your application—how you overcame your own struggles to plan such a successful protest."

How can my father be beaming with pride even after my mother found a bunch of pills in my trash can?

I told Tess it wasn't her fault that she didn't know me. There are so many parts of myself that I hid from her. But I'm not sure it's not *Dad's* fault, not after everything that's happened.

There is part of me that wants to plan rallies and make a difference the way he taught me. I believe in the causes he believes in. I *want* to help people.

But there's also a part of me that wants to go upstairs and pull the covers over my head.

I want both. At the same time.

I *am* both at the same time.

"It wasn't one goal, one voice," I say softly.

"What do you mean, kiddo?"

I raise my voice, just a little. "The protest today—it wasn't what I planned at all."

"What are you talking about?"

And louder still. "I wanted it to be about Maya and Mike, but it turned into something else. The protest got so much bigger—"

"Bigger is better for events like these."

I wish I could be calm and reasonable, like Mom. But that feeling in my belly, that twist I couldn't identify, makes its way up into my throat. I felt this same feeling last Monday, when Mom told me Maya came to school with a black eye: I'm angry.

"This wasn't a successful protest." I'm yelling now. "I'm not proud of what happened today. It got out of control. I mean, Mike Parker actually marched! How can I be proud of that?"

Dad doesn't shout back. My whole life, whenever Dad and I argued, it was never anger that motivated me. Our arguments were more like *debates* than actual fights. He liked arguing the opposite side, liked seeing me craft a counterargument. It was the lawyer in me, he said.

Now he says, "Maybe Mike's seen the error of his ways. We believe in second chances, Juniper. Mike surely has demons of his own to confront. Studies show that abusers often have problematic backgrounds themselves. You know that."

"Today wasn't Mike's second chance." I push my chair away from the table and stand. "What happened today, what it means for Maya, isn't the result of some study. She isn't a hypothetical person, a statistic, a fact I read about in a textbook. She's my best friend! Can you understand that? Of course I hope Mike gets the help he needs too, but today, right now, I'm more concerned about *Maya*."

I know I'll toss and turn over these words in bed tonight, worrying that I said the wrong thing—something that wasn't fair, wasn't kind, wasn't true. But then I remember that Maya still helped me today, even after I said unkind words to her last night. Maybe I don't always have to say exactly the right thing.

"Today was a lie," I continue. "Mike convinced half the student body that he had nothing to do with what happened to Maya." I grip the back of my chair, but my hands still aren't shaking.

"Maybe I have to fight for things in a different way than you do. Maybe—" I rack my brain for an example. "Maybe I want to *write* about the world, rather than fight in a courtroom." It's the closest I've come to telling him I don't want to be an attorney like him.

"Junie, don't let this setback—"

I cut him off. "I freaked out this morning. I was barely conscious during the protest." I thought I'd never tell my parents what happened, but maybe they need to know.

"What do you mean?"

I close my eyes, remembering how it felt to gasp for breath. I thought I was having a heart attack. "I was so out of it that I couldn't hear what Maya said, and I certainly didn't tell her to say it."

Before Dad can call *that* just another setback, I ask, "Why didn't we go to family sessions?"

Dad blinks. "What?"

"Mom said that Dr. Kreiter wanted us to do family sessions. Why didn't we?"

Dad throws up his hands. "Not you too," he moans. "Since when do you agree with everything that doctor has to say? She wanted you to go to group therapy, and I respected your opinion when you said you didn't need it."

"Maybe you shouldn't have." My stomach twists with anger again. "What did you think when you saw me in the hospital in February?"

"What kind of question is that? I was worried about you."

"I know," I say. "But when Dr. Kreiter said that cutting was a coping mechanism—"

"We all have ways of coping. We just need to find you a healthy outlet. Meditation. Exercise."

"But didn't you wonder *why* I had so much trouble coping in the first place?"

Dad doesn't answer.

"It's not a *setback*, Dad. Not what happened today, and not the cutting. I'm sick. I started hurting myself because it hurt *less* than not hurting myself. Can you understand that? Can you even imagine it?"

Dad opens his mouth to answer, but for once a counter-argument doesn't emerge. Instead, he shakes his head. "I can't."

"Okay," I say. Carefully, slowly, I push my chair back under the table. "Well, from now on, I'm going to try to explain it to you. Because I think you need to understand it if you're ever going to understand me." I think but don't add, *If I'm ever going to understand me.*

I take a deep breath, remembering what Maya said about good love. "And I have to hope that you'll love me even if I'm not exactly the person you want me to be." My voice shakes, of *course* it shakes. But I think I actually said the *right* thing for once.

I turn on my heel and walk toward the stairs. Mom's sitting on the bottom step, her head in her hands. She must have heard every word.

"I'm so sorry, Junie." I'm surprised to hear that her voice is shaking too—it's high-pitched, nervous. I've never heard her sound so anxious before. "Dr. Kreiter said you were scared to ask for help. Like you didn't trust that we'd love you no matter what."

I sink onto the steps beside her. Mom's dark brown hair is streaked with gray. Unlike my hair (I inherited Dad's stick-straight mop), Mom's hair is wavy. It's pulled back into a tight ponytail this morning, but Mom tucks a few phantom strands behind her ear, almost obsessively. Or maybe *precisely* obsessively, since the same trick of genetics that made me inherit Dad's hair could have made me inherit Mom's OCD.

"I noticed you were acting differently this fall, but I thought it was just the stress of junior year. I thought that if anything was really wrong, you'd have come to me to talk about it, but now—" She sighs heavily. "I thought I was being a good mother, giving you space. I didn't want to raise you the way my mother raised me. Overprotective. Overbearing."

"You *are* a good mother," I say.

Mom continues as if I didn't say anything, "Now, I think Dr. Kreiter was right. You were too scared to tell me you needed help. How could I have let that happen?"

"I didn't start cutting until December," I protest. "I was still okay in the fall."

Mom shakes her head. "No," she says firmly. "You weren't." I remember how pleased Mom had been when she thought I was taking baths, that I'd set aside time for self-care.

At our very first session, Dr. Kreiter explained that while the cutting was our most immediate problem, it wasn't our *only* problem. I nodded, because I knew she wanted me to agree (it made sense, given my diagnoses), but at the time, I didn't actually think the doctor knew what she was talking about. Like Dad said, I wasn't supposed to cut, and I haven't, so how could Dr. Kreiter say I wasn't making progress?

But that was before I knew how it felt to be flush with a false sense of well-being. I thought Dr. Kreiter was wrong when she said I cut (partly) for the endorphin rush, but now I'm not so sure.

I think back to the fall: studying SAT words and fitting in my homework between my extracurriculars. Falling for Tess months before she ever really noticed me. Even then, my hands sometimes shook while I typed my English and history papers, while I wrote out my notes from physics lab.

Mom's right: I was struggling even before the cutting started.

"A parent's most important job is making sure her child knows she's loved," Mom continues. "After that, it's keeping her child safe. And I didn't do either of those things."

"You kept me from cutting myself for months," I offer.

"That doesn't necessarily mean you felt safe, does it?"

I think about Maya, living day-to-day knowing that Mike might hit her. *That's* not feeling safe.

But when I think about the lengths I went to in order to hide my anxiety—not just the pills, but before that, playing it cool with Tess, insisting I could stop myself from cutting without extra help, too scared to even tell my father I didn't want to be a lawyer like him—I realize it's a different kind of not feeling safe, but it still counts.

Mom says, "I should have said something to you sooner. *We* should have said something. But I want you to know how proud you made me today."

I blink in confusion. Mom heard what I said to Dad—the protest was a disaster, I freaked out. How can she be proud of me?

Mom continues, "It was brave of you to stand up to your father like that. To ask him—to ask *us*—to see all of you. I'm just sorry you had to ask at all."

"I'm sorry too," I reply. "I shouldn't have lied. Not just about the pills, or about sneaking out last night." Mom's eyes widen in surprise (I forgot she didn't actually know about my sneaking out), but I keep going.

"I'm sorry I lied about everything. I'm sorry I lied about myself."

nineteen

MAYA

I imagine that he hears the phone ringing. I picture the surprise crossing his face when he sees my number on the screen. I exhale when I hear his voice say, "Hi, sweetheart."

"Hi, Dad."

"How are you?"

Sitting cross-legged on my bed, I feel my face crumple. I cry until my chest hurts. I cry until I can barely breathe. I cry until I have to put the phone down to wipe my face.

If it were Mom on the other end of the phone, I'd end up comforting *her*, trying to quiet her concerns with soothing nonsense promises that everything's going to be okay. But it's Dad, so he waits quietly.

"I have to tell you something," I manage finally. "Mike, Mike—Mike has been—" It's hard to say his name. "He hit me."

"Oh, sweetheart," Dad says. I wait for him to ask whether I've gone to the police. I wait for him to ask how long it's been going on, and then to ask why I didn't come forward sooner. I wait for his confusion that the boy I lit up around is also a boy who hurt me. But instead, Dad simply says, "I'm so sorry."

I blink and swallow. "You don't sound surprised."

"Your mother told me."

"Mom told you?" I sit up and wipe my eyes. Mom and Dad haven't spoken in months. They *can't* speak. Since the divorce—and for a while before that—any conversation dissolves into shouts. I'm already planning to have them sit on opposite sides of the school auditorium when I graduate next year to keep the peace. But I'm not sure that will be far enough, because they managed to fight even after Dad moved into the guest room, and after he moved to a hotel, and then after he moved across the country to New York.

"She called me Monday afternoon," Dad says. "I didn't tell you because—well, I guess I thought you'd tell me when you were ready."

"God, that's just like Mom," I say. "Making this thing that happened to me into something that happened to *her*."

"Not this time, sweetheart. She was worried about you. We needed to discuss it."

I almost laugh. "Come on, Dad. You guys never *discuss* anything anymore."

"I know we're not very good at it," Dad admits. "But your mom did the right thing, telling me."

It's the closest he's come to saying something nice about my mother for years.

"It's not just Mike," I begin, and my throat catches but I swallow hard, determined not to start crying again. If I'm really done with secrets, I have to say this too. Even if it's just as hard as telling the truth about Mike. "I've been making myself throw up. Pretty much ever since Mike and I got together. Even before he hit me."

Dad's quiet. Maybe he's thinking that Mom should have known, since she's the one living with me. Maybe he thinks a good parent would have known, that *he* would have known. I'm surprised by how much I want to defend her. "I've gotten good at keeping secrets."

"Sweetheart," Dad begins gently, "I hate to hear that you've been hurting yourself like that."

I almost object, thinking that throwing up is nothing compared to what Junie went through, but I stop myself. Maybe it's not the same thing as cutting myself open—but Dad's right. It's still a kind of hurting myself. Dad continues, "Your mom and I have been talking. I understand the school hasn't yet decided what Mike's punishment will be, whether he might be expelled."

"There's a board meeting tomorrow night."

"I know," Dad says, "but whatever they decide—if you don't want to go back to that school, it's okay."

"What do you mean?"

"I mean, you could come live with me. Finish high school in New York."

I shake my head, even though he can't see me. "Mom doesn't even want me going away to *college*."

At the beginning of junior year, before Mike and I were a couple, our high school's college adviser made all the juniors put together a list of all the colleges we're thinking of applying to. My list included Berkeley, Pomona, and UCLA, but also East Coast schools like Barnard, Columbia, and NYU, Vassar and Cornell.

When the adviser told Mom about the list at a parent/teacher conference, Mom freaked out. *How could you leave me alone like that?* she said. *Why would you pick your father over me?*

"Actually," Dad says now, "it was your mother's idea."

"What?"

"Maya, I'm the first to admit that your mother's not perfect." Dad sighs. "Maybe I should have been better about keeping a few secrets myself. I shouldn't have let you get caught in the middle of our issues. Neither of us should have. Maybe if we'd done a better job, you'd have felt safe coming to one of us sooner.

"Your mom loves you very much. She called me the other night because she—both of us—we don't know how to make this better for you. She wants you to feel safe. And I—she—*we* want you to be healthy too." I can't remember the last time either of my parents referred to themselves as *we.* "And if coming to New York will make things easier for you, then she wants you to be in New York."

I look around my room, imagining all the clothes in my closet packed into boxes, all my carefully arranged books shipped across the country. I have a room of my own in Dad's apartment, but it's mostly empty—I've never stayed there for more than a couple weeks at a time, during school vacations. I picture myself walking down his street to the high school around the corner, starting my senior year with a new set of classmates, but the image is fuzzy because there's so much I don't know. Will I be popular there? Will I be someone else's girlfriend? Will I stop throwing up? Will I end up a burnout, cutting class and sitting in someone else's car?

Then again, they probably don't drive cars to school in Manhattan. I wonder where the burnouts go to do whatever it is they do.

Which reminds me of another secret I've been keeping. "There's something else I should probably tell you."

"What's that?"

"I've been—" I pause. I'm not exactly sure how to say it. It's not like my limited experience with this kind of thing has been all that much *fun*. I mostly did it so I could forget about everything else for a little while. "I tried pot. A few times. With a friend."

I know for a fact that my dad smoked when he was in college—I've seen pictures in old photo albums of him with a joint in his hand. (In fact, that picture led to one of his bigger fights with Mom; she was worried it would make me think that using drugs was no big deal.)

"I'll have to talk to your mom about that too," Dad says finally.

"I'm not sure I even *want* to do it again," I explain. "But I didn't want to keep it a secret either."

"Well, I appreciate your honesty," Dad replies.

I uncross my legs and lie flat, leaning my head against my pillows. "Can I ask you something?"

"Anything, sweetheart."

"How come you never offered before?"

"Offered what before?" Dad sounds confused.

"Did it have to be something as bad at Mike hitting me for you to offer to let me come live with you?"

"Of course not," Dad answers quickly.

"Then why didn't you ever offer before?"

"Your mother—"

"Don't blame Mom," I interrupt. "I always knew Mom wanted me to live with her. I never knew if you did."

"Honey, divorce is complicated—"

"So complicated that you couldn't have asked me before moving across the country?" I'm so surprised by the question that I almost drop the phone.

I always envied my dad for leaving. I thought I understood how much he needed to get away—after all, I wanted to move away someday too. But right now, I wish he'd stayed. It would've been nice to know that however bad things were with Mom, however much he wanted to be three thousand miles away from *her*, it wasn't enough to make it worth being that far from *me*.

"You didn't only leave Mom," I say.

"Oh, honey," Dad says. "Say the word, and I'll be on the next plane."

I shake my head, imagining other fathers, fathers who'd *insist* on being by their daughters' sides at a time like this. I feel a shadow of the anger I felt this afternoon. Why do I have to ask? Why doesn't he *offer*? Why did he wait for me to call him, when he's known about Mike for days? Why hasn't he shown up?

337

"What if I needed you to move back here, to live close by?"

I hold my breath while I wait for Dad to answer. Finally, he says, "I can't make any promises, but if you need me there, I'll do my best to be there for you. Okay?" Somehow, I knew he wouldn't make any promises. "But you should know, your mom's there for you too."

I exhale. "I know."

Mom wanted to pick me up from school on Monday morning, but I begged her not to. Then, she left work early. Maybe it wasn't because she was upset. Maybe she wanted to be closer to me, in case I needed her.

"I know," I repeat.

"Then why did you tell me about the bulimia, not her?"

It's shocking to hear Dad call it *bulimia*. It's not as though I haven't thought about that word since I started throwing up. But I never called myself *bulimic*. Dad says it as though there's simply no other word for it.

At Kyle's house last night, I thought the words *domestic violence, dating abuse, relationship violence* were all too big, too *much* to apply to Mike and me.

But maybe those were the right words after all.

"Honey?" Dad prompts.

I didn't tell Mom I was making myself throw up because I knew she would freak out. Because she would yell and cry and tell me I'm beautiful the way I am. Then she'd call the nearest therapist and send me to an eating disorders support group, and I would think she was blowing the whole thing way out of proportion.

But maybe that's exactly *in* proportion. I mean, not the freaking out and yelling and crying, like I'd done something to *her* instead of to myself. But the therapy and the support group. Telling me I'm beautiful.

"Are you going to tell Mom?" I ask finally.

"I will," Dad answers. "Because she'd tell me. But I think you should tell her yourself first."

I sigh. "She's not always easy to talk to."

Dad chuckles. "She's always been a worrier."

Again, I'm surprised by how much I want to defend her, even though I was just complaining about her. Maybe there are things she can understand that Dad never will. Because he's never been a seventeen-year-old girl, and she has.

"You should talk to her," Dad says. "She's ready to listen."

"She'll lose it if I move to New York."

"No," Dad says firmly. "She won't. I promise. *We* promise."

Monday, April 17

twenty

JUNIE

I'm late. I promised myself I wouldn't be, I said this was too important, I even set my alarm for twenty minutes earlier than usual—but still, somehow the day (well, at least the morning) got away from me, and now I'm pulling up to Maya's driveway fifteen minutes past the time we agreed on. But I know that Maya won't be mad at me, even if I'm twenty, thirty, fifty minutes late. My hands aren't shaking.

In our first session, Dr. Kreiter asked me if I had anyone to lean on, anyone I trusted enough to see my weaknesses. Maybe I didn't, then. But I know I can trust Maya now.

Before I left the house, Mom reminded me that I'm scheduled for a special therapy session after school. Apparently what happened over the past few days is a big enough deal that the doctor moved her regularly scheduled Monday appointment to make time for me. Mom said she'd meet me at the office because she wanted to talk to Dr. Kreiter too.

I knew that Mom and Dr. Kreiter had already spoken (how else could Mom have secured this emergency session?), so I almost asked why Mom needed to be there this afternoon, but I stopped myself. Maybe it will help, her being there.

Instead, I asked, "Do you think Dad will agree to family sessions?"

"Of course," Mom began, but her voice faltered, because we both knew that despite everything that's happened, he might not. "*I'll* go to family sessions," she added finally. "No matter what."

Unlike me, Mom didn't need to set an alarm to wake up early this morning. When I came downstairs, the kitchen was even more spotless than usual. I suspected she'd been cleaning since about five o'clock, and I know she'll be waiting in Dr. Kreiter's office by three fifteen even though our appointment isn't until three thirty.

I wonder if that kind of OCD is better or worse than the kind I have. I don't mean is hers more severe than mine, I mean, which *feels* worse. Being late and disorganized means I always feel like I'm scrambling to catch up. But maybe it's just as bad to always feel like you have to put everything in precisely the right place, to give yourself thirty minutes to make a fifteen-minute drive. Think of all the time you'd spend cleaning or waiting, time you might have spent doing something else.

"What do you think Dr. Kreiter will say?" Maya asks as she gets into the car. (I already texted her about my emergency appointment.)

"No idea," I answer honestly.

"Do you think she's going to want to put you on antianxiety medication?"

"I'm pretty sure my mom wants her to."

"Okay, but what do *you* want?"

"I don't know." I'm still not sure if my actions on Saturday night (and Friday afternoon, for that matter) were my own or if the pills were the ones in control. I'm sure that anything Dr. Kreiter would prescribe would work differently than those red diet pills, but I can't help being scared of how medication—even *proper* medication, like Mom said—might change me.

I say, "A week ago, I would have done anything to avoid being medicated."

If my inner monologue hadn't been silenced by a *false sense of well-being* Saturday night, I might not have said the things I regret now, even though Maya forgave me. Maybe my inner monologue isn't all bad. I wonder if that's something *proper* medication could help with—not silencing my thoughts, but helping me not to be overwhelmed by them either. That doesn't sound scary. That even sounds kind of nice.

I guess I could ask Dr. Kreiter about all this, instead of refusing to talk about much of anything at all. I could even try using some of the tools she recommended to keep myself from spiraling—not only medication, but some of the thought exercises she suggested. Maybe they're called *exercises* because they take practice. It's not like anyone can do a pull-up on their first try.

"It's not fair to judge by the past week," Maya offers. "This wasn't a *normal* week."

"Yeah." I nod in agreement. After all, I never had a panic attack before yesterday. "But there were a lot of weeks before when I still wanted to cut, weeks when I *did* cut." I pause. "I think whether or not it was a bad week might be beside the point."

"What do you mean?"

"Other people get through bad weeks not just without cutting, but without *wanting* to cut. I mean, it doesn't even *occur* to them, you know?"

"You mean how it doesn't occur to other people to make themselves throw up when they want to lose weight?" Maya asks, and we both start laughing.

"This wouldn't be funny to anyone but us," Maya points out, and I know I'm right to believe I can trust Maya to love me no matter what side of me she sees.

As our laughter fades, I say softly, "Maybe someday it won't be funny to us either."

At school, I pull into my usual crappy parking spot and turn off the car. Even though we're late, neither of us is in a rush to get to homeroom.

"Let them try to scold us for being late after what we've been through." Maya grins.

"You've never broken a rule in your life," I protest, though now I know it isn't true.

My best friend shrugs. "And still, I managed to cause so much trouble."

For some reason, this strikes both of us as hilarious too. We're laughing so hard that I almost don't hear it when someone taps on the driver's-side window. I look up.

Tess.

"Can we talk for a minute?" she asks.

Maya and I get out of the car. I lean against the door. "I'll just go…over here," Maya says, wandering off in between the cars. I'm not sure if she lingers because she doesn't want to go into our school alone, or because she knows that after Tess and I talk, I might need her. Maybe both.

"I've been thinking about what you said yesterday," Tess begins. "That I never really knew you."

Her hair is back to its usual height. She's wearing tight blue jeans and a faded gray T-shirt that looks so soft, I'm tempted to reach out and touch it. Instead, I stuff my hands in my pockets.

"I'm sorry about that," I say carefully. "Like I said, it's not your fault."

"I was thinking that I'd like a chance to get to know you. The *real* you. Whatever that means." She smiles. "So I thought I'd ask you out on an official date. We could start over." She holds out a hand like she wants me to shake it. "Hi," she says. "I'm Tess Washington."

A week ago, I thought that Tess and I had done everything backward. We kissed before we dated; we called each other *baby* before we held hands. A week ago, if she'd asked me out on a real, official date, I'd have said yes before she had a chance to finish inviting me.

But a week ago, Tess had no idea how much of myself I hid from her.

"I'm not sure that's such a good idea," I answer finally.

Tess drops her hand.

"I'm not saying no," I add quickly. "I mean, I *literally* don't know if that's a good idea or not."

Maybe this is another thing I should actually discuss with my therapist. Did I ever tell Dr. Kreiter that Tess and I broke up?

"Do you mind if I think about it?" I ask. "I don't expect you to wait for me or anything, if someone less complicated comes along."

"Maybe I like complicated," Tess tries.

"That's really nice of you to say," I answer. "But I'm not even sure *how* complicated I am yet." Maybe Dr. Kreiter will add pathological liar to my diagnosis later, because of all the parts of myself I kept hidden. Maybe I'll walk out with a stack of prescriptions a mile high.

Tess nods and leans against my car beside me. "Just so you know, *everyone* is complicated. There's a lot I haven't told you about me too."

"There is?" I'm genuinely surprised. Tess always seemed like an open book.

"Of course there is." Tess grins. "I wasn't about to let you see what a weirdo I am. I wanted you to like me."

"I do like you," I say.

"I like you too." Tess's smile falters. "I guess I should get to class. Not everyone has your magic touch with the faculty."

"You know, they only let me get away with being late because my doctor told them I can't help it."

"Really?"

I nod. "OCD." I feel my hands shake in my pockets as I reveal this secret, but I keep talking. "Makes me late to everything. But I'm working on it. Or anyway, I'm going to work on it."

"Good luck."

"Thanks."

Maya approaches as Tess walks away. "You okay?" she asks.

I almost start laughing again. "I seriously don't know how to answer that question."

Maya smiles. "Fair enough."

I gaze at our school, knowing that Mike is probably somewhere inside. "*You* okay?" I ask.

Maya nods. "I kind of am. At least, I feel better than I did last Monday."

"You do?"

"Yeah." Maya pauses. "Don't you?"

I consider it. A week ago, I was determined not to let anyone see that I was an anxious basket case, even if that meant holding the people around me—from my therapist to my girlfriend—at arm's length. But how could I have been a good best friend—or girlfriend, or daughter—when I was so busy balancing the different parts of myself that I never got to actually *be* myself?

Maya's right. This—standing beside my best friend without hiding anything from her—feels better.

"Do you think Tess and I should get back together?" I ask, confident that Maya will have the right answer.

"I don't know," Maya replies. "I don't know whether a person has to sort out her own problems before teaming up with someone else like that." Gently, she bumps her hip against mine. "But I'll be your best friend either way."

It's not a yes or no, but still—Maya managed to find the right thing to say. Like always.

Maya takes a deep breath in, then out, and stares across the parking lot. I follow her gaze to the one car parked farther away from school than mine. Hiram is sitting inside his car, silently supporting Maya from his place in the background, just like he did yesterday, and maybe for a long time before that. I wonder if he and Maya will ever walk down the halls hand in hand the way she did with Mike. I remember his text on Saturday night: **I'm here if you need to talk.** Maybe he's supporting me this morning too.

I look back at Maya and say, "I'll be your best friend either way too."

Part of the reason I was late this morning had nothing to do with my OCD. Dad stopped me as I was racing out the door.

"I owe you an apology," he said. "I'm sorry I put so much pressure on you. If it weren't for me, you wouldn't have felt the need to plan that protest, you wouldn't have had that..." He paused, like he was searching for the right word. Finally he said, "That *episode* on the track."

I shook my head. "I *wanted* to plan that protest," I explained. "I wanted to do it for Maya."

"But you got…" Dad paused like he couldn't think of the word to describe what happened to me yesterday. "You got sick," he finished finally. "Maybe if your mother and I had raised you differently—"

"You mean by teaching me not try to make things better, not to be a good friend?" I interrupted. "That's the kind of person I *want* to be." My breath caught in my throat. "I just don't know if I'm strong enough to do all the things I want."

Dad nodded. "We all want to do more than we think we can." I could practically see him biting his tongue. Normally, that would be the moment when he'd encourage me to *try*, no matter how hard it is.

Finally, I took a deep breath and asked, "Are you going to come to Dr. Kreiter's this afternoon?"

"What?"

"Mom's coming," I explained. "She wants to talk to the doctor in person. You could come too. The appointment's at three thirty."

Dad hesitated. "I have a meeting," he began. "But I'll see if I can move it, okay?"

I nodded. I wanted to ask if he was still proud of me. I wanted to ask if I'd let him down, by admitting that I might need therapy and medication, that I might not be able to handle everything on my own. Actually, I didn't *want* to ask, but I couldn't stop the questions from bouncing around my brain. I knew Dad would have said *of course* he was proud, *of course* I hadn't let him down—that's the kind of father he prides himself on being. But I also knew that no matter what he said, deep down, he might still be disappointed. And I was scared that if I asked out loud, I'd be able to see the lie in his face when he answered. But this morning, Tess didn't look like a liar, asking me out even though I lost my cool with her twice in the last two days.

Maybe I haven't given her enough credit. Maybe Maya isn't the only person I can trust.

Maybe I haven't given myself enough credit either. Maybe I can be an activist *and* struggle with anxiety, even if that means no matter how badly I want to organize protests and attend rallies, sometimes my nerves will get in the way. And sometimes I truly feel cool and aloof, but there are also times when I feel needy and vulnerable.

Maybe I have to stop trying to be one thing or another. Maybe I need to accept the ways I contradict myself. Maybe that's what it is to be human.

I take my hands out of my pockets. They're still shaking, just a little bit. But I'm done hiding them.

I'm done hiding *me*.

twenty-one

MAYA

I glance at my phone—it's nine o'clock. Not only have we missed homeroom, but now we're about to be late to our first class.

I never told Junie this, but I don't actually mind that she's always late. It makes everything feel like an adventure—rushing to get to class, to a movie, to dinner. And, it means that she's never angry at me if *I'm* running late.

When Mike was the one picking me up and taking me to school each day, I had to be precisely on time. If I was even a few minutes behind schedule, he wouldn't talk to me the whole ride from home to school, or during the walk from the parking lot to homeroom. It was only at lunch, sitting at our table, surrounded by our friends, that he'd be himself again—holding my hand, laughing at my unintended jokes. Then again, maybe that wasn't being himself. Maybe his real self was the silent boy in the car, grinding his teeth because I made him late.

Actually, no—I don't believe that. Both versions of Mike are real, because both *exist*. Along with the competitive racer, and the spoiled son, and the dutiful big brother, and who knows who else. I think about his face when Hiram hit him the other day. He reset his features before I could figure out if he was angry, frustrated, or surprised. At the time, I thought it looked like he was putting on a mask. But now I think maybe he was all of those things: angry, frustrated, surprised, but also calm and collected. Mike could be different things at once too.

"You ready?" Junie asks as we approach the steps that lead into school, toward Mike and everyone else.

I nod. Maybe in a few hours, the board of trustees will decide to expel Mike, or Hiram. I glance back and see Hiram leaning against his car.

"You think Hiram's gonna go inside today?" Junie asks.

I shrug. "He doesn't always go to class even on days when he isn't waiting to find out if he's expelled."

"He'd go if you wanted him to."

"What do you mean?"

"I mean, if you thought you'd feel better with him at your side, or whatever. He'd do it for you."

I smile. If I brought Hiram home with me, Mom wouldn't approve—he looks like trouble. Then again, Mike looked like a dream.

My bruise has faded so much that you might not notice if it you didn't know it was there. It would have been easy to hide all traces of it under makeup before I left the house this morning. But today, I didn't even consider covering it up.

Maybe the board will open an investigation, interviewing everyone who knew Mike and me—our teachers, our parents, our friends. Maybe they'll put a process in place so they'll be prepared if this ever happens again: next time, the accuser will fill out an official complaint; the accused will be put on probation, and suspended or expelled if there are witnesses or additional accusations. Or maybe the board will say I have to go to the police and press charges, letting law enforcement take charge.

Maybe they'll simply say *case closed*, since they can't technically prove who hit me. Maybe they'll secretly—or not so secretly—think I'm a slut for being with two boys at once. I imagine Junie lecturing the board members about the perils of slut-shaming.

Mom and I talked for a long time last night—a nice, thoughtful, surprisingly calm conversation. We both cried, but I didn't have to comfort her once. She apologized for not noticing sooner; I told her I hid it. She asked about the smoking (she called it my *experimentation*), but she didn't seem angry, more concerned that I'd needed something to dull the pain. She said she'd understand if I wanted to move away; I said I hadn't decided yet. She said no matter what, she'd support my decision. She said she was so proud of me for coming forward.

"I'm not sure I could have been so brave," she said, and for the first time I didn't feel like I'd been a coward for waiting as long as I did.

"But if I do decide to move," I asked, "isn't that just running away?" Running away isn't brave.

Mom didn't answer immediately. She cocked her head to the side and chewed her lip, the same way she does when she's trying to work out the answer to Final Jeopardy each night.

"No," she answered finally. "You'd be leaving a bad situation behind. That's not running away. That's an act of strength."

I blinked in surprise. Did Mom actually *want* me to move away? "Are you saying you think I *should* leave?"

"Oh, honey, if it were up to me, you'd be living under my roof for the rest of your life." Mom smiled sadly. "But it's not up to me. And it's not as though I did such a great job protecting you while you were here."

"It isn't your fault," I began, but Mom held up her hand.

"Parents can't help believing that everything that happens to our children is our fault. All I've wanted all week is to march over to Mike's house and smash his car with a baseball bat."

I couldn't help it—I laughed out loud. The image of my mother trashing Mike's car was too funny not to laugh about.

"I thought you loved Mike."

Mom looked horrified. "I love *you*," she said fiercely. For the first time, it occurred to me that I did have the sort of parent who'd say things like: *If you ever lay another finger on my daughter, I'll kill you.* It just wasn't my dad.

"Why didn't you tell me that?" I asked. "About wanting to smash Mike's car?"

"I would've if I'd known it would make you laugh like that."

She smiled. "But I didn't want you to see how upset I was. I know—" She paused. "I know you think I make everything that happens to you about me."

I shrugged. I couldn't deny it.

"But that's another thing about being a parent," she explained. "I love you so much that sometimes I can't always tell where I end and you begin."

"Oh," I said softly. I never thought of it like that. Maybe she acts the way she does because when bad things happen to *me*, it feels like they're happening to *her* too.

"Promise me something," Mom added. "Whether you go to New York or stay here, I want you to attend a support group for survivors of abuse."

Survivor. Another word I hadn't thought applied to me. But when Mom said it, I thought maybe it was true. Maybe it was a part of myself I hadn't even met yet.

Now, I tell Junie about Dad's offer to let me come live with him. "It was my mom's idea," I add.

"Really?" Junie sounds incredulous. "Your mom's okay with you moving across the country?"

"Well, she's not *happy* about it," I concede. "But she said she'd let me go."

"Are you waiting until the board meets to decide?" Junie asks.

"I think it's more complicated than whether Mike's going to be here or not, you know?" Junie nods. We both know that even if Mike's gone, Kyle and Anil will be here. The track coach will still be here. Eva Mercado will still be here. To some of our classmates—and to some of our teachers—Mike will always be golden, and I'll always be the girl who hurt him.

"Maybe it doesn't matter whether or not Mike gets expelled." I wave toward the school in front of us. "There will always be kids in there who believe *him*, not me."

Junie shakes her head. "It matters," she says firmly, and I nod. She's right, of course.

It matters.

But, still—even the people who believe me may always see me as the girl whose boyfriend hit her. Maybe the guys will give me a wide berth when I walk down the hallways, as though I might accuse them should they get too close. Maybe some girls will be scared to hug me too tightly, worried they could trigger an unpleasant memory. Maybe the teachers will go easy on me in class because they know I went through a hard time. They'd think they were being nice, but it would just be another reminder. Not that I want to—or ever could—forget. But to these people, I'll always be Mike's girlfriend.

And yes, that's part of who I am. It always will be.

But it's not *all* I am.

"Mom and I agreed that I need help—you know, professional help. Whether I go or stay. Not just because of what happened with Mike, but because…" I trail off.

Because it happened for as long as it did before I told anyone, even if that's not my fault. Because coming forward was traumatic. Because of the bulimia. Because my relationship with my mother is complicated. Because my parents had a messy divorce, and my father moved far away. Because I'm tired of being different things to different people. Because I sought refuge in Hiram's car, choosing to go numb rather than deal with what was going on. Because I want to be with Hiram, but I'm also scared of being with *anyone* ever again. Because Hiram's going away next year, and I'll miss him, and I'm scared that if I move to New York, I might be following him, which would be letting another guy determine my future, even if it's one who never tried to control me the way Mike did.

Junie doesn't rush to fill the silence, but after a beat, she grins and says, "I can get you Dr. Kreiter's number." I put my arm around my best friend and squeeze.

"I love you," I say.

"I love you too. Whether you go or stay. Whether you need therapy every day of the week or drop it after a month."

I grin. "Ditto."

Junie puts her arm around me too. We walk toward the school holding each other close.

I am a girl who loved her boyfriend.

And a girl whose boyfriend hit her.

I am a girl who loves picking out her clothes each morning.

And a girl who struggles to accept the way she looks.

I am a girl who was charmed by Mike.

And a girl who is disgusted by Mike.

I am a girl who wants to escape.

And a girl who wants to stay in the here and now.

I suspect there are more pieces I have yet to discover. Maybe the survivor will be next, like Mom said. Or maybe some other part of my personality will surprise me by bubbling to the surface, the way a fighter came out at the protest yesterday.

Whatever it is, I'll accept that part too.

If you or someone you know maybe
suffering from dating abuse, help
is available. Please visit:
https://www.refuge.org.uk/get-help-now
Or call: 0808 2000 247

If you or someone you know is
engaged in self-harm, please visit:
https://www.supportline.org.uk/
problems/self-injury-and-self-harm/
Or call: 01708 765200

ACKNOWLEDGMENTS

Thank you to my wonderful editors, Kate Prosswimmer and Eliza Swift, and thanks so very much to the extraordinary team at Sourcebooks: Chris Bauerle, Sarah Cardillo, Margaret Coffee, Christa Desir, Stephanie Graham, Cassie Gutman, Sara Hartman-Seeskin, Steve Geck, Sarah Kasman, Ashlyn Keil, Kelly Lawler, Lizzie Lewandowski, Katy Lynch, Sean Murray, Beth Oleniczak, Valerie Pierce, William Preston, Dominque Raccah, Jillian Rahn, Stefani Sloma, Todd Stocke, Heidi Weiland, Shane White, and Cristina Wilson, and thanks to Nicole Hower for the beautiful cover.

Thank you to my brilliant agent, Mollie Glick, and to Berni Barta, Lola Bellier, Austin Denesuk, Julie Flanagan, Kayla Shore, Jamie Stockton, and the entire team at CAA.

Thanks to Samantha Schutz, and thank you, Jocelyn Davies, Anne Heltzel, Jackie Resnick, and Danielle Rollins, for a conversation that helped spark this story. Thanks also to Rachel Feld, Caroline Gertler, and Julie Sternberg.

Thank you to my sister, my parents, my friends, and my teachers. And again, thank you, JP Gravitt, for everything.

"I can't imagine life without a dog. They constantly remind me of the art of being well-and-truly present, and they also show me how to be joyful, how to concentrate on joy."

—KATE DICAMILLO

ABOUT THE AUTHOR

Alyssa Sheinmel is the *New York Times* bestselling author of several novels for young adults including *A Danger to Herself and Others* and *Faceless*. Alyssa grew up in Northern California and New York, and currently lives and writes in New York. Follow Alyssa on Instagram @alyssasheinmel and Twitter @AlyssaSheinmel or visit her online at alyssasheinmel.com.